C. F. Roe was brought up in Scotland and graduated from Aberdeen University Medical School with a gold medal in Surgery. He has practised and taught surgery in the U.S., travelled the world as a ship's surgeon and worked in Afghanistan before becoming a full-time writer. C. F. Roe now lives in London and Albuquerque, New Mexico.

He is the author of *The Lumsden Baby* and *Bad Blood*, both Doctor Jean Montrose whodunnits and available from Headline.

Death by Fire

C. F. Roe

HEADLINE

First published in 1990
by HEADLINE BOOK PUBLISHING PLC

First published in paperback in 1991
by HEADLINE BOOK PUBLISHING PLC

10 9 8 7 6 5 4 3 2 1

ISBN 0 7472 3504 X

Printed and bound in Great Britain by
Collins, Glasgow

HEADLINE BOOK PUBLISHING PLC
Headline House
79 Great Titchfield Street
London W1P 7FN

This book is for my sister
Isabelle and her family.

Acknowledgement

I would like to thank Lady Lesley Smith for her help in reviewing the proofs: any remaining errors or solecisms are mine.

Chapter One

Visiting parents usually had trouble finding St Jude's Academy; not that they came in droves, as most of the boys had been sent there by parents who wanted to see as little of their offspring as possible. Seven and one tenth miles out of Perth, on the Dunkeld road, said the brochure; there was a sign warning of a sharp bend in the road, and just beyond that, on the left, was the narrow side road, unrecorded in AA maps and marked only by a white placard with black letters which read 'St Jude's Academy', and below, in smaller letters, 'est. 1978'. The road was about a quarter of a mile long, now grey and dusty from the drought, lined on the left by a low drystone dyke, crumbling in places, and surmounted by occasional splashes of yellow whin. Beyond the dyke was a scruffy wood of mixed pine and spindly silver birch, which thinned out to be replaced by furze and some scattered clumps of heather nearer the gates.

The gates of St Jude's Academy dated back to the original construction, when the house had the grand-sounding name of Muirs of Strathtay. Their iron tracery was elaborate, but even when fully open there was only a narrow space between the gates, barely wide enough for a small van to pass through. The overall first impression was of a constrictive meanness, well beyond the normal prudent economy that was always well respected in these parts.

The narrow gravel drive up to the front of the house was lined on each side by a two-foot-wide strip of dried brown grass; the tracks of cars and vans left shallow, elongated ruts on the edge of the crumbling drive, now dried out and crazed with the heat and drought, with tyre marks emerging from the dried puddles like dinosaur tracks coming out of a mesozoic lake. The drive expanded into a cramped court-yard at the front of the house, leaving barely enough space for a vehicle to turn without backing into the dark, ghostly rhododendrons surrounding the yard. To the right of the house, a few Douglas firs had been cut down to make room for a parking area, and the spaces were jammed together so closely there was barely room to open the car doors.

The finest feature of the house was undoubtedly the facade; built around 1890 by a Dundee industrialist, it incorporated granite turrets, crenellations, and all the use-less but impressive embellishments of the full-blown Scottish Baronial style. Inside, however, it was a different story: the house was crammed with a multitude of mean, dark rooms with low ceilings and ancient and unreliable plumbing. It was just the kind of house a man brought up in the slums of Dundee might build, a small mill-owner suddenly made rich by a fortuitous combination of tight-fisted exploitation and economic factors over which he had neither understanding nor control.

It was in every way the ideal place to turn into a private school.

At the back of the building, on the second floor, Mr Morgan Stroud was taking a class in intermediate physics. Mr Stroud was only about thirty years old, but the lines of petulance and failure were already on his face, and self-indulgence was evident in his corpulent figure. Not that Morgan Stroud didn't enjoy his work as a teacher; indeed he did, and he was particularly enjoying himself now.

'Mackay, if you think you could stay awake long enough to give us the benefit of your wisdom . . .' Mr Stroud's eyes flickered over his eight pupils and landed on Neil Mackay, one of the few day-boys, who had come to the school only that term. Neil had a stammer which surfaced only when he

was under stress; Morgan Stroud was well aware of this.
'. . . And give us your definition, and I expect an erudite
and thoughtful one, of the term *energy*, as it applies to
physics.'

Neil, a tall lanky boy who had difficulty fitting into the
cramped, old-fashioned wooden desks, went red in the
face, not from ignorance, but because of the effort he
would have to make to get his words out in a coherent form.

'Energy is the capacity to do work,' he started, confidently
enough. 'There are three kinds, mechanical, chemical, and
p-p-p-potential . . .'

'I suppose *p-p-p-potential* would be your favourite,' cut
in Mr Stroud with a sneer that looked as if it had been
etched into his face. 'If you define "potential" as "in the
future, with no present sign of activity".'

There was a mild giggle from Dick Prothero, the class
sycophant, and Mr Stroud glanced benignly at him.

'Well, is that all? Mechanical, chemical and p-p-p-
potential?' He mimicked Neil's stammer and stared at the
boy with an expression of overt disgust before addressing
the rest of the class. 'Anybody?'

'Thermal?' suggested Billy Wilson, sitting next to Neil,
hoping to get Stroud's malignant focus away from his
friend.

'Well, finally we have someone who pays attention during
my classes,' said Stroud, with an expression of bored
surprise. 'Yes, indeed, thermal energy, the energy of heat
and light, including the beneficent radiations from the sun
and other warm bodies . . .' He paused for a moment. 'We
shall ignore for a moment, no doubt to your deep distress,
other forms of energy such as electrical, nuclear, etcetera,
and concentrate on thermal energy . . .'

'I'd like to concentrate some thermal energy on him,'
muttered Neil, looking sideways at Billy. Stroud heard him
and, quick as a viper, turned, then very deliberately walked
down between the two rows of desks and stopped in front of

Neil. He paused, his eyes fixed on the boy with a vicious intensity.

'Stand up, scum!' he barked.

Neil, his face white, stood up.

'And what makes you, a day-boy, think you can interrupt my class at will?' he asked. 'Is it because your father is so far behind on the payment of your school fees, perhaps?'

Neil stood stone-still, his lower lip quivering in spite of himself.

'Well, aren't you going to answer? Are you proposing to compound insolence with that stubborn impertinence which you have no doubt inherited?'

Billy made a quick move to grab Neil's arm, which he was about to raise, and Morgan Stroud smiled.

'Now then, don't interfere, Wilson,' he said, quietly, but with a chilling intensity, not taking his eyes off Neil. 'I'll deal with you later. Meanwhile, if Mackay here wishes to strike me . . . Go ahead, boy, go ahead!' He stared at Neil, taunting, daring him. Neil didn't move, but his fingernails dug hard into his palms.

'We hear that your father is having some business problems, is that it?' went on Stroud, relentlessly. 'And perhaps he has these problems because he's like you.' He still didn't take his eyes off Neil's face; he was positively relishing the boy's humiliation. 'Mendel's laws of inheritance, as I'm sure you will agree, have a great deal of validity. Are you aware that stupidity is an inherited factor, recognisable by a low brow and small, ill-shaped head such as yours?'

There was a silence, a painful stillness in the class.

'Sit down, you . . . Darwinian reject!' said Stroud finally, and returned to the front of his class. 'Now, for those of you provided by nature with adequate neuronal equipment, let us get back to the mysteries of thermal energy . . .'

Stroud felt better now; the venting of his feelings on Neil Mackay had relieved some pent-up tension within him, and the rest of the class went smoothly enough, although he was aware of a simmering hatred emanating from the direction of Neil Mackay.

At this point Stroud had to refer to his notes. Recently he had been having headaches and some difficulty concentrating, and occasionally lost his place or the thread of an argument; he really would have to do something about it.

'Transfer of heat energy,' he said, almost talking to himself, then recovered his normal hectoring tone. 'You there, in the corner, what's your name, Drummond. How is thermal energy transmitted from one object to another?'

'Conduction?' asked Terry Drummond, a small, bright boy who blinked frequently behind his round National Health glasses.

'Good. Conduction is transfer of heat by direct contact, right, correct.' Stroud felt Neil Mackay's smouldering eyes fixed on him, and they were beginning to make him feel uncomfortable. 'Any other methods of heat transfer? Anyone? Mackay? You look surprised, as if a thought had somehow inadvertently entered your head . . . No?'

'Radiation,' said Neil, still looking at Stroud. 'Transfer of heat energy from a distance.'

'Very good!' said Stroud, oozing sarcasm. 'Can anybody give me an example?'

'The sun,' said Billy Wilson.

'Wonderful!' said Stroud. 'Maybe you two boys should form a travelling brains trust, touring Africa, perhaps. Just as long as it was far from these . . .' he looked around the cramped room with disdain, 'these hallowed halls, whose ancient traditions date back to, when was it, 1978?'

'How about psychic energy?' asked Neil, suddenly seeming to come to life. His eyes were glowing in a way Stroud had never seen before. 'Can one or more people concentrate enough energy from their minds to heat up an object? Even make it burst into flames? I read in a book that . . .'

'Of course not! Nonsense! Pure rubbish!' said Stroud, irritated at the intrusion of such an unscientific notion. 'This is a *physics* class we are conducting here, not some kind of . . . supernatural . . . seance!'

'But if it *can* happen, doesn't that bring it into the world of physics, of reality?' Neil Mackay was standing up now, and his voice was loud, with a strange, resonant quality to it, and no trace of stammer. Everyone there could feel the power, the energy radiating from him.

At that moment the bell rang for the end of the period, and the boys instantly poised themselves to leave the room, waiting for his word. Stroud looked at them with an expression of undisguised contempt.

'Saint Jude's . . .' he said slowly, his eyes moving from one boy to the next. 'I can see why your parents would send you to a school named after the patron saint of lost causes.'

He paused, still looking at them. 'Now get out,' he said. 'You all disgust me more than I can tell you.'

After the boys had gathered their books and left the classroom, Stroud felt suddenly tired, used up. Teaching was an exhausting business. Psychic energy, forsooth! Actually, he thought, I could use some of that myself. He looked at his watch and hesitated. There would be just time to go into Perth and see the doctor before his next class, which started in an hour. If there was a queue at the surgery, he'd ask to be seen first. After all, he had a job to do, unlike the layabouts and smelly women who normally frequented her surgery, with their hordes of dirty, snuffly, disgusting children . . .

Neil Mackay and his friend Billy Wilson walked to their next class and waited with the other dozen or so boys for the teacher to arrive. Billy felt anxious, sensing Neil's boiling rage. 'Don't pay any attention to him,' he said. 'Everybody knows what a pig he is . . .'

'It doesn't bother me,' said Neil, 'but it's going to upset my father.'

'Then don't tell him,' suggested Billy sensibly.

'We have a deal,' replied Neil slowly. 'We tell each other everything that happens, the good and the bad. We've done that ever since my mother died.'

'I'd still not tell him,' said Billy. 'My God, if it was *me*, my father would come to the school and kill Stroud with his bare hands.' Billy was exaggerating; his father, a distinguished actor and the most gentle of men, wouldn't have dreamt of taking direct action of that kind, however severe the provocation. But Neil's father was not gentle, not by any means. He was an ex-boxer, unsettled by a failing business, and saddled with a very short temper . . .

Two men stood at the window of the teachers' common room on the second floor.

'There goes that bastard Stroud, slipping off early,' said the younger one, a muscular, athletic-looking man with carefully styled hair. Without even realising he was doing it, he cracked the knuckles of his left hand, one after the other. The men were looking down at the portly, prematurely balding figure hurrying across the yard to the car park.

'Now then, George,' said the other, a sturdy, middle-aged man. 'It's really time you got over your resentment.' He puffed a great cloud of smoke from a well-worn cherrywood pipe. 'It's doing *him* no harm, but it's eating you up. Forget it; you're wasting your time and your energies.'

'It's easy for you to say, Angus,' replied George Elmslie. 'He didn't do it to you, and anyway you could leave here today and go and teach anywhere you wanted.' George looked over at Angus Townes. 'You know, it really beats me why you ever came to work in a rat-hole like this.'

Almost as if he sensed that he was being discussed, Morgan Stroud looked up at the window of the common room and saw the two men. For a moment a strange expression flickered over his face, an ugly combination of dislike and fear, but at that distance, no one could have told at which of the two men the look was directed.

Angus Townes and George Elmslie watched Stroud get into his car and start it, and their eyes followed as his dusty blue Ford Escort negotiated the sharp turn into the drive. The car vanished between the dark rhododendron bushes, one back wheel sliding momentarily off the narrow drive and raising a cloud of yellowish dust. Both men stood there as the dust slowly settled, but neither of them said anything; they were too deeply immersed in their own thoughts.

Chapter Two

When Jean Montrose got to the surgery that afternoon she found that her parking place had been taken by a blue Ford Escort, and she had to go over two blocks to Logie Crescent before she could find another. Most of her regular patients respected her need to park outside the surgery, as she occasionally had to drop everything and rush out for an emergency. Jean walked back, turned the corner into Williams Street, feeling oppressed and irritated by the dry, airless heat that had been hanging over the country for so long. She really needed to get more exercise, she thought; as usual she'd put on a few pounds when they were away in Tuscany, and as she was short it showed up immediately. All that good Italian food . . . And every year it was getting harder to lose it again.

The car was still there in her spot, and the shimmering heat over the bonnet showed that it hadn't been there very long.

At the door of the surgery, Jean turned and pushed it open with her back; both her hands were full, one with her little black bag, and the other with a cardboard box of NHS forms she was bringing back to the surgery.

'*Good* afternoon, Dr Jean,' said Eleanor, the secretary she shared with Helen Inkster, her partner. Eleanor looked up at the clock on the wall opposite her desk, and Jean felt a flicker of amused annoyance. Why did she always feel she had to answer to Eleanor?

'I had two extra calls,' she said, sounding apologetic in

spite of herself. 'And they both took longer than I expected.'

'Well, you have twelve people in there,' said Eleanor composedly. 'And half of them have been waiting over an hour.'

Jean put her things down on the desk and noticed a small hole in the left seam of her skirt. It wasn't even a tear, just a gap where two pieces of material met, nothing much: the thread had broken and run. She could fix it in a minute, just as soon as she *had* a minute . . .

Jean left the cardboard box on the desk; it was Eleanor's job to send the completed forms to the central office in Dundee.

'Would you like a cup of tea?' asked Eleanor as Jean opened the door to her office.

Jean nodded gratefully. 'Yes, and a couple of biscuits, if there are any, please. I didn't have much lunch.'

Jean decided to look into the waiting room first. It was really a shame to keep these poor folk waiting all this time. She opened the door; there was the usual odour of hot humanity, and all the eyes turned towards her.

'I'm sorry to keep you all waiting like this,' she said contritely. 'I was out on emergency calls; I came back as soon as I could.'

There was a general comforting murmur.

'That's a' right, Doctor. They needed you worse than us,' said Mrs Dornoch, an old lady who came to the surgery almost every week because of her unstable diabetes, and the others seemed to agree.

Somebody got up and came towards her, a rather fat young man, balding, with sweat showing in beads on his forehead. Jean recognised him; he was one of the school-masters out at St Jude's. Jean's practice had a package deal with the school's administration; she and Helen took care of all their personnel, teachers, pupils, coaches, together with the kitchen and other staff.

Jean had an excellent memory for names. She smiled. 'Well, Mr Stroud, can't you wait any longer? I shouldn't be more than forty minutes or so, unless you were the first in.'

Jean was very conscious that everybody was watching, and that there was an unusual tension in the air.

'I have to get back to the school,' he said in a high-pitched, aggressive voice. Jean got the impression that he had rehearsed his words. 'I have a class starting in exactly thirty-eight minutes, and I formally request to be seen first.'

There was a low murmur from the watching patients; they wanted to see how Dr Montrose would handle this arrogant fellow.

Jean looked around the room. Every eye was on her.

'Well, now,' she said, still smiling. 'How many people are here ahead of you?'

About nine or ten of the patients raised a hand, and Morgan Stroud made a movement of annoyance. 'These people . . . Do they have work to go to? I . . .'

'How long does it take you to drive to St Jude's?' she asked, nicely, not sounding as if she were interrupting, and just loudly enough for everybody to hear. 'Keeping to the speed limit, of course.' There was such a twinkle in her eyes that even Stroud hesitated, and smiled faintly. 'Twenty-two minutes . . .'

'Right,' said Jean, brisk again. She looked over the patients once more. 'I'll see Mrs Dornoch first, because she's needing some insulin, then Mr Grover, because I can see he's having pain in his leg ulcer . . .'

Mr Grover grinned; it sounded like a fair enough solution to him. '. . . And then I'll see you, Mr Stroud. Is that all right with everybody? We don't want all those boys up at St Jude's to tear the place apart because Mr Stroud's not there to keep them in order, right?'

There was another murmur of reluctant approval; the wee doc had managed the situation without ruffling too many feathers. Ten minutes later, a tight-lipped Eleanor told Mr Stroud to go through into the Doctor's room. Jean looked up at him from her chair, and her smile was gone.

'Well, Mr Morgan, you'd better be deathly ill, after that disturbance you caused out there,' she said. Jean was not amused; if everybody insisted on being first, it would cause chaos, and she liked things to be neat, tidy, and well regulated.

'I've been getting headaches,' he said. 'Sudden, like needles sticking in my head . . . Just for the last few weeks, usually worse when I'm ready to go to bed. And I'm having trouble concentrating.'

Jean took his blood-pressure and pulse. They were normal. She listened to his chest, but everything sounded the way it was supposed to. She picked up her ophthalmoscope and drew the curtains. 'Sit down there,' she said, 'and focus on the letter "A" on the chart on the back of the door.' She examined the back of his eyes carefully, checking for narrowing or pinching of the bloodvessels on the retina, then sat back on the examination table and watched Stroud thoughtfully for a moment. 'Everything looks fine to me,' she said, then looked at her watch. 'You're going to have to get back to the school now. Take a couple of aspirins for your headaches, and if they aren't any better in a week, come back and we'll go into it more thoroughly. But don't expect to be seen out of turn again, all right?'

Just over an hour later, after dealing with her last patient, Jean went in to see Helen Inkster, whose office was on the opposite side of the waiting room. Helen had just come in, although it was officially her afternoon off.

Jean told her about Morgan Stroud, and how he'd wanted to jump the queue. Helen shook her head when she heard how Jean had handled the problem. 'I'd have just let him wait,' she said. 'Just because he's aggressive and thinks everybody has to kow-tow to him because he's a teacher at a private school . . . Anyway, what was the matter with him, that he needed you to see him so urgently?'

Jean hesitated for a moment, and Helen's eyebrows went up. 'Something . . . private?'

'No, certainly not!' said Jean with some asperity. 'He was having headaches . . .' She hesitated again. 'You know how people describe headaches – throbbing, or like a band around their head, or something of the kind . . . Well, he said it was like needles sticking into his head. Have you ever heard a description like that before?'

'Well, I don't know . . . people often describe their symptoms in odd ways,' replied Helen, with a trace of a grin. 'There was this lady I saw last week. She said her pain felt like a camel sitting on her chest. Not a horse, or even a donkey, but a camel . . .'

'Have you seen Morgan Stroud? I mean in the surgery? I really don't like to say it, but there's something . . . well, dislikeable about him.' Jean blushed. 'Oh dear, I shouldn't be saying things like that. He's never been anything but polite to me.'

Helen stood up. She was wearing her thick walking shoes, and Jean knew she was going to walk around the North Inch, the big, grassy park on the West bank of the Tay, beyond the old bridge. Every Wednesday afternoon Helen could be seen striding along the riverside path, whatever the weather. She made an impressive and determined figure, swinging her walking stick in a way that made passing joggers and strollers give her plenty of room. Sometimes she took Red, her Irish setter; he'd jump out of the car, chase a few pigeons, to show he could catch them if he wanted to, before settling down to a dignified trot by her side.

'Well, I'm off to the Inch,' said Helen. 'I'll see you in the morning.'

'Fine,' said Jean. 'And I'm off to the nursing homes. I have two at The Elms, old Mrs McDonald and Major Buckley, and then I need to see that poor girl at Seacrest.'

'You mean Deirdre Townes?' Helen stopped on her way

to the door and turned to face Jean. 'Isn't there any way we can get her out of there? The poor kid, only eighteen years old, with all those senile old people around her . . .'

'Helen,' said Jean firmly. 'Deirdre can't talk, and as far as I can tell, can't understand who she is or where she is. They take good care of her there, and there's simply no other place for her.'

'Isn't there any kind of rehab unit that she could go to? It's such a tragedy . . .' Helen's homely face was the picture of sympathy.

'Her father's taken her everywhere. She spent some time at the Cambridge plastic surgery unit when her father was teaching there, and they did the best they could. There was too much tissue lost, they said.'

'Well, it's a sad thing,' said Helen, opening the door. 'In this day and age . . .'

Billy Wilson was sitting on his narrow bunk bed, bending forward so as not to bump his head on the bunk above. The boy who owned the top bunk, Dick Prothero, was not to be trusted and had been sent packing. Neil Mackay, still smarting from his encounter with Mr Stroud, stood with his back to the door.

'Why doesn't your father take you out of this place?' asked Billy. 'Are the state schools so bad around here?'

'It's not that,' said Neil, hesitating. 'They're actually quite good. It's just that he thinks that private schools . . . well, that they give you something . . . something you can't get at the local schools.'

'Well, I could understand if it was Eton, or Harrow, or even Gordonstoun, but here?'

'Dad was brought up in Glasgow, and he's always had that accent, and it makes him furious. He wants me to have a cultured voice, he says.'

'Why didn't he just send you for elocution lessons or something?'

'Why don't you ask him yourself?' said Neil, tiring of the conversation. 'By the way, you and Terry are invited over for dinner tonight, did I tell you?'

'No, you didn't,' said Billy, scrambling to his feet. 'Are we going to do some magic after dinner?'

'Yes we are, Billy. And for what we're going to do, the three of us are going to have to concentrate like we've never concentrated in our lives before.' He put a hand on Billy's shoulder, and his intensity made Billy flinch. 'Billy, this time, I'm really serious.'

Chapter Three

It was late, almost seven o'clock, by the time Jean finished seeing her nursing home patients, and as always after seeing Deirdre, she felt sick and thoroughly wretched. But life goes on, she said to herself, and mentally braced her shoulders and put it behind her. If she let her patients' problems get to her she would crack up and not be any use to anyone.

Let's see, she thought, do I need to get anything on the way home? She decided against doing any shopping now; for one thing it was almost seven, and most places would be closed. Anyway, the girls would have made the dinner, or so Jean fervently hoped; Steven liked to eat at seven, prompt.

She drove her little white Renault down South Street towards the Queen's bridge; even at this late hour, it was still hot enough for her to need all the windows open. Jean didn't remember weather like this; it had been so hot and dry that it was getting on everybody's nerves. Even normally placid and friendly people like old Mrs Farquarson, their next-door neighbour, were getting bad tempered and irritable (she had thrown some misdelivered post over the front fence on to Jean's doorstep) and tempers around town flared without provocation, resulting in a spate of assaults and other violent crimes. The *Perth Courier and Advertiser* had said that it was the longest spell of hot weather on record, and showed no signs of breaking. Steven said it was due to a stationary anticyclone, but declined to discuss the matter further when Lisbie and Fiona asked him what that meant.

Even South Street looked limp and exhausted; the awning outside Kennaway's Bakery sagged dispiritedly, and a stray dog crossed the street in front of her, panting, searching for a cool place to lie down. Looking back from the bridge, Jean could see the grass of the North Inch, dry and yellow for the first time she could remember.

After the bridge, she turned left past Bridgend, then right at the lights, up Argyll Crescent past the sturdy sandstone semidetached houses with their neat front gardens, to the top of the hill, to number 12, the house she and Steven had chosen when they first came to Perth fifteen years before. At the time, it had been the last house on the row, and still was. Beyond the house was a field where Mr Forrest kept a small flock of border sheep; the grass was dry as tinder, and for weeks now he'd had to bring water and hay for them. Half a dozen of the sheep were by the gate, a couple with half-grown lambs; they watched Jean park the car behind Steven's Rover.

Even the roses in the front garden were drooping from the heat.

The front door was open to let some air into the house. 'Hello!' Jean cried in the hall. She put her bag down on the hall chair and looked for messages on the pink pad by the phone.

'Mum?' It was Lisbie's voice, coming from the direction of the living room. They were probably all there, watching the news on television.

'God, I hope they're not waiting for me to make dinner,' thought Jean. She opened the door. Steven was in the green easy chair opposite the TV; that was his chair when he was home. Lisbie was in her favourite position, flat on the floor, facing the television, chin cupped in her hands, and Fiona was sitting on the old wing chair, the beige one that had belonged to Jean's mother. She was sewing a strap on a rather frilly bra, and watching the news with one eye.

'Fiona did the fish and I did the vegetables,' said Lisbie.

'I said we should have a salad because it's so hot, but who ever listens to me?'

'There's a big forest fire burning up by Crieff,' said Steven, getting out of his chair. 'They say everything's so dry, anything could have started it, lightning maybe, or somebody's cigarette.' He went over to Jean and kissed her on the cheek. 'You smell of nursing homes,' he said, but not unkindly. 'Let's have dinner. OK, girls, let's get going!'

Fiona and Lisbie got up slowly, Fiona saying they hadn't seen the local news, but their complaints were more out of habit than from feeling they were being imposed upon.

The routine in the Montrose household was that whoever made the main dish put it on the trivet in front of Steven, who then served everyone. Fiona positioned the steaming platter, and took the glass lid off.

'What is it?' asked Steven, as usual.

'Oh Dad, you know perfectly well what it is!' said Fiona. 'You were with me when I bought it.'

'Well, you can tell *me*,' said Jean, passing the plates, '*I* wasn't there.'

'It's halibut, Mum,' said Fiona, and Lisbie groaned. 'God, halibut *again*!'

'Now look here, young lady,' said Steven sternly. 'Halibut is a fine, nutritious fish; do you ever think of the dangers the fishermen run to bring this to you? If only . . .' Steven saw the two girls grinning across the table at each other and stopped speaking abruptly. Sometimes he had the feeling they were just leading him on.

'How were things at the glass works today?' asked Jean quickly, seeing what was going on, and anxious to avoid any potential row.

'Not great,' said Steven, still eyeing the girls with some disfavour. 'It was so hot I almost had to shut the place down. Even in the office, it was almost unbearable. Angela, you know, the book-keeper, well, she fainted and had to go home. You'd think we were in the Sahara, or something. I've never seen anything like it.'

'It's the Russians, with all the heat from their nuclear plants,' said Lisbie.

'More likely the Brazilians,' added Fiona, not to be outdone. 'Cutting down all the rain forests. I saw a programme . . .'

'Eat your fish, dear,' said Jean. 'Your father likes a bit of peace and quiet after working all day long.'

'Well, I was working too,' said Fiona indignantly. 'And I had a terrible day. Mr Pratt, the one in sales, tried to put his hands up my skirt when I was up a ladder, getting a box down . . .'

'Come on, Fiona,' said Lisbie, 'you loved every second of it. I know about you and Mr Pratt!'

A piece of buttered bread flew across the table and landed in Lisbie's fish.

Steven put down his knife and fork, and was about to yell at the girls when Jean caught his eye. In spite of himself, he couldn't stay serious, as if Jean had *forced* him to see the humour of the situation, and he grinned momentarily. That defused the tension, and everybody laughed.

After that, Fiona and Lisbie calmed down, and Jean asked Steven about the big order he'd had recently from the States. It was for reproduction Victorian coloured glass paperweights which had done very well with the local tourists.

'Do you make crystal balls?' asked Fiona suddenly. 'I mean at the glass works.' Lisbie giggled, and Steven looked across the table, surprised. 'Crystal balls . . . You mean the kind fortune-tellers use?'

'Yes, you know, for telling the future, who you're going to marry, stuff like that.'

'No, we don't, but there's no reason why we shouldn't, if there was a demand for them. Why?'

Fiona was about to answer, but suddenly she felt Lisbie's eyes boring into her. 'Nothing,' she said. 'I just wondered.'

Steven shook his head and looked at Jean. Those kids . . .

'I don't care,' said Lisbie in the stubborn voice that always infuriated her older sister. After dinner they had gone down to Fiona's room in the basement.

'But he's *two years* younger than you,' insisted Fiona. 'When did you get into baby-snatching?'

'He's no baby, let me tell you,' said Lisbie, with a superior lift of her nose. 'He's really *old* for sixteen.'

'For God's sake, Lisbie, he's still at *school*. What would your lawyer friends in the office think? Does he still wear shorts and a little cap?'

Lisbie, furious, jumped on her, and the bed moved, bumping into the standard lamp which teetered and then fell over with a crash.

There was the noise of a chair being pushed back upstairs, and Steven's voice came to them from the top of the stairs. 'What the devil are you two girls doing down there?'

'Nothing, Dad,' replied Fiona. 'Lisbie just sneezed.' For some reason, that answer made both the girls laugh so hard they clung to each other, hardly able to breathe. The door at the top of the stairs slammed, and silence reigned in the house once more.

Usually the girls did the dishes in the tiny kitchen, but Jean was feeling guilty about having left them to make the dinner, so this time she washed up herself, without drawing too many complaints from either Lisbie or Fiona. Steven stood sideways in the doorway talking to her, one hand up on the lintel. He was looking tired, and older than his fifty-odd years.

'I don't know,' he was saying. 'We haven't been back a month from Tuscany, and I feel as if we'd never been away.'

'I know it,' said Jean. 'And it's twice as hot here as it was there, and we went to get some sun, remember?'

'They were talking at the works about the strange things that are going on with the heat,' said Steven. 'Here, give me a dishtowel, I'll dry up.'

Jean passed one over. 'What sort of things?'

'I don't know; silly sort of things, like Gus's cat that left home for the first time a week ago and never came back, and Angela's boyfriend who wrecked her flat . . .' Steven examined a spoon critically, and returned it for reprocessing. 'It's actually more of a feeling that there's something in the air, something . . . I don't know, but I'll be glad when the weather breaks and things get back to normal.'

'Come on, Steven,' said Jean sensibly. 'That's what everybody's doing, blaming everything on the heat.' She handed him the rewashed spoon. 'Will that pass your inspection, Sir?'

Steven flicked at her posterior with his teatowel. 'A little less impertinence in the ranks,' he said, then suddenly he remembered. 'Jean, I forgot to tell you! We've been put up for an award!' he said, his voice alive with excitement. 'The Queen's Award for Industry. I got a letter today from the Secretary of State for Scotland . . .'

Jean wiped her hands on her apron and put her arms around him. 'Steven, why didn't you tell me?' Her eyes were shining with pleasure.

'I just did,' he murmured, putting his hands around Jean's waist.

'That's marvellous.' Jean was so excited she wanted to do something to celebrate, but Steven, cautious as ever, said they would celebrate as soon as they had something definite to celebrate, but not before. Meanwhile Jean wasn't to breathe a word of it to anyone.

It wasn't until after they'd gone to bed and Steven had fallen asleep that Jean's mind returned to her patients. Always, around this time, she thought about the patients she'd seen earlier that day, especially the ones who had some major ongoing problems, or where the diagnosis wasn't entirely clear.

'I've been getting headaches,' Morgan Stroud had said, 'sudden, like needles sticking in my head . . .' But Jean hadn't been able to find anything the matter with him. Not *anything*, and it really bothered her.

Chapter Four

The next morning, Jean got up early as usual. Ever since her medical student days she had been able to set her internal alarm clock, and could wake up within a minute or two of the desired time.

She got out of bed carefully, although she knew that nothing short of an explosion would waken Steven at this hour. As manager and part-owner of the Scone Glass Works, he could get to his office when he wanted, and that was usually around nine o'clock. For Jean it was different, and she'd worked out a routine over the years that rarely varied. She padded out into the bathroom, holding up her pyjama bottoms; the elastic had stretched and died, probably from the heat of repeated launderings. For running repairs of this kind, Jean waited until there was a big enough backlog, then she'd get them all together and do everything at once. Jean noticed some sweat on her forehead; it had been hot all through the night, and Steven had pushed all the bedclothes off himself, moving restlessly around until about three, something he didn't usually do. In spite of all his pleasure at being put up for an award, Steven worried a lot about his work; his biggest furnace was out of commission, and that would cause problems filling the large order he'd just received from the States. And he needed that order; unlike mass-produced ware, the glass from the Scone Works was hand-made, hand-shaped and blown by skilled artisans, and the whole operation was very expensive to run.

Jean didn't spend long in the bathroom; life was too short to be fussing with makeup. The house was silent and still when she went downstairs, carefully avoiding the creaky place on the second step from the top. She opened the back door to let in the cat, then she put on the kettle for a quick cup of tea. Although Steven had bought her a microwave the Christmas before, Jean still preferred to make it the old way. The tea seemed to taste better, and somehow it made a more satisfactory start to the day, with the sensible comforts of the old china teapot and its brown knitted cosy. Fulfilling the routine of heating the teapot with boiling water, then putting in the dry tea, with its dusty, aromatic smell and crunchy texture, infusing it with enough water to cover the bottom of the pot, letting it sit for exactly three minutes before putting in the rest of the water . . . All these familiar actions were necessary to start Jean's day off right. It was like a prayer.

The bathroom door upstairs opened and then closed. That had to be Lisbie, because Fiona hadn't appeared from the basement. Jean glanced up at the old, square-faced clock on the kitchen wall. It was time for Fiona to get up; she was a trainee manager for one of the big department stores, and today she was supposed to go to the Dundee branch to learn about personnel management.

At that moment, Fiona appeared, looking as if she'd slept in a haystack. Her black hair was sticking up all over her head, and there were dark rings around her eyes. Fiona always looked like this first thing in the morning, and every time, Jean was amazed at the transformation which would occur in the next thirty minutes, when Fiona would emerge from the bathroom as from a chrysalis, elegant in her grey business suit, hair in an immaculate short cut around her pretty, pixie-ish face.

The phone rang in the hall just as Jean was pouring out her tea, so Fiona went to answer it. She came back a moment later, her eyes shining. 'It's my sweetheart,' she said. 'Only it's you he wants to speak to, unfortunately.'

Jean put down her cup, and went into the hall, closely followed by Fiona, who didn't want to miss a word of the conversation. She watched her mother's face for some indication of what they were talking about. Detective Inspector Douglas Niven called her mother from time to time, mostly about dull enough things, but sometimes when something really exciting was going on.

'Oh my God,' said Jean, suddenly clutching tightly on to the phone. Fiona hopped up and down, desperate to hear more. Jean's mouth opened slowly, and a little shiver went through her entire body, in spite of the heat that was already building up inside the house.

'Where?' Jean wrote down an address on the pad by the phone. 'Have you told Dr Anderson?' Malcolm Anderson was the pathologist at the hospital and also the local police surgeon.

'Doug, there's a few things I *must* do first, like get dressed, then I'll come over. I'll be as quick as I can.'

Fiona saw that her mother's hand was shaking when she put the phone down.

'Mum, what's happening? Did he ask how I was?'

'No, Fiona, he didn't.' Fiona now saw the concern which had spread across her mother's face like a cloud. 'There's been some sort of an accident, that's all.'

Jean dressed fast, her mind in a whirl. The man had seemed perfectly all right yesterday, except for those headaches, which probably didn't mean anything; lots of people got headaches from stress and other things that were difficult to measure or evaluate. Whatever could have happened?

She left in such a rush that she forgot to wake Steven, and realised it only after she'd climbed into her car and set off. A familiar wave of guilt hit her again. Poor Steven! He always seemed to get taken care of last. You'd better watch out, said a quiet inner voice as she drove slowly down Argyll

Crescent. Have you forgotten what happened one other time, not even that long ago?

The address Inspector Douglas Niven had given Jean was luckily not too far away, on Pitcullen Lane, in a pleasant new development near the lower slopes of Kinnoull Hill. Jean knew the area; she had several patients who lived in that neighbourhood. At East Bridge Street she turned left, and went up Lochie Brae, a short but steep hill which could get very slippery and dangerous in winter. Morgan Stroud's house was easy to find because of the number of police vehicles outside. Looking in the rear view mirror, Jean saw a small van with two slender radio antennae on the roof following her. She sighed. That would be the advance crew from Grampian Television – Jean had heard that they listened in on the police and fire brigade frequencies, so they could get to an interesting story almost as soon as the police themselves. If it turned out to be something important, they would then call on their radio for the mobile TV team, which used a much larger truck.

Jean parked beyond the police and emergency vehicles, remembering to leave the sunroof partly open to let the hot air rise out of the car, and walked back towards the house. The TV van was double-parked right outside the front door of the house, and the two reporters, a man and a woman, were being kept at bay by Constable Jamieson from the local police; Jean knew him quite well. Nobody paid much attention to Jean, although she moved along deceptively fast; short and a tiny bit dumpy, certainly not dressed to attract attention, Jean could have passed for one of the neighbourhood ladies going down the road to the Bridgend Bakery for her morning butteries and rolls.

There was another uniformed policeman standing on the top step in front of the closed door, a man she didn't know, and he watched her as she walked with a determined step up to him. From the bottom step, he looked about seven feet tall to Jean. 'Well, Madam?' he asked, looking down at her as if from the heights of Mount Olympus.

'I'm Dr Montrose,' said Jean rather timidly, overawed by his size. 'Inspector Niven asked me to come over . . .'

At the mention of her name, the policeman moved with surprising alacrity. 'He's expecting you, Dr Montrose,' he said, and rang the doorbell. A few moments later Douglas Niven came to the door, looked through the window at the side, then opened it. He looked grey, as if he were about to be sick.

'Come on in, Jean,' was all he said. The first thing that struck Jean inside the house was the smell, which got stronger as they went along the narrow corridor to the living room, at the back of the house, facing the small garden. The smell was sweetish, acrid, like burned fat, but there was a suggestion of something else, another odour, and the hairs on the back of Jean's neck bristled. Could it be the pungent smell of ozone, the gas which was produced where lightning struck? Feeling suddenly sick to her stomach, Jean followed Douglas through the open door into the living room. Here the smell was stronger, almost unbearable, and now mixed with the odour of burned flesh and bone. There were several people in the room; the forensic team, missing only Dr Anderson who, Doug had told Jean earlier, was on his way in from Glasgow. There was the photographer, a young woman with a short skirt and long straight blond hair, taking Polaroid pictures from every conceivable angle. Two plain-clothes policemen had set out a grid of orange tape criss-crossing the room, and were laboriously marking down the location of all the items in each square. Jean's first thought, looking at the photographer, was that she'd have a lot of trouble getting the smell out of her hair when she washed it later.

Unwillingly, Jean turned her eyes to what was on the floor, and couldn't help letting out a gasp, although she put her hand quickly up to her mouth. Lying in the middle of the floor was a mass of charred material, some fragments of clothing, mostly burned beyond recognition. The only thing that identified the remains as human were two feet, in black, well-polished shoes and socks, the lower legs and trousers intact up to halfway to the knees, where they abruptly became unrecognisable black char. And then Jean saw the hands, apparently normal, still clutching at the carpet. With a sense of utter horror, Jean saw that they too were attached to normal looking forearms, which turned into black unrecognisably burned flesh and bone somewhere about the elbow. The centre part of the body was charred beyond any kind of recognition, and the obviously intense heat had also charred the carpet and the wooden floor beneath. Feeling suddenly very sick, Jean turned away. Then she saw Constable Jamieson come in, and that gave her courage. Jean would rather have died than have him detect any kind of weakness in her.

'I've never seen anything like this in my life before,' Jean said to Douglas, trying to keep the tremor out of her voice. Douglas put a reassuring hand on her arm although he was feeling pretty sick himself. He'd come across a few truly dreadful things in his time, but this one was completely outside his experience. And he was feeling concerned and protective towards Jean; he could see how badly she was taking this.

'Jean I'm really sorry to call you for . . . such a thing,' he said quietly, 'but I know you take care of the St Jude's people, and I thought maybe you could help us.'

Jean took a deep breath, then regretted it. She looked around the room. The body was lying approximately in the middle of the floor, and the only object near it was a chair with some papers strewn on it. She pointed wordlessly at them.

'They're no help,' he said. 'They're school essay papers he must have brought home to correct . . .'

'That's not what I mean,' said Jean, finally regaining the use of her voice. 'Douglas, how is it they're not even singed?'

Now it was the turn of Douglas's neck hairs to rise. He'd noticed the papers, of course, and the fact that they were intact, but he hadn't put it together in quite the way Jean had.

'Yes, aye . . .' he said, quickly looking around again. 'You're right. And nothing else seems to be touched . . .' In fact, there was no sign of fire damage anywhere else. The curtains in front of the window on to the garden were untouched, although Jean noticed a yellowish film on the window glass, the wallpaper and other surfaces. The only other window, which faced the garden wall and the neighbour's house, was open just a few inches at the top.

'There's smoke on the wall outside,' said Douglas, back to his normal Glaswegian accent. 'Above the window, like from a house fire. Mrs Rankine, the neighbour who lives over on that side, saw it first thing this morning, tried to get Mr Stroud on the phone, and when he didn't answer, that's when she called us . . .' Douglas hesitated, and Jean could sense the intensity of his discomfort. 'This house is alive with burglar alarms,' he said slowly. 'Automatic locks on the doors, sensors on the windows, doors, under the carpet . . . We set off all the alarms when we came in here . . .' Douglas was really rattled; he was looking at Jean with a strange expression, as if asking her, please, Jean, find a rational answer to this ghastly business, because I can't believe there's any supernatural element in this case . . . unless I'm absolutely compelled to.

Jean forced herself to bend down and examine the unrecognisably damaged body; from the closer position she could see some of the charred bones in the arm, the blackened skull and jawbone, but that was about all. The overwhelming impression was that Mr Stroud, if indeed it was he, had been subjected to some source of unbelievable heat, enough to entirely destroy the centre, the living core of his body. Jean had worked in a hospital burn unit for several months, had seen severely burned bodies pulled out of house fires, but nothing, ever, even close to this.

'Are you sure who . . . that is?' she asked Douglas, indicating the remains.

'I was hoping you might be able to identify Stroud from the hands, maybe, or the feet, Jean. There's a ring on the third finger of his left hand . . . Do you know if he happened to be married?'

'I'd have to check the records to be certain, but I don't think so,' replied Jean, trying to remember if she'd seen him wearing the ring at the surgery the day before.

At that moment, there was a noise at the door, and Jean and Douglas turned to see the large figure of Dr Malcolm Anderson approaching, sweating heavily in a lightweight suit. He nodded a brisk hello to the forensic staff, who had gratefully withdrawn to the furthest corner of the room when Jean appeared, and his face took on an expression of growing incredulity as he came towards the remains on the floor.

'Jesus God, quine,' he said to Jean in a startled voice, 'what in the name of heaven happened here?' Jean shook her head and pointed to Douglas, who gave him the essentials of the story.

Jean could see the growing excitement in Malcolm's eyes as he listened. He fell on his knees and examined the charred body, paying particular attention to the unburned parts of the arms and legs, and the sudden contrast between the charred, unrecognizable area and the weirdly normal looking hands and feet.

While he was doing this, Jean walked round the room, stepping over the grid of coloured tape, memorizing every detail, the position of every piece of furniture, every curtain, book and lamp. The strange thing was that there was nothing close to the body which could have set it on fire, no electric heater, no fire, no gas stove. There was a big, old-fashioned wall mirror with an ornate gilt frame leaning against the wall near the door. It looked quite out of place, and Jean wondered briefly why it was there. Jean went over to the chair and looked at the essay papers. Those poor kids, she thought, they'll never know whether they did well or not; the papers will be gathered up and put in a brown manila envelope and sealed for evidence; by the time they get them back they'll be out in the world, earning a living or at university . . . Jean glanced at the top paper, and to her surprise saw the neatly written name of Neil Mackay, the boy whom Lisbie had recently been seeing, much to the amusement of her sister and friends. Jean had not met him yet, but she was so taken aback at the sight of Neil's name that she barely noticed Dr Anderson creakily getting to his feet. But she certainly paid attention when he came over and said to her, in a voice of unaccustomed awe, 'Quine, this is without doubt a case of spontaneous human combustion. This is my first case, and the first one I know of in this area; I've heard of it, read a few things about the condition, but, believe me, I never in my life expected to see one.'

Chapter Five

Jean's voice was apologetic; and in fact she was feeling thoroughly embarrassed. 'I can't imagine how I didn't notice,' she told Douglas Niven when he called her at the surgery later that day. 'Yes, he was married, and the wife's name is Renée. She's one of our patients too, lives at a different address, so I assume they were separated . . .' Jean was using Eleanor's phone; Eleanor, as usual, was making no attempt to disguise her interest in the conversation, and that irritated Jean. She tried looking sternly at her, but it had not the slightest effect.

Jean turned the file card around in her hand. 'She's still listed as the next of kin. Her address here is 55 Don Street, Flat 4. Now that was a year ago. Maybe she's moved, I don't know.' Jean paused for a second. 'Not quite as nice a part of town as where *he* lived, is it?'

Douglas said something Eleanor couldn't hear, although she was stretching her head as far across the desk as she could.

'Yes, I know he has a sister,' replied Jean. 'Her name's Gwen, she's on our NHS list.' She was certain that neither one had ever spoken to her about the other, but it was stupid of her not to have mentioned it to Douglas. She had been so upset with the finding of Morgan Stroud's body that she hadn't even thought of it. Poor Gwen! She was on their list of patients, and occasionally came in to the surgery. Gwen Stroud was pretty well known around Perth, by the way she swept through the streets with that long, intense

stride, always in a tattered brown skirt that trailed around
her ankles, and always with a black, soft-covered bible
clasped in her rough, reddened fingers. Children sometimes
followed her, shouting, and she'd turn and shout right back
at them. Gwen was a tough, rather frightening young
woman, but thought locally to have a kind heart; it was
rumoured that she sometimes took care of sick people and
brought them little gifts, bunches of wild flowers, or fruit
from the hedgerows she'd gathered herself. Jean didn't
envy Doug Niven; he would certainly have to interview
Gwen Stroud concerning her brother, and that would be
quite an undertaking in its own right.

Jean had gone home as soon as she could decently leave
the scene of the incineration, but felt guilty about abandon-
ing Douglas, Malcolm Anderson and the other workers
who still had a job to do there, and who couldn't get away.
Not that most of them seemed to mind too much; it was a
clean enough situation, without blood or loose body parts.
It was just that dreadful smell.

Jean showered for longer than she could remember, and
even then she still felt contaminated – her hair felt as if it
had been permanently impregnated with the odour of that
awful house. When she finally got back to the office, she
watched to see if Eleanor or Helen picked up the smell of it
on her. But they were far more interested in hearing about
Morgan Stroud. Eleanor of course was panting for news
and made no bones about it. Helen, nice, discreet Helen
waited and said nothing. Jean finished her work and finally,
when she was about ready to go home, brought herself to
talk about it with Helen.

'Damn it, girl, you've had me bursting with curiosity all
day,' grumbled Helen in that deep voice of hers. They were
in Helen's office, with the door shut. 'That was the man
who came in yesterday with headaches, wasn't it?'

Jean nodded miserably. All day she'd been trying to work
out if she'd missed something, something that could have

warned her of today's tragedy. She felt such a weight of guilt about it; surely there would have been some way to tell that something dreadful was about to happen to him. And of course, she *had* missed so many things she should have picked up on, like his wedding ring, the fact that he had a wife she knew nothing about, and of course his sister, Gwen . . .

'Helen,' said Jean, very quietly and humbly. 'I don't suppose you ever feel the way I'm feeling right now, because there's no reason why you should . . .' Jean paused and looked at her friend's honest, direct face; she felt close to tears.

'Like what? Are you having hot flushes or something?'

'No . . . I tell you, Helen, sometimes I feel so useless, so . . . incompetent. I miss things *all the time*, things that I'm sure any normally observant doctor would pick up instantly. Helen, I feel I'm letting you down – I'm not up to your standards . . .'

To Helen's total astonishment, she could see tears in Jean's eyes.

'I've never heard such damn' rubbish in my life,' said Helen, in a very firm voice. 'Take a hold of yourself, Jean. I'm not going to start telling you how wonderful you are, because that's not my style, but I will tell you one thing.'

Jean, overwhelmed by her feeling of inadequacy, gulped, looked up at her, and waited. This would be a good opportunity for Helen to tell her about all her deficiencies, all the things about Jean that had disappointed her over the years. She cringed, waiting for the blow.

Helen looked at her for a few moments, struggling with a number of emotions of her own. 'I'll tell you this, Jean Montrose, and this is all I'm going to tell you, but if I had my pick of anybody in the entire world to be my partner, I'd still take *you*, so there!'

Suddenly feeling embarrassed herself, Helen got up and walked over to the filing cabinet. 'And as for missing things

. . . You miss less, in your own quiet way, than anybody I
ever met.' Her face broke out into her familiar open, honest
smile. 'Now we've got that little matter out of the way, did
you hear what was on the news at one?' she asked. 'Aside
from your . . . case, there was a car that went up in flames
on the Dundee Road this morning, and a man and his dog
were burned to death inside it. There's another forest fire
out of control up near Glen Rothes, and two kids were
pulled out of a house here in town early this morning just
in time; they were lucky; they just suffered some smoke
inhalation.'

Helen's face was full of concern. 'Maybe it's all coincidence,' she said, 'but I've lived here these many years, Jean,
and aside from this heat, and I've never seen anything like
that either, I get this strange feeling that there are things
going on in this town that I truly don't understand . . .'

Jean looked up at her in astonishment; Helen was absolutely the last person she would have expected to talk in this
way. For Helen, for good old solid commonsense Helen
Inkster, who had as much contempt for the supernatural as
anybody Jean had ever met, to suggest, even in this roundabout way that some influence, something beyond the
ordinary was at work, that the town was in the throes of
some kind of fire epidemic . . .

Thinking about it, Jean felt the hairs on the back of her
neck crawling again, just as they had when she was looking
at the mortal remains of Morgan Stroud.

Back at Pitcullen Lane, after all the photographs had been
taken, after the floor had been swept with a high-powered
vacuum cleaner for minute fragments of clothing, hairs and
other material, and specimens of the charred clothing put
into special containers for testing for petrol and other
possible inflammatory agents, Dr Anderson and Douglas
Niven finally gave the order for the remains of the body to
be removed to the police mortuary. All that was left now

was an irregular black hole in the middle of the floor, with ragged, charred edges of carpet. Even the floorboards had been charred and blackened.

'I don't see how the whole place didn't go up in flames,' said Douglas, eyeing Dr Anderson as he locked the padlock on the outside door. 'The heat focused on that body must have been incredible.'

But Anderson didn't seem to be listening. 'There was some story about a calf that was found incinerated like that in its byre, just a week or two ago,' he said, almost talking to himself. 'And that wasna too far fae here, out a few miles beyond the Lossie Estate . . .'

'Well, what was supposed to be the cause of that?' asked Douglas.

Dr Anderson looked uncomfortable. 'I didn't see the creature mysel',' he said. 'And you know how folks talk when something like that happens . . .'

Douglas gave a little snort. 'I can guess what they said.' He grinned suddenly. 'I bet they said it was black magic, or some stuff like that.' He laughed disbelievingly, and looked sideways at Anderson as they walked over towards their cars, which were both parked on the other side of the street.

To his surprise, Dr Anderson stopped, and turned to face him squarely. 'You're quite right,' he said. His usual jovial expression had been replaced by one of serious concern. 'That's exactly what they're talking about, black magic. Not that I believe a word of it,' he went on quickly. 'But certainly, in this case . . .' he pointed a thumb back to the house, 'you'll admit that there's not very much else to go on, is there, especially with all thae burglar alarms and all?'

'What was it you said to Jean Montrose?' asked Doug, his hand on the door of his car. 'Spontaneous something or other?'

'Spontaneous human combustion,' replied Anderson. 'It's supposed to occur when the fuel in the human body is suddenly ignited . . .'

'What fuel are you talking about?' asked Douglas, his Glasgow accent suddenly becoming strong. 'I've never heard of . . .'

'Fat mostly,' said Dr Anderson. 'But there's methane, an explosive gas found in the bowel, and then there's quite a bit of phosphorus distributed in the body . . .' He paused for a second, doing some calculations in his head. 'Actually,' he said, in a tone of voice that astonished Doug, 'there's as much potential energy in a human body as in a briefcase full of TNT.'

Doug's mouth opened slowly in shock as he watched Dr Anderson go slowly and thoughtfully back to his car, then he shook his head; he'd never come across a case anything like this either, or even heard of such a thing, but until they could prove all this stuff about combustion, he was going to treat this as a case of suspicious death, probably murder. There certainly didn't seem to be any way that the man Stroud could have inflicted such injuries on himself; Douglas and his team had spent over an hour searching for matches, a lighter, an electric fixture such as a radiator; they even checked the house for petrol, lighter fluid and paint thinner, anything that could have started a fire, but they had found nothing. Absolutely nothing.

Inside his car it was so hot that it was difficult to breathe, and Doug took off his jacket and drove back to the police station in his shirt-sleeves, feeling thankful he wasn't in the uniform branch. His radio crackled; there had been a fire in the prison; not a big one, and it had been put out quite quickly. There was no indication of how it had started.

Once he was away from Pitcullen Lane, his mind seemed to clear; maybe it was the terrible odour of burning that had affected him. Anyway now there was a lot to do, people to interview, the neighbours, Stroud's estranged wife, the sister, that odd, half-crazy Gwen Stroud, the people at the school . . . And, of course, the body, or what was left of it, would have to be positively identified, and that was

something for the forensic pathologists, not for the relatives,
whatever they might say. Maybe there was enough left of
the jaw for them to use the teeth for proof of identity . . .
And the ring on his finger hadn't helped; it was a plain gold
band, without engraving or any distinguishing marks.
Around the country, there must be millions just like it.

Chapter Six

It didn't take long for Jean to recover from her moment of weakness in Helen's office. It must have been the heat, she thought; it seemed to be affecting everybody. Jean shook her head in wonderment. Of course she knew that she wasn't nearly clever or attentive enough, that was one thing, but blurting it all out to Helen, that was another. Anyway, Helen wouldn't mind; they'd worked together and been friends for a long time now. As Jean got into her car to go home, she remembered with some surprise that Helen herself had occasionally been known to weaken and let out her own feelings of failure to Jean. So they were about even, Jean reckoned. She checked the rear view mirror and drove off into the street, suddenly feeling much better.

She stopped off at Marks and Spencer's, leaving her car in the car park down the road from the museum, and ran in to the food section.

'So it's chicken for dinner tonight, Dr Montrose?' said the girl at the checkout counter, putting the groceries in a bag. 'I don't know how you manage to do it all, busy the way you are.'

'Chicken's easy,' smiled Jean. 'That's what I like best about it.' She held out her charge card. 'And how's your mother doing, Elsa? She was looking a wee bit better last week.'

Elsa put the card in the little machine and pulled the lever across it, then back. 'If you'll just sign . . . Actually my

mother's nae doing so great. She was making chips yesterday and she got some hot fat on her hand and burned it
enough so she had to go up with it to the hospital. There's
aye something, isn't that right, Dr Montrose?' Elsa
laughed. 'And who knows that better than you!'

When Jean got home, she found a guest for dinner,
Lisbie's friend Neil Mackay, but that didn't surprise Jean in
the least. In the Montrose household there were always
friends dropping in for a meal, or sometimes even staying
for a few days. Both Lisbie and Fiona had long since got
used to meeting strangers on the stairs or coming out of the
bathroom in pyjamas, or round the table for dinner.

Lisbie made the introductions; she was looking a little
pink in the face, and Fiona was making rude faces at her
behind Neil's back.

Neil was a nice-looking boy, Jean thought. Tall, a bit
gangly perhaps, but he seemed bright and well brought up.
She had been in his father's dry-cleaning place on South
Street a couple of times. Ken Mackay and his son had come
to Perth less than a year before; he had travelled for a large
chemical company after retiring from a moderately successful career in the ring, and decided to settle in Perth after his
wife died. Jean had taken in some clothes for cleaning; both
she and Steven made a point of patronising new establish-
ments in town – they both knew from personal experience
that it wasn't always easy to start in a new town, especially if
one wasn't from the area.

The chicken would take too long to cook, Jean decided,
and anyway everybody seemed to want Indian food in spite
of the heat, so they called down to the Star of India, and
after a few minutes, Lisbie and Neil went down to fetch it.

'It's ridiculous, Mum,' said Fiona heatedly as soon as the
door closed behind them. 'Do you know how old that boy
is?'

'I don't know, dear, about the same age as Lisbie, I
suppose.' They were in the kitchen, getting things ready,

while Steven sat in the next room watching the news. 'Fiona, would you mind smelling my hair?'

'He's almost *two years* younger than her!' said Fiona furiously. 'Your hair smells all right,' she went on, coming over to sniff it. 'Why?'

'Good,' said Jean. 'You know how I hate it when your father comes over and says that I smell of something, like the hospital . . . Now, if you'll take through the big plates, I'll take the glasses . . .'

When in the course of the meal Neil said something about St Jude's, Jean put her head down, and Lisbie noticed. 'There's nothing wrong with St Jude's,' she said defensively.

'I didn't suggest there was,' replied Jean. She turned to Neil. 'I was thinking that you must all be very upset about what happened to poor Mr Stroud,' she said. The story had been on the news, and they all knew about it.

'Not really,' said Neil, very coolly, to Jean's astonishment. 'Everybody hated him. Even my Dad.' Neil told them about the way Stroud picked on him, how he sneered and imitated his stammer. And his father nearly had a stroke, he told them, when he heard about his son's latest run-in with Stroud in class.

There was a stunned silence around the table, broken hastily by Jean. 'I was called to his house this morning,' she said, 'and I saw a pile of essay papers including yours . . .' Almost before the words were out of her mouth, Jean was sorry she'd mentioned it.

'Mine was at the top, right?' Neil had stopped eating and was looking at her with a strange expression. Jean stared at him.

'Yes, it was,' she said, slowly. 'How on earth did you happen to know that?'

There was a sudden tension in the room. Everybody stopped eating and looked at Neil.

'Two reasons,' he said, smiling, and apparently completely

at ease. 'One is that if you saw a *p-p-p-pile* of papers, you'd only see the name on the top one, right?' Lisbie laughed, a nervous laugh of relief.

'And what was the other reason?' asked Steven, very quietly, his fork poised in the air.

'It's very simple.' Neil had started eating again, quite unconcerned about the shock waves he'd sent around the table. 'At school, I c-c-c-collected the papers, and put my own on the top.' He smiled across the table, a rather charming, diffident smile. 'Fiona, would you please pass the mango chutney?'

After that, the conversation became general again, and Jean was careful not to allow any further discussion of Mr Stroud.

'Miss Farnham resigned today,' announced Fiona. 'She's the head book-keeper. She was just working away, seemed perfectly normal, then suddenly she got up from her desk and shouted "I've had enough of all of you!" and walked out.'

'Oh my!' said Jean. 'And what did Mr Jones say?'

'Oh, he just shrugged his shoulders and said she'd be back tomorrow. It's just the heat, he said.'

Neil had to go home soon after dinner as he had homework to do, and it was a week day. He was just leaving when they saw Douglas Niven's car pull up outside. Fiona ran out before Jean had time to stop her. Jean hoped Doug didn't mind her; she didn't want him to think that Fiona was making a fool of herself. When she turned round, Neil had already gone.

Douglas came up the short path with Fiona hanging on to his arm; as usual when Fiona was around, he looked pleased and a bit astonished, like the owner of a new and rather exotic pet.

When he saw Jean, his face reverted to the sombre expression he'd had when he got out of the car. The whole Morgan Stroud business had shaken him up more than he'd thought, and it must have shown, because his wife Cathie had watched him all through dinner with that funny look she had when she could see he was upset about something.

'I had a feeling you'd drop in,' cried Jean. Sitting in the living room, Steven heard her, sighed, put his glasses in his top pocket, folded his paper and took it upstairs into his bedroom before Douglas, preceded by Jean and Fiona, came through the door. At least Jean had taken the trouble to warn him; she didn't usually raise her voice without a very good reason.

Jean led the way into the living room.

'Fiona, I'm sure you have things to do,' said Jean in her no-nonsense voice.

'But Mum . . .' pleaded Fiona, but Jean was quite inflexible. 'Doug, would you like a cup of tea?' called Fiona in desperation over Jean's shoulder. Doug grinned, and gave her a friendly, conspiratorial wink. 'Maybe later, thanks, Fiona,' he said. Fiona made a face at her mother and left. Jean closed the door firmly behind her. 'I don't know what it is you do to my daughter, Douglas Niven,' said Jean, 'but it's just as well for you that you're safely married. How's Cathie, by the way?'

'She's fine. Her mother's coming over next week, though, from Skye, and that's always a stramash, when she's here . . .' Doug sighed.

Jean watched him, waiting. Doug rarely got to the point immediately, and that sometimes irritated Jean.

'And of course she'll be coming over to see you,' he said. 'She doesn't trust her doctor over there; she says he's aye drunk.'

'There wasn't much wrong with her last time I saw her,' replied Jean. 'She looks as if she'll outlive all of us. Did you tell her about the heat wave?'

'I did that,' said Doug placidly. 'And she said that was fine with her, and it was cheaper coming here than going to the Riviera.'

'Well, that's a good way of looking at it, I suppose.' Jean picked up a large envelope and started to fan herself with it. When was all this going to end? Was all of Perth, including her, going to curl up at the edges and start to smoulder?

Douglas settled back in his chair.

'A very interesting problem, Mr Morgan Stroud,' he said. 'What do you make of it, Jean?'

'Well, as you know, that kind of thing's a bit out of my range of competence,' Jean replied, twisting in her chair, looking for her crochet work. Finally she found it, the hook stuck like a harpoon into the ball of thread.

'Didn't you work in a burn unit for a while?' asked Doug.

'Yes, I did,' said Jean quietly. 'But I never saw anything like that.'

'Dr Anderson was talking about "spontaneous human combustion",' said Douglas. 'And I'm no' too sure about that, although I looked it up in the book this afternoon.'

'I don't know much about it either,' said Jean. She was having trouble withdrawing the crochet hook, and finally just pushed it right through the ball of thread. 'But I remember seeing a documentary on it a few years ago, an American one, I think. It was quite frightening, as I remember.' Douglas suddenly had the distinct impression that Jean was not telling him everything she knew on the subject.

'But how could a human body just burst into flames like that? And if it could, why doesn't it happen more often?'

'I don't know,' said Jean. 'Why don't rare diseases happen more often?'

That silenced Douglas for a few moments. He gently patted the box with one cigarette in his breast pocket, knowing that would be as close as he'd get to smoking in *this* house.

'Malcolm Anderson's all excited,' he said. 'Says he's going to write a paper about it for the *Lancet*.' Douglas let that hang in the air for a while. 'You see, normally I'd be thinking of this as a murder inquiry . . . But if it's really due to something, well, natural, then I shouldn't be wasting my time and the department's money on it. There's plenty ither crimes I could be investigating in this area.' He sat up very straight, as if he should be on his way immediately to solve them.

'What about all these other fires and things around here?' asked Jean, finding the place on her crochet-work. Her fingers started to move, very fast. Douglas could imagine her brain cells working away just as industriously, but not on the crochet work, which was almost automatic.

Douglas shook his head. 'We only get called if the firemen think it's a criminal situation,' he said. 'Right now, they're so busy putting the fires out that I don't believe calling us even occurs to them.'

Jean stopped her crochet for a moment and looked at Doug over her half glasses. 'What I'm wondering, Doug,' she said, 'is whether Morgan Stroud is really an isolated case, or whether he's just part of a pattern . . .' She smiled, rather a forced smile, Douglas thought. 'But of course there might be someone who wants us to think that way.' This time she laughed, more like the usual cheerful Jean Montrose laugh. 'I said "*Us*", but who cares what *I* think about it? It's what *you* think . . .'

'There are certainly plenty of people who hated Stroud,' said Doug. 'Everybody I've talked to so far, including his wife, said it was good riddance when he died!'

'That doesn't prove he was murdered,' said Jean. She stopped her crochet suddenly. 'Which reminds me, one of his pupils was here for dinner, Neil Mackay . . .' Jean told him about Neil's hatred of Stroud, and his comments about the essay papers.

'He's an unusual lad, that Neil,' mused Jean, almost to herself, and took up the crochet hook again.

Soon afterwards, Douglas got up, slowly, and unstuck the back of his shirt from his skin. 'Well, I'm awa', he said. 'I have a lot to do yet.'

'Who do you have to . . . talk to about this?' asked Jean, putting her crochet work on the table and getting up too.

'Well, his wife, for a start,' said Doug. 'She's in Tomintoul now, and won't be in until tomorrow. Then some of the teachers at St Jude's, his sister Gwen . . . and some of the boys, maybe even that Neil Mackay you were talking about. It depends a bit on what happens. Maybe the very first one I talk to will burst into tears and confess . . .'

'Don't count on it,' said Jean smiling. 'Anyway, as you said, there's always the possibility that this was a strange but entirely natural phenomenon.'

Fiona just happened to be in the hall, looking up something in the telephone book.

'I was about to make some tea,' she said. 'Would you like some?'

'Thanks, Fiona, but if I don't get home soon, Cathie'll string me up by the thumbs,' he said. 'Next time, OK?' He wiped the sweat off his brow; it was incredible how hot it still was, so late in the day.

Going down Argyll Crescent in the car, Douglas thought again about the extraordinary charred appearance of the corpse. He couldn't imagine how it could have happened, or what could have produced that vast concentration of heat. It certainly wasn't a routine case where somebody had poured petrol over a body and lit it. In fact, it wasn't a routine case at all. Well, he thought, turning right at the lights to go across the old bridge, by the time he'd talked to all the people who knew him, he'd have a better idea. Of course, Dr Anderson might be right, maybe the body had simply burst into flames. He seemed to know about it, even had a name for it. 'Spontaneous human combustion', he'd called it. It all sounded very fishy to Doug; meanwhile, he was going to go ahead and treat it as a possible homicide, until he got some better information.

Chapter Seven

Mr Wardle, the headmaster, made the announcement to the assembled school some hours after the discovery of Morgan Stroud's body. All the teachers were there, together with the eighty-odd boys, and to most of his listeners, the Headmaster seemed more concerned about the continuity of teaching than about his colleague who had died in such horrific circumstances.

George Elmslie, he announced, would now be in charge of the Science Department *pro tem*, the appointment to be made permanent in due course.

'Congratulations,' whispered Angus Townes to George Elmslie, after the Head had finished speaking. 'But was it worth killing him for?'

George spun violently round in his seat. 'Is that what people are saying?' he asked. To Angus's astonishment, George was white with concern.

Angus patted him gently on the arm. 'Don't overreact, old chap,' he said. 'I was only joking.'

'Damned bad taste, Angus, if you don't mind my saying so,' grumbled George, subsiding into his seat, but for a few moments Angus watched him interestedly out of the corner of his eye.

Two rows behind the masters, Neil Mackay sat between Billy Wilson and Terry Drummond. All three were unusually silent, and they didn't look at each other.

As they filed out after the announcements, Terry grabbed

Neil's arm and whispered, 'Don't you think we should tell them? Because . . .'

'Don't be a fool, Terry,' Neil hissed back. 'It would just cause more trouble than there is already.'

'He's right,' whispered Billy urgently, grabbing Terry hard by the shoulder. 'One word from you, and I'll personally slit your throat from ear to ear.'

Terry Drummond shook himself free. He didn't know whether he could keep quiet about it all for ever and ever, but on the other hand . . . he didn't want to finish up dead, either.

'Come on,' said Neil. 'We're going to be late. I wonder if Big George will start where Stroud left off?'

'Where was that?' asked Terry from behind his round glasses.

'Transmission of energy from a distance, idiot!' said Billy. 'I can't imagine how you'd have forgotten *that*!'

The boys raced up the narrow wooden staircase as fast as they could, and when they reached the top, the three friends leaned against the banisters, breathless but laughing.

A few minutes later, George Elmslie came bounding athletically upstairs, his shabby black gown trailing behind him like the cape of the masked avenger. The rest of the class came straggling up behind him, and they waited in the dark hall while Big George searched for the key to unlock the door.

'We're going to start on a new topic,' he said heavily, after the boys had told him how far they'd got in Mr Stroud's last class. 'Today, we're going to learn something about the elements of atomic structure. If you would kindly open your books at page fifty-nine . . .'

'Are we going to meet again?' whispered Billy out of the corner of his mouth. 'Because . . .'

'Friday night,' said Neil from behind the open cover of his desk. 'In that deserted tower on the top of Kinnoull Hill.

I talked to Gwen. And we're going to have a new member. Her name's Lisbie Montrose.'

'Quiet, back there!' barked George Elmslie, banging the end of the pointer on the floor. 'You, Wilson, and you, Drummond! This is no time for hilarity . . .'

Dr Malcolm Anderson felt much more comfortable in the cool, spacious police morgue than in Morgan Stroud's house. For one thing, there wasn't that ghastly smell. Also, there had been a strange atmosphere there, something he couldn't quite put his finger on; in fact, he hadn't really thought about it until after he'd driven away from the house; it felt like coming out of a fog.

The carefully collected remnants of the body were now brightly lit on a clean white enamel post-mortem table; the attendant, with an innate sense of order, had placed the hands and feet approximately in the correct position, where they would have lain had they been attached to the rest of the body. Bits of charred body had fallen off during transportation, and the pieces had been placed on a separate table. Under the lights, Anderson could confirm that there was enough of the teeth and jaws left for a positive identification.

He shook his head, then donned a pair of thick red rubber gloves before touching the charred fragments. Even the main piece, which had been the trunk and chest, was incinerated all the way through; Malcolm Anderson had seen many fatal burns, from burning houses, petrol bombs, even one little boy whose drunken stepfather had killed him with a blowtorch, but, like Jean Montrose, he had never seen anything like this. The degree of charring represented an unimaginable concentration of heat, as much as in a crematorium. But then, why had the rest of the house not burned down? How had the papers next to the body not been even singed? The more Anderson looked, and the more he thought about it, the more he was convinced that this had to be a case of spontaneous human combustion, where the body's store of fuel had, in some inexplicable way, been ignited.

There was no question in his mind that this should be reported in the medical literature, and Dr Anderson was going to make sure that every detail was covered. Once a colleague of his had given a medical paper in Edinburgh, at the Royal College of Surgeons, and he'd been ripped apart by the other doctors there because he had failed to make some basic observations; well, Malcolm Anderson was damned sure that wasn't going to happen to him. Every detail, every little aspect, he'd have the answers for the most critical listener.

Once the lighting was properly adjusted, he had Brian Thomson, the technician, photograph the remains from every possible angle, until he ran out of film. Then Dr Anderson took samples for biochemical testing from every part of the body, samples from the totally burned part, samples from where the burned flesh joined the virtually undamaged ankles and wrists, samples from the hands and feet. As he poked and delved at the grisly fragments, he dictated his findings into the voice-activated microphone suspended over the table, and all the while he was getting more and more excited about the paper he was going to write. Spontaneous human combustion was extremely rare, and he would thus become an instant authority on the subject; he'd be invited to give lectures around the country, and they'd fly him out to see doubtful cases, maybe abroad, maybe even to the States. As he carefully sliced a piece of heat-coagulated vein from the body's left wrist and placed it in a plastic bag, Malcolm Anderson had never in his life felt so happy.

Angus Townes negotiated the tight turn from the school parking area, and drove his old Humber away towards the school gates. It wasn't easy keeping the wheels from sliding

off to either side of the narrow, ill-surfaced drive. As he
stopped to pull open the gates, their old hinges squeaked
and creaked from lack of oil and the iron was rust-red where
the black paint had flaked off. A brief feeling of disgust
came over him, then passed; all his instincts rebelled at the
stinginess, the pettiness of the whole institution, neatly
symbolised by the narrow drive and the rusting gate.

The drive down to the main road was deserted, and that
was fortunate; if a vehicle happened to be coming up the
other way, one of them would have had to reverse back to
the gates or the road or risk scraping either against the
dry-stone dyke or the fence.

Angus was tired; the teaching schedule was demanding,
and although he was popular with the boys, and didn't have
to put up with the treatment they accorded some of the
other teachers, it was still a wearing job. Also he was more
accustomed to teaching university students, so he found
that he had to continually readjust his sights; even the clever
boys didn't have the breadth of knowledge he had come to
expect.

At the end of the road, he waited while a heavy lorry from
Bell's distillery roared past towards Perth, then Angus
almost got clipped by a car which came round the corner
too fast; as often happened, the driver had ignored the
'sharp bend' sign, and before he knew it found himself on
the wrong side of the road. Thirty seconds sooner and he'd
have gone straight into the lorry, thought Angus, as he
pulled out quickly into the road; and that would have added
yet another tragedy to the local count.

He put a cassette into the tape deck; it was one of his
favourites, some piano pieces by Erik Satie, played rather
better than he ever could, but then the pianist was Claudio
Arrau . . . There were times when Angus really missed his
piano, but it wasn't as painful now as it had been. It had
really hurt when he'd had to sell it, that old but lovingly
maintained Pleyel, to a woman who never even tried the

keys, and was more concerned about her drawing-room curtains matching the colour of the wood. Angus shrugged. None of these material things were of any real importance, now. He got enough pleasure just listening to the effortless way that Arrau's fingers danced and weaved the patterns of Satie's whimsical, iridescent music, but his own fingers still moved, still played, even if it was now only on the rim of the steering wheel.

Soon he came to the big roundabout on the outskirts of Perth, and the distillery came up on his right, after he negotiated the turn. And that he did with care; the front shock absorbers weren't absorbing very much these days, and that in turn affected the steering.

As often happened, Angus was glad that his mind was fully occupied keeping his car on the road; the alternative was to go again over the tragedies of his life, and he had already gone over them more times than he could remember. His mind followed a track, like a well-used record, the first scratchy groove starting all those years ago. Before the accident, there was nothing, nothing he could remember without a major effort of will; for instance he could not remember a single time when he had been happy, although he must have been, at least occasionally, like everyone else. It was as if his life's journey had started on that dreadful day, and since then every step, every yard of the way had hurt.

Angus followed the traffic along the Dunkeld Road for a mile or two, then turned left down Atholl Street towards the centre of town. When he had time, he liked to park down by the North Inch and walk back towards Kinnoull Street and the little side streets with the antique shops. Although now he couldn't afford any of the fine things he saw in the windows, he had learned to enjoy them anyway, even when they reminded him of things he had once owned. Angus had found that when he stopped wanting to possess things, whether it was beautiful furniture or fine clothes, he inherited a huge, limitless freedom, the freedom from 'I want', as he called it to himself.

Today he was late, because of all the excitement at the school, so Angus drove on through the thickening traffic of Kinnoull Street, then up past the Station Hotel to the supermarket, where he stopped to buy some seedless grapes and some fruit juice. Somehow he'd developed the idea that Deirdre liked mango juice, although there was no way he could be sure, so he bought two tins. Ten minutes later, he parked in the visitors' car park at the side of the nursing home. He sat there for several minutes, looking at the blank brick wall in front of him, gathering himself together, summoning up his reserves of strength and courage as he had done outside different hospitals and plastic surgery units and treatment centres so many times before.

Finding Gwen Stroud didn't turn out to be as difficult as Doug Niven had expected. Within a couple of hours of the discovery of the body, one of the patrol cars found her down by the harbour trying to convert a small, astonished group of Finnish sailors to Christianity. The officers picked her up quietly, without fuss, probably leaving the sailors with a slightly warped view of the fair City of Perth and its inhabitants.

The police should have known that it wouldn't continue to be so easy. They put Gwen in the back of the car, behind the wire fence, where she read silently from her bible. From time to time, as they drove back towards the main police station, she laughed uproariously at what she was reading. The constable who had helped her into the car looked over at the sergeant, who was driving, and said, 'Do you think she's reading some Jesus jokes there in the back?'

The sergeant, a staunch member of the Free Church, didn't think that was funny, and said so, so for the remainder of the trip the only sounds heard in the car were from Gwen herself.

She had gone into the car willingly enough, but like a lobster caught in a lobster pot, was much less amenable when it came to getting out. As the officers found, it is very difficult to remove a passenger who wishes to remain in the back of a car. After about five minutes the sergeant retired with a bitten thumb, and it took the combined efforts of the constable and two policewomen to extract her. While the policewomen tried to get to her through one door, the constable crept around the back of the car and suddenly opened the other, whereupon Gwen, who had backed up against it, fell out, bible and all.

After that demonstration of independence, Gwen was cooperative enough.

'We'd like to ask you a few things about your brother Morgan, if you don't mind,' said Doug. One of the policewomen stood behind Gwen's chair, just in case.

'He was spawned by the devil,' said Gwen. 'And he that thinketh evil, and he that doeth evil, that one verily shall burn in the fires of hell.'

'You made that up, Gwen,' said Douglas, who knew his bible.

Gwen said nothing; her big grey eyes moved restlessly around the room. Douglas wondered what the woman was seeing, and then had a brief vision of the impression she'd make giving evidence in the witness box. No, that wouldn't do at all; anything she said could be so easily held up to ridicule. He was about to get up and tell the policewoman to take Gwen back to her Finnish sailors, when Gwen said something that made him sit quietly back in his chair.

'My brother Morgan was struck down by a ball of lightning, sent by the Lord to destroy him,' she said.

'A *ball* of lightning, Gwen?' he asked, but that was all Gwen was going to tell him at this time. He couldn't even get her to say how she'd heard of Morgan's death: nobody had ever seen her reading a newspaper, and she certainly didn't possess a radio, let alone a television.

Doug sent her off without really working on her very hard; maybe he'd bring her in again, later, but right now there was no way he could tell whether there was any truth or substance to the little Gwen was saying.

Chapter Eight

'How does it look?' asked Lisbie, spinning round. The blue-and-white striped skirt twirled up around her thighs, for a second showing her white underwear.

'It looks fine,' said Fiona from the bed. 'And your legs are okay too, but your bottom's too big.'

'I can't do anything about that,' said Lisbie. 'I just thank God it isn't as big as your mouth.'

'My, my!' said Fiona, sitting up. 'And who trod on *your* tail today?'

'Nobody,' said Lisbie. 'I just feel a bit nervous about tonight. One of the girls at work . . .'

'Well, what?' asked Fiona after letting the pause grow to its full size. 'If you only knew how maddening it is when you start off a sentence like that and don't . . .'

'Don't what?' asked Lisbie guilelessly.

'You don't FINISH it, you cuckoo!' screamed Fiona at the top of her voice.

There was a familiar noise from upstairs, and they both heard the basement door open. There was a silence while the two girls held their breath. Then the door closed again, very quietly.

'Marianne Donald said Neil once went out with her sister Claire,' said Lisbie. 'Just once, though. Claire wouldn't tell her much about it, but it sounded as if . . .' Lisbie hesitated, and took off the skirt.

'If you do that one more time I'll throttle you!' said Fiona, jumping off the bed and advancing on her sister, who grabbed her skirt and backed into the corner. 'Do WHAT?' she shrieked. 'Have you gone completely crazy, or what?'

'YOU DIDN'T FINISH YOUR SENTENCE! AGAIN!'

'Oh, sorry, Fiona. What was I saying?'

Fiona's mouth opened slowly, but she'd forgotten what Lisbie had left unsaid, and jumped back on the bed.

'Anyway, I'd advise you to wear jeans,' she said, sounding very worldly. 'By the time he's undone the buttons and pulled down the zip, even you will have had time to work out what he's up to.'

'Fiona! He's not like that at all! How can you say such things? You saw him when he came for dinner. Didn't he seem okay to you?'

'I don't pay too much attention to kids that age,' replied Fiona haughtily.

'Right!' Lisbie yelled, really out of patience. 'What you like is old married men like DOUGLAS NIVEN!' She finished the sentence at the top of her voice, and from upstairs came the sound of heavy, determined footsteps. The door opened at the top of the stairs.

'What are you girls shouting about? I'm trying to do some work . . . What's going on down there?' Steven did his best to sound angry.

'Nothing,' said Fiona in her mildest voice. 'Lisbie's just trying on a skirt . . .' Lisbie put her hand up to her mouth to stop from laughing, and Fiona put her fist under Lisbie's nose, mouthing that she'd smash her with it if Lisbie made a single sound.

They waited a few moments in total silence; they could feel Steven's presence at the top of the stairs, then he sighed and closed the door.

'What was that you were telling me about magic?' asked Fiona, as if nothing had happened. 'Something Neil was fooling around with?'

Lisbie shrugged. 'He told me he'd learned how to project

energy at a distance,' she replied. 'I think that's what he said. Anyway he's been doing it with a couple of his school friends.'

'That sounds exciting!' Fiona sat up again. 'How did he learn that stuff?'

'They have a class in it at school,' said Lisbie in a mocking, sing-song voice. 'It's called Introductory Black Magic . . .' She turned to see Fiona advancing on her. 'If you touch me I'll scream the house down,' she said loudly, retreating towards the door, holding her blue-striped skirt in front of her.

'A fine sight you'd look, running up there in your knickers,' said Fiona, but she went back to her bed and sat down again.

'He said he learned from some woman he met in the park. He was just walking along and made friends with her. He's like that. He'll talk to anyone.'

'I don't know if I'd want to fool around with that kind of thing,' said Fiona, sounding serious and big-sisterly. 'I hope he's not trying to get you involved in it, is he?'

'Could I try on your Calvin Kleins?' asked Lisbie.

'If you like,' said Fiona. 'But what makes you think you'll get into them *this* time?'

When Jean came down into the basement, she found Lisbie lying on her back on the floor, legs up in the air, trying to get into Fiona's blue jeans.

'Neil's upstairs waiting for you, dear,' said Jean. 'Why don't you just wear your blue-and-white skirt?'

That evening, Doug Niven was not in the best of moods; the Morgan Stroud case was very confusing, and quite unlike anything he'd ever had to deal with in the past.

'So why don't you just give it up?' asked Cathie. They were sitting in their tiny garden after supper; it was the only place where there was a breeze. 'It's making you very bad-tempered.'

'So you think that's how the detective unit functions, do you,' said Douglas, his voice heavy with sarcasm. 'Oh, yes! I can just see myself going up to Bob McLeod and saying, "Hey, Bob, I've decided to drop that Stroud case, because my wife says it's making me bad-tempered." Aye, that would go down very well with Bob, I can tell you that, very well indeed.' Doug glowered at Cathie and angrily swatted at a fly. 'Yes, he would really like that, would Bob!'

'Would you like some more tea?' asked Cathie, the pot poised over his cup. Doug nodded, rather sulkily. It really didn't help him to make important decisions when Cathie made comments like that.

'You see, if there hasn't been a crime, I've got no business wasting time on it,' he said. 'And Dr Anderson's got himself convinced that somehow Morgan Stroud's body just burst into flames.'

'What does Jean Montrose think? I'd listen to her more than anybody.'

'She isn't saying much,' replied Douglas glumly. 'She says she doesn't know anything about spontaneous human combustion, and she'd rather leave it to the experts.'

'Like Dr Anderson?' asked Cathie.

'Aye. He's going to write a big paper about it, he says. So by now he probably knows a fair bit about the subject, and he's no' a fool, you know.' Doug took a sip of his tea.

'What I like about Jean Montrose,' said Cathie thoughtfully, 'is that she's not just a doctor, she has a lot of common sense, you know, the kind that cuts through all the
. . . the . . .'

'Bullshit?' asked Douglas.

'I'm sure there's a better word than that,' replied Cathie primly, 'but yes, that's exactly what I mean.'

Douglas grinned at her; somehow Cathie had the knack of making him feel better, more confident about things.

'What time's your mother arriving?'

'Ten in the morning. She'll be tired, because it's a long

bus ride for her, and she'll probably want a rest.'

'Yes, well, I'll try to stay out of the way, then.'

'You don't have to. She likes you, you know.'

There was a long, comfortable silence, broken by the sound of a police siren, far away. Cathie could see Doug's ears prick up, like an old warhorse.

'Another fire, do you think?' she asked.

'Maybe,' said Douglas in a slightly odd voice. 'But there haven't been quite as many this week, did you notice?'

Cathie laughed. 'Sometimes I really think you're totally superstitious, though I know you'd never admit it,' she said, getting up and putting the tea things on a gold-coloured metal tray.

'That's not superstition,' he protested. 'It's a matter of fact.'

'I was just thinking about what you were saying earlier on,' she said, 'about Morgan Stroud . . .'

'I'll take the table in,' said Douglas. 'Do you think it's getting any cooler?'

'Is there anybody who would benefit from his death, or who hated him enough to kill him?'

'You're beginning to sound like Jean Montrose,' said Douglas. He looked at his watch. 'What's on the telly tonight, d'you know?'

George Elmslie sat in his small eighth-floor apartment in the Altus Towers, one of the very few high-rise buildings in Perth. Although officially within the city limits, the Towers was situated north of the Tay, on the Bridgend side, and commanded a spectacular view of the City, Kinnoull Hill, or the mountains, depending on which way one's windows faced.

George was lucky; he had a corner flat, and the bedroom had a pleasant view to the north, while the living room faced west, over the river. But this particular evening, George was not feeling lucky; he was feeling frightened. He tried to concentrate on the homework he'd brought home with him, and sighed. Those boys . . . It was so discouraging. He thought he had a good class, then when he saw their papers, it became clear that they hadn't understood a word of what he was saying. But even while he was thinking these things, a small voice kept relentlessly saying to him, 'What if Stroud wrote down that information and hid it somewhere? He could have put it in a safe-deposit box, or with a lawyer, and how do you know that it won't be opened by his executors when they read the will, or even by the police?'

That bastard! He was still causing problems, even after he was dead, and maybe it was even worse now. At least he hadn't told anybody while he was still alive, not as far as George knew, anyway. So maybe Stroud was getting his revenge on a *post mortem* basis . . . What a thought! George shivered involuntarily.

And all because of what was essentially only a hobby.

George got up from the comfortable easy chair by the window and paced round the room. He should stop doing it, he knew that, but there were two very strong reasons why he couldn't. First, it brought in enough money to eke out his miserable salary at St Jude's, and secondly, it was one of the few things in his life that brought him any real pleasure, although it also brought a feeling of self-loathing, afterwards.

The funny thing was that when Morgan Stroud first mentioned the matter, he'd just about given up. In fact, he was thinking of selling the equipment, which had only been gathering dust for some months.

Morgan had telephoned him on a Saturday morning a few weeks before, and suggested they have coffee at Strathdee's about eleven. George had demurred; for one thing he needed to go to the cobbler to have new cleats put on his rock-climbing boots, and for another, he didn't care for Morgan, although he was his colleague.

'I was talking to a friend of yours,' said Morgan in a

casual voice. 'He knew you a few years ago, he said, in Exeter, I believe . . .'

There was a long silence; George gripped the phone tight, and felt the blood draining out of his face.

'Eleven, then, at Strathdee's . . .' George's hand was trembling when he put the phone down. Ever since that time in Exeter, although he had been found not guilty on a technicality, George had known that it was an incident in his life that couldn't be erased, and that sooner or later it would catch up with him.

And that sooner or later was now.

Morgan Stroud was waiting for him inside the restaurant, at one of the small tables by the window that looked out on South Street. He stood up when George approached, something George would never have expected him to do.

'Well, George, I'm glad you could make it!' he called out in a voice of spurious bonhomie. 'Have a seat, have a seat!'

George sat down, trying to look as much at ease as possible. There was no point in showing Stroud how close to panic he was.

'I ordered coffee and cakes,' said Stroud. 'Is that all right?'

'What's on your mind, Morgan?' asked George. But Stroud was enjoying himself, and didn't want to hurry things along too much. He ignored the question.

'I'd have thought you'd be up in the hills climbing,' he said. 'On a fine day like today.'

George said nothing. The waitress approached with a tray and set out the coffee and cakes.

'Very fattening, full of cholesterol, I know,' said Stroud, taking one and biting into it. 'But we'll all have to die of something some day, I suppose.'

George watched him, making little attempt to hide his distaste. Even though, as far as he knew, Stroud was barely into his thirties, he was fat, the kind of sloppy, wheezy, unhealthy fat that bespoke total self-indulgence and equally total lack of exercise. George would rather be dead than look like that; he paid a great deal of attention to his physique and his appearance. It must feel so awful, he thought, to be obese; like carrying a sack of coal around on one's shoulders all day long. And it looked so unhealthy and disgusting. But at this moment George wasn't feeling sorry for Morgan, not by any means.

'Yes,' said Morgan finally. 'I met a friend, well, an acquaintance might be more accurate . . .' He smiled at George, like a cat might smile at a bird. 'Oh, look!' he said, pointing out of the window down at the crowded South Street pavement. 'You see those two little boys, the ones in shorts crossing the road? How do they appeal to you, George? I mean, *photographically* speaking?'

The post of senior science master was coming up at the end of the term, when Mr Spinks, the incumbent, was due to retire. Morgan Stroud wanted the job, but George was better qualified, had been at the school longer, and would probably get it. Unless, of course, he withdrew his name from consideration. Morgan was very helpful in suggesting reasons why he might want to do that; after all, the job carried a lot of tiresome additional responsibility, and involved more work, committees, that kind of thing. But the most appealing reason, as Morgan carefully pointed out, was that it was preferable for George to keep the job he had now than to have no job at all.

Seething with silent anger, George had withdrawn his application, but as a kind of retaliation, and also because he was running short of cash again, he dusted off his cameras and his lights, and sent the backdrop sheets to the laundry. There were only a couple of other things he needed to do to get back in business; one was to get a new exposure meter, and the other was to make a couple of phone calls to Glasgow. That was two weeks ago, and this evening they were bringing some kids over for a photo session.

George looked at his watch at the same moment as the

door buzzer sounded. He put the door on the chain and cautiously opened it a crack. It was Alec and Sally, his Glasgow contacts, accompanied by three silent children between the ages of seven and ten, two boys and a girl.

'No parents?' asked George.

'Just the mother,' said Sally, a worn-looking woman with tobacco-stained fingers and the scars of long-healed acne on her face. 'She didn't want to come up. She'll be at the Lithgow Arms when you're done.'

'Hello, children,' said George. 'Come on in. We're going to have some fun together this evening . . .'

'Don't bother with that shit,' said Sally. 'They know what it's all about. They've done it before, lots of times.'

George felt relieved; he didn't like to make anybody do things they didn't want to do, although sometimes it was necessary. Just as it was sometimes necessary to do quite distasteful things to protect oneself.

Chapter Nine

Because of the publicity which had been given in the papers and the TV and radio coverage of the horrific death of Morgan Stroud, Detective Chief Inspector Robert McLeod had instructed Doug to put aside his other cases and work full time on this one. Accordingly, and with secret reluctance, Doug parcelled out his other work and got on with interviewing all the people on his list.

He'd already spoken to Stroud's neighbour, who had originally called the police. She had been as helpful as she could, but was very deaf, and the high-pitched whistle of her hearing aid had set his teeth on edge. Apart from seeing the smoke on the wall above the window, and not being able to reach Stroud on the phone, she had nothing to add, except that she'd seen some lights go on in Stroud's house late in the evening. When Doug pressed her, she thought it was about ten thirty, when she was about to go to bed. No, she grinned suddenly at him, she hadn't heard anything. She only used her hearing aid when there was company and when she went shopping. Didn't he *know* how much those little batteries cost?

The morning after discovering the body, Doug sat in his tiny office and wished that a breeze would come in through the open window. He looked at his watch; Renée Stroud was supposed to be here by now. Douglas had traced her to Tomintoul, a rather remote village up in the highlands, a few hours' drive from Perth, where she was staying with her parents. On the phone, she told him she hadn't lived with her husband for over a year, and had only seen him a few times when she came to his house to pick up items of clothing or furniture. She had been in Tomintoul for two weeks with her parents who worked a farm there. She hadn't been further away from there than Dufftown, where she'd gone to do some shopping.

'Good,' she said when Douglas told her of her husband's death. When he gave her more details, she sounded shocked. 'That's what his sister Gwen said would happen to him,' she said. 'God would heap coals of fire upon him, until he was dead. That's what she said, lots of times. My goodness gracious, that is odd.'

She would come back to remove a few things, Renée said, and then she'd put the house on the market. 'But don't wait for me,' she said. 'Go ahead and cremate whatever's left of him.'

'Excuse me for asking,' said Douglas, still on the phone, 'but do you know of anybody who might have . . . done such a thing?'

'Just about anyone who was more than a passing acquaintance,' she replied. Renée Stroud had a quick, decisive voice, and Doug tried to visualise her. She sounded quite a bit older than her husband's thirty-odd years.

'Would you think that he left much money?' Douglas persisted, although he could feel that she wanted to get off the phone. No doubt to open a bottle of champagne with her parents, he thought sardonically. For a second, he wondered how Cathie would react to *his* death.

'I've no idea,' she said. 'But as far as I know, he never had any money to leave. Apart from his car, and the house, that is, and the house mostly belongs to the building society.'

Douglas whistled softly when he put the phone down. Morgan Stroud certainly didn't have much of a fan club.

Coals of fire . . .

Balls of lightning . . .

Maybe even God had hated Morgan Stroud. A shiver passed through Doug's frame, a shiver which had its roots in his early religious education, in which the emphasis had been heavily on the Old Testament. A phrase came to mind instantly, because it was so visual: *'I beheld Satan as lightning fell from heaven.'* In his mind's eye, Douglas saw the horrified figure of Morgan Stroud, devilishly outlined and illuminated by that final bolt of lightning, hurled at him by an exasperated deity . . .

Douglas sat back in his metal chair, pulled out the single cigarette he'd been carrying around with him since he stopped smoking four weeks before, looked at it and put it back in his pocket.

Renée had told him that she was coming back to Perth anyway that evening on the bus. Doug wondered vaguely why she needed to take the bus; didn't the woman own a car?

He pressed the buzzer by the phone and Constable Jamieson came in.

'Go and see if there's a Mrs Stroud in the waiting room,' he said.

'Oh, aye,' replied Jamieson in his slow way. 'She's there all right, been there over fifteen minutes. She's quite a looker,' he added.

Doug took a deep breath, but decided this was not the moment to get angry.

'Send her in,' he said.

Renée Stroud was indeed quite a looker, although she seemed pale, and her eyes were a little puffy; from lack of sleep, Doug guessed, certainly not from weeping, judging by what she said to him over the phone. Doug estimated that she was maybe eight or nine years older than her late husband, in her mid to late thirties. She was wearing a loose grey dress and matching shoes.

'Would you care for a cup of tea?' Douglas asked.

'That would be nice,' she replied, and Doug nodded to

Jamieson, who went out.

'Well, I gather you're not too upset about your husband's death,' Doug started.

'I'm only worried about getting the house cleaned up,' she replied. 'If it's as bad as you said . . . When can I get in?' She had a rather attractive husky voice, and Doug couldn't identify where she was from.

'Not for a while,' said Doug. 'The forensic people still have things to do there, and nothing must be disturbed.'

There was something strange about her eyes, Doug noted; they didn't seem to look straight at him, but moved around in an odd kind of way. It was only noticeable when she was addressing him directly.

'Forgive me asking,' he said, 'but is there something the matter with your vision?'

'I have no central vision,' she said. 'I can see everything except what I'm looking directly at.' Renée folded her hands together.

Doug frowned with compassion. 'How do you manage to read? Or drive?'

'I can only read very large print,' she replied. 'I can't tell you what that's like . . . I used to be a librarian . . .' She bit her lip. 'And obviously I can't drive now.'

There was a long pause, and Doug fiddled with his pen.

'You told me that you had been in Tomintoul for the last week,' he said, his voice casual.

Renée nodded.

'Mrs Stroud,' said Doug, his voice changing suddenly, 'I spoke to your mother on the phone this morning.'

'Well?' Renée's voice had changed too.

'She told me a car came for you at the farm in the early evening, two nights ago, and you didn't get back until the next morning.'

'That's quite true,' said Renée, not appearing at all confused or embarrassed at having been caught out.

'May I ask where you were?'

'I was visiting someone,' replied Renée, with a trace of defiance in her voice.

'May I ask who and where that person was?' Douglas's pen was poised.

'You may ask, but I'm not going to tell you,' said Renée.

Douglas put his pen down, feeling frustrated that his intimidating tricks of body language and facial expression didn't seem to be working with Renée. He had now only his voice to rely on, so he did the best he could with that.

'You realise that your refusal to cooperate with the police may be interpreted as guilt,' he said, his voice loud and harsh.

'Guilt?' asked Renée calmly. 'Are you accusing me of something? And by the way, I can hear you quite well; my *hearing* is excellent, I'm happy to say.'

'A crime may have been committed in regard to your husband's death,' said Douglas heavily. 'And if you persist in hindering our investigations . . .'

'Now you're just being silly,' said Renée in a sensible voice. 'I'm not hindering you in the slightest. I'm simply not telling you who I was with because it's none of your business and has nothing whatever to do with Morgan's death.'

'That's for us to decide,' said Douglas, his voice still loud, deliberately keeping up the pressure. She was a good-looking woman, he thought, checking out her legs and her body with a look he knew would have been offensive if she could have seen his gaze. He felt like a voyeur, and was suddenly ashamed of taking advantage of her in such a way.

'No it isn't,' she replied, and to his increasing annoyance Douglas thought he detected the trace of a laugh in her voice, 'because *I've* already decided.'

Douglas tried a different tack, and asked her about Morgan's enemies, about reasons why anyone might have wanted to kill him.

'I'm quite a religious person,' said Renée. 'And I truly believe that God killed him because he was such an evil man. But if you're looking for reasons why a *person* might have killed him, I have as good a reason as any. He . . . Never mind, it doesn't matter now.'

Douglas was unable to get another word out of her.

The interview ended soon afterwards; Douglas was left with a reluctant but strong feeling of admiration for this woman, who hadn't let herself be defeated by her blindness or by what must have been an appalling married life with Morgan Stroud. He wondered whom she had gone to visit, but unless something turned up that really implicated Renée, it was mere curiosity on his part. Just as Renée had said.

'What d'you think of that boy?' Steven asked Jean. 'He seems very, well, sort of sophisticated, don't you think?'

'Lisbie says he's very clever,' replied Jean, not taking her eyes off her crochet, which was reaching a critical stage.

'I met his father, Ken. He came in to buy a pair of paperweights. He's not tall like Neil, but he's got a tough look about him . . .'

'He used to be a boxer,' said Jean. 'I don't know how well his dry-cleaning business is going. It's a bit like bringing coals to Newcastle, starting that kind of a business here, isn't it?

'I had a chat with him about that while they were wrapping his paperweights. He said Pullars could use a little competition.'

'Well, Steven, I hope he'll do as well as we did here, for both their sakes.'

'I said I'd help him get into the Rotary Club, if he wanted, and told him about the Chamber of Commerce people . . . They were a big help when we came.'

'It must be tough on him, trying to run a business and take care of Neil at the same time,' said Jean.

'I suppose that's why Neil's at St Jude's,' replied Steven. 'Anyway I've heard that he's seeing somebody around town . . .'

'Who is?' Jean was always interested in the social comings and goings in Perth.

'Ken. I don't know who . . . Some young woman. Somebody mentioned it at work.'

There was a silence after that, while Jean concentrated on her crochet, and after a few minutes Steven wandered off, feeling restless and rather irritable. He went into the living room and turned on the television. Even when the programmes weren't very good, at least they took his mind off his work and the other things that bothered him.

The next time Jean Montrose forced herself to visit Deirdre Townes in the nursing home, she found her father there, sitting by the bed, holding the girl's hand and talking softly to her. The room was tidy and clean, with a rather pathetic little bouquet of wild flowers and a glass containing some tired-looking blackberries on the bedside table. Jean couldn't help looking at the dreadful wreckage of Deirdre's face, and for the hundredth time wondered how it was that in this day and age the plastic surgeons hadn't been able to do anything better. Maybe it was because she couldn't cooperate, couldn't communicate, and because she'd never be able to look at herself in a mirror . . .

Angus stood up when Jean came into the room.

'I was just about to leave,' he said. 'There's not much change . . . She had a small fit earlier, the nurse said, but it wasn't severe and didn't last very long.'

Jean felt so sorry for the man; his face showed all the years of anguish, an anguish that would last until the day he died.

'I need to check a couple of things here,' said Jean, her voice full of sympathy. 'Then let me take you across the road for a cup of coffee. You look as if you need one.'

Angus smiled briefly; Jean could see from the way his face moved that he didn't smile often. 'That would be lovely,' he said, and Jean felt sure he meant it.

Jean got him to help turn Deirdre over while she checked for bedsores; there was a small red area on one buttock. They rolled her back, and Jean found a drop of pus coming out of the left eye socket. On the way out, Jean asked the nurses a few questions, gave some instructions and wrote a progress note in the chart.

Jean could sense Angus Townes' discomfort as they sat down in the small cafe opposite the nursing home, and she wondered when was the last time he'd really talked to anyone, let alone sat down in a cafe with another human being.

But Jean, without even knowing it, was an expert at making people feel comfortable and at ease. She talked about her holiday in Tuscany, and wondered if Angus had ever been there.

'The closest I've been to Tuscany is Turin,' replied Angus awkwardly. 'And that's not too close. Susan and I drove there from Menton, soon after we were married, through the Maritime Alps . . . God, that was a wonderful time . . .'

It was as if a door had just opened in Angus's mind, a door which had been closed for a long, long time. And Angus didn't stop. He told Jean about his early married life, when he was doing his doctorate in chemistry, about the little house they had in Cambridge when he was appointed a tutor at New College. Suddenly Angus put his hand in his inside pocket and pulled out a stiff brown envelope. With great care, he extracted a photo and passed it carefully across to Jean. His eyes never left it, and Jean sensed that this was the first time for many years that he'd shown it to anyone. It was a colour print of a young, blond, tanned and very beautiful woman in a white winter coat holding a child, the most adorable-looking girl, with hair that was so blond it was almost white. Already she had the look of a beauty about her, the confidence and even the bearing.

'Deirdre was just five, then. That was taken two weeks before . . . before . . .' Jean handed the photo back to him, averting her eyes. She didn't need to look at him to see the trembling lower lip.

'You'd never think to look at her that she was epileptic, would you?' Angus smiled; he had quickly recovered his composure. He put the photo back in his pocket. 'Not that it was severe; she only had a very occasional attack, once every few months, after they put her on treatment, and the doctors fully expected she'd grow out of it.'

Jean said nothing, and filled Angus's cup from the coffee pot. Angus looked at her with a slightly puzzled smile. What was it about Jean Montrose? How was she able to project such sympathy, such a human warmth and yet say so little? And what was it about her that had allowed him to say things to her that had been buried so deep in his inner self that even he thought he had forgotten about them?

Angus took a deep breath and prepared to rip off the last, most tender scab. 'One afternoon, it was December the eighteenth, I came home from the college. It was a cold, raw kind of day, with some wet sleet and a lot of wind . . .' Jean listened with a fearful fascination. She could see how hard it was for Angus to say what he had to say; he was circling around it, trying to delay the horror of reliving those dreadful moments. 'I took out my door key; I was wearing my old RAF greatcoat, and the key was in the right-hand pocket.' Angus absently tapped the pocket of his jacket. His eyes were far away; he was coming up the wet steps of his house, putting the key in the lock . . . 'The first thing I noticed . . . I thought Susan must have left something on the stove, so I ran into the kitchen, but everything seemed all right there. I called for Susan, then for Deirdre . . .' Angus stopped speaking, as if to gather his strength for the worst part.

Jean sat very still, as if hypnotised. She couldn't bear to hear the end of the story, and yet she couldn't stop listening; she had to hear him out.

'Deirdre was in the living room; she'd had an epileptic attack, because her underclothes were soiled, and she was unconscious. She'd fallen with her face in the electric heater . . . and there was smoke, a column of smoke going up straight up from it . . .'

Jean couldn't repress a long shudder. She had never really heard what had happened; she was familiar only with the grotesque end-results.

A question was on her lips, but Jean didn't dare to ask it. Angus supplied the information anyway. 'Susan was over at the neighbours'. . . She never forgave herself. She . . . needed treatment in an institution for several months, and a few days after she came home . . . she went missing. They found her in the river Cam two days later.' Angus straightened himself up. 'I'm sorry to have burdened you with all this,' he said. 'And I thank you for listening so patiently.'

Impulsively, Jean got up and gave him a hug that was so full of friendship and sympathy that their eyes filled up again.

Jean sat in her car in the nursing home's car park and watched as Angus's old car backed out into the street then disappeared down the road. It seemed to be leaning over to one side more than it should, and it trailed a thin cloud of bluish smoke behind it.

Feeling as if she herself had been struck by lightning, Jean slowly started her car and headed back to the surgery. In the rear view mirror, she had a glimpse of somebody going quickly into the nursing home, and thought she recognized Gwen, but wasn't sure. Anyway there were more important things on Jean's mind. One thing about being a doctor, she thought as she turned the corner towards South Street, was that whatever happened to you, however bad things got, you knew that there were always folk worse off than you.

Chapter Ten

'He's just awesome!' said Lisbie at dinner that evening. 'I've never met anybody like him in my whole life!'

'What did you do when you went out, dear?' asked Jean, throwing a quick, amused look at Steven. Only half an hour before, the two of them had been discussing the changes in teenage vocabulary since their time.

'Well, first we went down to McDonalds . . .'

'Right after dinner?' asked Steven, astonished. 'Don't we feed you enough here?'

'We went to get a *Coke*,' went on Lisbie, ignoring the interruption.

'When I was your age,' said Steven, 'coke was something you put on the fire when you couldn't afford coal.'

'Dad!' said Fiona. 'Would you let her get on with her story? Can't you see she's in L-O-V-E?' Her voice finished on that high, mocking note that Lisbie had learned to hate above all else.

In a flash, Lisbie's hand was raised to throw a hard roll, but Jean caught her wrist just in time and gently lowered it to the table.

'You mustn't throw food, dear,' she said. 'Where did you go after McDonalds?'

'We sat in there for a while,' said Lisbie, 'and he was telling me all about different kinds of magic.' She turned to her father. 'Dad, have you ever heard of Aleister Crowley?'

Steven shook his head.

'Well, he was a great English magician, and he wrote some of his secrets in a book . . .'

'Did he happen to write spells on how to have peaceful non-combative meals?' asked Steven. 'Because I would certainly like to hear about that.'

'Maybe we can skip the magic,' said Jean. 'What did you do after McDonalds?'

'We went to his house,' said Lisbie curtly. 'And now I'm going to eat my dinner . . .' She grinned at her father, '. . . quietly, like a good little girl.'

And nothing would make her say anything more about her evening with Neil Mackay until after dinner, when she followed Fiona down to her room.

'Are you glad you wore the skirt?' was the first thing Fiona asked, her eyes shining. Lisbie blushed. 'It didn't make any difference,' she said. 'He's not like that . . .'

'All boys are like that,' said Fiona. 'I could tell you a few stories . . .'

'Well, I don't want to hear them,' said Lisbie, 'because I know you'd make up a story to make them sound like . . . like some kind of animals, and they're not. Anyway he's not.'

'So what happened with the magic?' asked Fiona. 'Did he do any on you?'

'Of course not. It's very exciting, with secret signs, *cabalistic* signs, he called them. Anyway, he wants me to meet his friend, the crazy woman, Gwen something, you know who I mean, you've seen her going around town holding a bible . . . Neil says she *really* knows about black magic.'

'Aren't you scared?' asked Fiona, grabbing a pillow. She held it like a dancing partner and swayed rhythmically with it, standing on the bed.

'Not as long as Neil's there,' answered Lisbie, her eyes going dreamy again. 'I wouldn't be scared of *anything* as long as he was there . . .'

'My hero,' said Fiona, addressing the pillow. 'With thee I will fear nothing!' She fell on her knees, still on the bed, and held the pillow out at arm's length in front of her. 'Never leave me, hero of my dreams!' she said, and went on like that until Lisbie finally jumped on her and pushed the pillow in her face.

Malcolm Anderson discovered that most of the information on spontaneous human combustion was to be found in the older literature, and in the more obscure journals; even there the reports tended to be anecdotal and unscientific. There was almost nothing about it in the medical textbooks since the war. And this knowledge filled him with a marvellous excitement; his paper would rekindle the spark of interest . . . My God, he thought, backtracking on his words, 'rekindle the spark of interest!' What a phrase to start a paper on this particular topic!

He walked towards the librarian's desk, past medical students ensconced in the tiny cubicles, past the high bookshelves loaded with centuries of distilled information on every conceivable medical subject. It had been a long time since he'd spent much time in a medical library; usually it was a brief visit to the forensic medicine section, or the pathology shelves when he needed to look up some finding he'd come across during an autopsy, or some abstruse post-mortem diagnosis.

The woman at the desk was very helpful. She was middle-aged, free of makeup, with a healthy, intelligent appearance.

'Mrs Lockhart, I'm writing a paper . . . But I dinna really have that much experience in medical writing. Would you have a book, something I could refer to . . . You ken what I mean, that would tell me how to set it out, like?'

Within a few moments, Mrs Lockhart came back with a slim bound volume and put it on the desk. 'Elements of Medical and Scientific Writing', it was called.

'Would you like to take it out?' she asked.

'Aye,' said Malcolm, trying to contain his excitement. 'Aye, I would that.'

He went back to his car, clutching the book as if it were the Holy Grail.

But once he got home and had settled himself in at his writing desk, he found that it still wasn't as simple as he'd expected. The book appeared to be mostly about the best way of presenting experimental data, the importance of statistical evaluation, and why it was important not to have tables with too many numbers.

Still, there were some things in it which he could use, points that made perfectly good sense. Start off with a review of the pertinent literature, it said in the first chapter, then describe to the reader the aspects which have not already been covered, and why these are important.

Well of course it's important, said Malcolm to himself, otherwise I wouldn't be bothering to write it. But actually putting that thought down on paper wasn't as easy as it sounded.

After that, he found in the second chapter, you describe the materials and methods you propose to use, then you will report, in a separate section, the actual scientific findings. It sounded so clear and concise, but somehow it didn't seem to fit in at all with that Malcolm wanted to say. And he *knew* what he wanted to say . . .

After over an hour of struggling with the inoffensive-seeming book, which left him feeling as if he'd been battling with a multi-coiled boa constrictor, Malcolm gave up, and went to the pantry where he took a tumbler out of the cupboard and poured himself a very large Glen Dronach. He was all set to go away on holiday the next day, and would grapple with that damned book again in Blackpool, just as soon as he got settled into the hotel. And this time, he promised himself, this time he'd break *its* bloody back.

Over the last several years, Douglas Niven had developed the habit of dropping in to Jean Montrose's house every few days to discuss cases that she was involved in, or which had aspects he needed her help with. Although Jean was not a native of Perth, having been born in Aberdeen, she had lived and worked there for long enough to be regarded as a native. Probably more important was that she had a remarkable ability to get on with almost everybody without in any way compromising her direct and sometimes blunt manner. Doug had only been in Perth for just over four years, and used that excuse repeatedly, sometimes to Jean's annoyance.

'You see, being just a lad fae Glesga puts me at a bit of disadvantage here,' he said, sitting back comfortably in Steven's chair and emphasising his Glasgow accent. 'Whereas you know everybody, and they all know you, and tell you everything. And of course when they see me coming, they say, "Here comes the cop", and run.'

'You puir wee thing,' said Jean, with a hint of sarcasm. 'I hae my ain problems, an' I'm nae aboot tae greet for yours! Now just keep quiet for a few minutes. I can't talk to you and write a letter to a surgeon at the same time.'

While Jean concentrated on her correspondence, Douglas looked round the room. They must be doing all right, the Montroses, he thought. The furniture was all very good quality, not flashy, but solid, the kind of things they could hand down to their kids. There was an ornamental display cabinet with curved glass windows in a light wood that looked like walnut. Inside were dark blue and gold plates and cups, a silver milk jug, and a few other items. Photos of the children, two bigger ones of Steven, a snap of two people Douglas assumed were Jean's parents, and over by the window a formal portrait of Steven's parents, stiff in their Sunday best.

'Why is there no a picture of *you* on the wall, Jean?' he blurted out, forgetting that he had been enjoined to silence.

Jean looked up. 'Who would want to look at me?' She smiled and went back to her letter.

Douglas idly turned the pages of the expensive-looking art book on the glass coffee table between Steven's chair and the fireplace, now closed for the summer by an ornamental brass screen. It showed pictures of Venice, with gondoliers and palaces and strange-looking peaked bridges. Doug turned his head; behind him, over the upright piano which still stood despite the years of pounding it had received at the hands of both girls, was a smiling photo of Steven and Jean taken a few years before when the Queen Mother visited the Glass Works.

Finally Jean put the letter in an envelope, licked it and put it in the cardboard box which held the forms and papers she would take back to the surgery in the morning.

The door opened, and Fiona stuck her head in.

'I'm making some tea – would anybody like some?'

'That would be lovely, yes, thanks,' said Douglas, keeping his face straight.

'Well, now that I can give you my undivided attention, Douglas,' smiled Jean, 'what's on your mind?'

'There's a couple of people I need to talk to about the Stroud business, and I'd like to know a bit about them first,' began Douglas. 'The teachers up at St Jude's for a start.'

'Douglas Niven, if you think I'm going to sit here and go over the life histories of all the teachers up there, you're mad. I don't even *know* all of them.'

'No, no, of course not,' said Douglas, surprised at her emphatic tone. 'The one I was thinking of was a chap by the name of George Elmslie, who works in the science department, where Stroud was.' He glanced over at Jean, hoping she knew him. 'I heard that the two of them, I mean Stroud and Elmslie, weren't on the best of terms.'

'I don't know about *that*,' said Jean, 'but I've seen George Elmslie a couple of times. Once he strained a tendon, and another he got a gash on the leg while he was rock-climbing.'

'Very athletic sort of chap, eh?'

Fiona came in with a tray loaded with tea things and two plates of biscuits, Penguins and wheatmeal. Jean eyed the Penguins and smiled at Fiona. 'You always know how to get around me, Fiona, don't you!'

Fiona smiled too, but at Douglas. 'I know what you take,' she said to him. 'Milk and no sugar, right?'

Douglas nodded, and glanced at Jean.

'You met George Elmslie, didn't you, Fiona? At the Choral Society concert?'

Fiona handed Douglas his cup. 'Mr Body Beautiful? I remember him.' She made a face. 'But I also remember that he was more interested in talking to the boys in the choir than to me.'

They all laughed. 'There's no accounting for tastes, is there?' said Douglas, getting up to pass the plate of Penguins to Jean.

'Why do you want to know about George Elmslie?' asked Fiona, turning to Douglas. 'Has he done something awful?' Then her eyes got big suddenly. 'My God,' she breathed. 'Do you think he killed that Mr Stroud?'

'Fiona, you do jump to conclusions, rather,' said Jean. 'Now I'm sure you have other things to do, and I don't want to keep you.'

Fiona couldn't prevent herself from brushing against Douglas on her way to the door.

'I'm still having problems working out what really happened to Stroud,' said Douglas. 'Malcolm Anderson's so wrapped up in the spontaneous combustion idea that I can't get a balanced idea of the different possibilities here.'

Jean had an idea.

'You know Angus Townes?' she asked. 'He's also at St Jude's. He's a really nice man, who's had some terrible tragedies in his life. But he's a chemist, and very well qualified, and I'm sure he'd have some intelligent ideas on the subject.' The Montroses' tabby cat came in, looked up at Doug and boldly jumped up on his knee. 'Throw him off if he bothers you, said Jean. 'Angus Townes . . . He's become a real expert on burns, too, after something that happened to his daughter. Also he could maybe give you some insight about the school, and about Stroud.'

Douglas mumbled something. Angus Townes was one of the teachers on his list to be interviewed.

'I know what we can do,' said Jean, picking the cat up and putting him outside the door, 'Angus is coming over for dinner tomorrow, Tuesday. If you and Cathie would like to come and have dinner too, you could meet him and talk in an informal kind of way here. He's very nice, you'll like him, and I think he might be able to tell you a lot.'

Renée Stroud's parents lived on a farm called 'Fordmouth' near the river Avon, which the local people call the A'an so that they can laugh at the way the visiting Sassenachs and American fishermen pronounce it. Renée's limited vision made it difficult for her to get around; she couldn't drive even the half mile up to the main road, so she walked. She could see most things well enough, but she couldn't read, which was a torture, or even enjoy the television, which now gave her a headache if she tried to watch it for more than a few minutes.

She often listened to cassettes of books, but was forced to lead a much more restricted life than before her vision was damaged. The worst part, and the main reason she hated Morgan so bitterly, was that since the 'accident' she had completely lost her self-confidence.

Renée had never fully explained to her parents what had happened, but they knew she had sued for divorce not long after, and the few comments she made about her husband were enough for them to get a grasp of the seething hatred she felt for him every waking moment of her day. It frightened them, particularly her mother, who would come upon Renée, sitting, looking down at the river with an expression which showed what she felt better than she could have said it.

And they were even more afraid now, but they didn't know quite what of. First there had been the phone call for Renée, then several hours later they had seen a car come bumping down the road to the farm, and Renée had gone out and into it without saying anything to them, except that she would be coming back the next day. They had been sick with worry, and when they heard on the radio that Morgan Stroud had died in suspicious circumstances that same night, they had held on to each other with a dreadful fear. They knew what hatred was in their daughter's heart. Had she killed him? They felt that she was quite capable of doing such a thing; she certainly hated him enough.

The worst was that she wouldn't talk to them about it; she went on her way as before, obviously happy that Morgan was dead, but, as she said, that wasn't going to restore her sight.

What could they do? Of course they couldn't approach the authorities; after all, Renée *was* their daughter. They obviously couldn't discuss it with their few friends . . . The two old people just huddled together in their big hand-carved bed, sleepless, wondering who that person sleeping in the next room really was, that person so consumed with hate that she was apparently capable of risking her own safety and freedom.

But Renée didn't sleep as soundly as they thought. Lying in her bed, she relived, night after night, that awful violent flash of light.

It had been an ordinary enough afternoon; although Renée had a librarian's degree, Morgan had never allowed her to work, reminding her that a woman's place was not out gallivanting around, but in the kitchen cooking his meals and doing his laundry. Not that it stopped him complaining about how much she cost him . . .

The day before, he had come in furious about something or other that had happened at the school, and then ten minutes later came storming out of his study, accusing her of snooping through his letters and papers.

It wasn't true, and she had denied it vigorously; Morgan seemed to accept her denial, and Renée thought the incident was forgotten.

The next afternoon, Morgan had a half-day, and spent the afternoon in his garage lab. She had no idea what he did there, except that it had to do with lasers, intense light beams, which he was using in experiments to accelerate some complicated chemical reactions.

Morgan came round to the house in the middle of the afternoon.

'I need a little help in the lab,' he said. 'Do you have a minute?'

Renée was astonished – he'd never asked for her help before – but she wiped her hands on her apron and accompanied him outside, then down the short, sloping drive to the garage.

'Here, hold this,' he said, putting a long black cylinder in her hand. 'Hold it like this . . . As soon as you see a faint red light in there, tell me, okay?'

And then it was as if the whole world exploded with a white flash inside her head. But through the excruciating pain she could still hear his soft, mocking voice saying that perhaps this would keep his correspondence private . . .

The lawyer she saw the next day was horrified and sympathetic, but said that in court it would be just her word against his, and of course Stroud would say it was an accident. So she started divorce proceedings against him, and as she could have predicted, he made the whole business as acrimonious as possible. There were certain items in the house that belonged to her which he had kept – silver, and some pieces of jewellery, a few items of furniture – and he'd phone from time to time saying she had to come and get the item immediately or he would throw it out with the rubbish. In spite of everything her lawyer could do, he kept her on a string. She could expect such a summons every few weeks, at any odd time of day, and the fury it aroused in her lasted for days.

She still had a few possessions in the house, but they were impounded until after the police had finished their investigation. Then she'd be able to sell the place, and try to forget about Morgan, about that school, about all these people, including that filthy pederast, George Elmslie, Morgan had once told her about. Morgan had been so happy recounting the story, rubbing his fat little hands together as he told her . . .

At the thought of George, Renée unexpectedly started to laugh until the tears rolled out of her eyes. Her parents, sitting in the next room, heard, and held their breath, wondering if Renée was losing her mind.

Of course things were different and much better now she had her new friend, but recently she'd been getting a bit nervous about him too. He was loving and kind most of the time, in spite of all his worries, and had been so supportive. He'd been profoundly angry at Morgan when one day she told him why she couldn't read the newspaper. And somehow he brought out the gentleness, the maternal instinct in her . . . What had frightened her was an occasional glimpse of a hard streak of brutality in him. It was evident only occasionally, but when it surfaced it was like a dark cloud blotting out the sunlight. Renée laughed again, without humour; maybe she'd just become suspicious of all men.

Chapter Eleven

The packet of reports from the Central pathology lab in Dundee appeared on Malcolm Anderson's desk the next morning, sooner than he expected. The lab did the forensics for Central and Eastern Scotland, and had the usual problems of too much work and too few workers, and it often took weeks for the reports to come through.

First was the spectrometer report from the chemical section; all the samples of clothing, carpet, human skin and hair had been tested for flammable hydrocarbons such as petrol, paint thinners and lighter fluids. There was no sign of any such substances. There was a handwritten note from the chief technician asking if the samples could have got mixed up, because the other indicators pointed to an intense fire started by some highly flammable substance.

Anderson shook his head, felt a tingling at the back of his neck, and laughed at himself. He was too old and too experienced to get caught up in this superstitious nonsense.

He turned to the other analyses. The next report was from general pathology (microscopic); 'A segment of vein,' he read, 'consistent with attached description of antecubital vein R forearm. Microscopic examination reveals preservation of gross structure with heat coagulation of tissues and blood within the vessel. The findings are consistent with severe thermal or electric burns.'

Dr Anderson considered that for a moment. Electric burns . . . There had been nothing near the body, certainly no loose wires, broken lamps, anything electrical. In suicide attempts he had seen which involved electrocution, the victims were usually naked, having stepped into the bath holding a single bare wire in one hand before grasping the other once they were in the water. And the burns were nearly always small, and localised to where the wires had touched the skin.

Lightning? The thought came into his mind against his will. Douglas Niven had mentioned that as a possibility, in an uncomfortable, hesitant sort of way. Malcolm suspected that somebody else had given Niven that idea and he was just trying it out. Ball lightning, he'd said. Again that was something Malcolm thought he'd heard about, but he couldn't remember much about it. He'd called the meteorologist at Grampian television who kindly went to look it up for him. 'Ball lightning,' he told him, 'is a rare and mysterious form, a sphere of luminosity that moves horizontally a few meters per second, can penetrate closed windows, often ends in an explosion and leaves an odour of ozone or smoke.'

Malcolm shook his head and turned back to the reports. Ball lightning!

From the dental section, the identification of Morgan Stroud was confirmed. Impressions from both upper and lower jaws had been taken with wax, and although these were incomplete because of charring and disruption of the bone, they conformed almost exactly with impressions taken by a Perth dentist a year before. There was one discrepancy, one missing molar, upper left. The dentist had confirmed by telephone that he had removed this tooth since the impression was taken.

Samples of intact and charred tissue from various parts of the body had been tested for the usual battery of common poisons, including alcohol, barbiturates, arsenic, and cyanide. Negative. A secondary test had been run to exclude the less common poisons such as digitalis and other toxic alkaloids, and that had likewise been negative.

The autopsy room technician came into the office. 'We're ready,' he said. Malcolm Anderson looked at the typed post-mortem list on his desk. There were three scheduled for today, and two of them were old people who had apparently died from heat exhaustion. It was hard to believe that people could die from that in Perth, of all places. But this summer, Perth felt like Death Valley and the weather still hadn't broken. The farmers were desperate, the crops wilting and drying up in the drought-stricken fields.

There was one more report that he hadn't read; the analysis of the greasy film on the windows of Morgan Stroud's house. On his instructions, the technicians had taken swabs off the windows with sterile cottonwool and placed some in an alcohol solution, some in formalin solution, and a third sample in a dry sterile container. He'd insisted on all this because he had no idea what the substance was and didn't want a sarcastic call from the lab asking why he hadn't put it in such-and-such a solution.

But the report didn't reveal very much; the film contained fragments of carbon, mostly in small aggregates, triglycerides and stearic, oleic and smaller amounts of other as yet unidentified free fatty acids, plus a small amount of cholesterol.

Malcolm sighed, and got up out of his chair. Then it struck him that all the lab reports he had just read completely supported his diagnosis of spontaneous human combustion. Hugely pleased, Malcolm braced his shoulders, grabbed his long apron from behind the door and stepped briskly into the autopsy room, whistling.

Gwen Stroud lived in an abandoned railwayman's shed along the tracks towards the west side of town. Only a few people knew this, and they were mainly railway workers; being generally a kindly lot, they sometimes left food for her outside the door: nothing fancy, maybe a sandwich or an apple left over from a lunch pail. Inside the shed, there wasn't much: a thin mattress, covered in tattered striped ticking, rescued from a skip and dragged there by Gwen. It now lay on the floorboards along the side of the hut, under the boarded-up window. Opposite the mattress was a pile of old newspapers, some of which seemed to have had sections removed with scissors. On the mattress was a sheet, grey with age, and an old army greatcoat was spread out over the sheet for the cold days. In the present hot weather, Gwen slept on top of the coat.

From her makeshift bed, Gwen could lean over and reach into the cardboard box that held all her earthly possessions: a metal mug, two old willow-pattern china plates of different sizes, half a dozen unmatched woollen socks and some lisle stockings, some underwear, a couple of shapeless garments stuffed unfolded into the corners, a framed photo of two girls in a sunny garden, one a few years older than the other, a few yellowed press cuttings. Near the top of the box were a few basic toilet items, a faded photo of herself with her parents and her brother Morgan. Morgan's image had long ago been heavily inked out, making deep furrows in the paper, and a large inked arrow pointed down on his head. Propped up against the wall opposite the bed was a reproduction of a bearded and haloed Christ, staring out at her from his cardboard frame. There were two books on the floor by the bed: a bible, old, black and tattered, next to a thick, well-thumbed volume of extracts from Aleister Crowley's *Equinox*, which, when talking to her young disciples, she called the book of God's magic.

Gwen looked through a crack to see if there was anyone around, picked up her bible, then pushed the door open and strode off along the track, back towards the station. Half a mile further, she crossed the tracks and headed for the bridge. It should be getting dark by the time she reached Kinnoull Hill, and completely dark by the time she got to the top.

'Have a good time, both of you!' said Jean.

'We will!' replied Neil, but for some reason Lisbie just mumbled something and went out quickly. Jean didn't notice, but Fiona, who was also at the door, did, and resolved to ask Lisbie later what was going on.

'I don't really like this,' said Lisbie, driving her ancient Morris Minor down the hill. 'I always tell my parents where I'm going, and they trust me.'

The sun had gone down over the hills, and although it had been a hot day again, a breeze sprang up and the air cooled suddenly.

'If you'd told them where you were *really* going,' said Neil, matter-of-factly, 'they wouldn't have let you go, so you didn't have any choice, right?'

'Well, I still don't like it,' repeated Lisbie. 'Where are we supposed to meet them?'

'At the top, in the tower,' said Neil. 'Actually, Billy and Terry Drummond aren't coming, so it'll be just us and Gwen.' Maybe it was the sudden chilling of the air, but Lisbie shivered.

'Did you bring a sweater or something?' Neil was smiling at her with those big eyes of his, and Lisbie's fears melted away. How could she be worried, when she had Neil taking care of her? Maybe he *was* younger, but he was a lot bigger, and very strong.

Lisbie had tried to tell Fiona how she felt about Neil, but it was so difficult; when faced with strong emotions, Lisbie ran out of language. Yes, of course he's nice, she'd said, and no, he didn't try anything when they were in the car together, or any other time, for that matter. Fiona had *laughed* . . . Better luck next time, she said, except you've probably already turned him right off. Then there was another of those interruptions during which both of them landed on the floor. They sat up, out of breath, shook the hair out of their faces and resumed the conversation, still sitting on the floor.

'It's really funny,' said Lisbie thoughtfully. 'You know

how it is with Mum and Dad. Basically she decides what's
going on, and he grumbles and goes along with it, right?'

'Not always,' said Fiona in a funny kind of voice, and
Lisbie knew what she meant. They both remembered the
time when her father had gone off for a while with that
woman from his office.

'You know what I mean,' said Lisbie, annoyed. She
hated to be reminded of that time, which was one of the
saddest in her life. 'Anyway, with Neil . . . I couldn't
imagine having that kind of relationship with him. He says
what we're going to do, and that's it. And he's *younger* than
me, I know. I just can't help it. Do you think I'm just weak,
or something?' Fiona looked at her with a slightly puzzled
expression, and the conversation had stopped there, because
Neil arrived to pick her up.

'Turn left here,' said Neil. 'There's a car park about half
a mile up the road, on the right, and we'll walk up from
there.'

Lisbie was beginning to get into the spirit of the thing,
and she laughed. 'I couldn't count how many times I've
been up Kinnoull Hill, but never in the dark. Did you see
any ghosties or bogles when you were there the last time?'

'Just an owl,' said Neil. 'And I think he was more scared
than I was.' Darkness was falling already, and the tall pine
trees at the edge of the gravel car park looked dark and
menacing. The breeze rustled the branches, and Lisbie fan-
cied they were talking to her, but she refused to listen to
their message. No, this was going to be fun, she told herself
firmly, an adventure she'd enjoy telling her friends and
family about. Her parents wouldn't mind as long as she
came back safely, but Lisbie knew that her father would be
strict, and tell her sternly that in future she was to tell them
where she was going, before, and not after the fact.

It was getting hard to see things now. Lisbie walked
straight into the wire fence and let out a little squeal of
surprise. If Fiona had been there, she would have just about

died laughing, but Neil quietly held the wire up while she went underneath, then she did the same for him. Everything was so quiet . . . Lisbie tried to remember the last time she'd been there; they'd all been on a picnic with their uncle Charlie, who lived in the States. Had it been so quiet then? Lisbie couldn't remember; she certainly hadn't been aware of it at the time.

It was really dark among the trees, and even though Neil was there right beside her, she couldn't help feeling a bit scared. What if there were animals in the undergrowth? Maybe there were some that only came out at night . . .

Suddenly there was a loud crack, and Lisbie's hand leapt to her mouth. For a moment she thought her heart had stopped. But it was only a rotten branch that Neil had stepped on. Neil was very quiet; he seemed preoccupied, as if he were thinking about what was going to happen up there in the old stone tower. And what *was* going to happen? Neil had been rather vague about it.

'Well, you know Gwen Stroud? She . . . Well, she reads . . . mostly the bible, but sometimes from other books, and she makes it sound very weird, and she brings this stuff and lights it and the smoke makes you feel funny and light-headed . . .'

'Is it pot?' asked Lisbie sharply. 'Because if it is, I'm not interested.'

'No, of course not,' said Neil in a superior way. 'I don't know what it is exactly, but it's nothing bad, I know that.'

How he knew, Lisbie didn't ask. She didn't even think of questioning him. Neil had said it wasn't anything bad, and that was the end of it, as far as she was concerned.

'Then what happens?'

'Then we all recite some stuff together, and that brings the aura into the place . . .'

'Aura?' asked Lisbie, fascinated.

'It's a feeling that comes into the room, and you're sharing it with everybody there, a kind of magic, I suppose.'

Neil took a big breath; his words were not coming easily, because like Lisbie, he had difficulty articulating feelings.

Finally he said, 'It's like a spirit coming into the place, and it fills it . . . and seems to enter right into you and makes you able . . . to do things you normally couldn't.' Neil finished his sentence in a rush.

'What kind of things?' asked Lisbie. It all sounded so exciting, so wonderful.

'We concentrate on something, and if you concentrate long enough and hard enough, you can make things happen.'

'Like moving mountains, you mean? Is it like faith, where you can make good things happen if you have enough faith?'

'I suppose so,' said Neil, but Lisbie could see that he didn't think it was at all the same. 'You *can* make good things happen,' he said, and then he looked Lisbie straight in the eye. 'Sometimes,' he went on, and Lisbie could hear the intensity in his voice, 'if you have a good enough reason, you can make bad things happen too.'

The sounds in the woods around Kinnoull Hill were rather frightening. The branches creaked, and every so often there was a sudden, terrifying scuttling nearby as some nocturnal creature was disturbed. Slowly they worked their way up the hill. Suppose he ran off, thought Lisbie, just ran off down the hill and left me here. What on earth would I do? She grasped Neil's hand tightly and walked on, trying to feel as if they were just going out for a walk together. After all, she knew Kinnoull Hill like the back of her hand.

When they reached the peak, a crescent moon was coming over the horizon, and its thin light made the trees seem darker and more mysterious than ever.

The tower, long deserted and empty, showed up faintly against the sky a few hundred yards away, and as Lisbie watched, a light flickered there, just for a moment, then died.

Lisbie could almost feel the silence that followed that momentary flash. 'I'm really a bit scared,' she said to Neil. Without meaning to, she spoke in a whisper, clinging on to his arm.

'There's nothing to worry about,' he said, and at that moment, listening to his voice, Lisbie realised that Neil hadn't expected to see that light, and that he too was very frightened indeed.

Chapter Twelve

When Lisbie and Neil looked again, the light in the tower had gone. All that remained was the silhouette of the ancient turret, standing stark, forbidding and sombre against the night sky.

'Let's go home,' said Lisbie, shivering. 'I'm really scared.'

Neil hesitated for a fraction of a second.

'Gwen must have got there ahead of us,' he said. 'She has a lantern, and that's what we saw.' He held Lisbie's hand with a reassuring pressure, and again Lisbie felt that nothing very dreadful could happen to her as long as Neil was there. She held on tight as they slowly approached the tower, walking along the twisting path at the crest of the hill.

It *must* be Gwen, Neil thought, although she always liked them to get there ahead of her. Who else would come up here at night? The old wooden door had a heavy padlock on it, and only Gwen had the key, because she'd cut the original one off and put on one of her own.

They stopped at the door; everything was eerily silent, as if the world had stopped breathing, and was watching, and waiting. Neil looked up at the narrow, empty window high above him. Nothing. With Lisbie hanging on to him for dear life, he gently pushed the door, and it opened a fraction. The creak was terrifyingly loud. He pushed it further, expecting to see a faint light from Gwen's lantern, but inside there was only darkness, hard, impenetrable. Neil took a step forward, and then another, with Lisbie clinging tightly to his hand.

'Eeeeeeeee!' The piercing shriek came from about a foot away from them, and both Neil and Lisbie leapt back, terrified, and crashed into the door, which slammed shut with them inside. A lamp shone right in their faces, blinding them, and Lisbie found herself screaming at the top of her voice from sheer panic and terror.

'Och, shut up, you,' said a female voice. 'Neil, why didn't you do the owl hoot? Are you trying to frighten me to death?'

'Gwen!' Neil, almost speechless, could barely get her name out. Lisbie stopped screaming and was now sobbing quietly, her face in her hands. She had never been so frightened in her entire life.

'Well, you'd better come upstairs, then,' said Gwen. 'My, what a scare the two of you gave me!'

Numb, Lisbie followed them up the spiralling stone stairs; for a brief moment she thought of making a dash for the door, but she was sure she'd get lost trying to get down Kinnoull Hill, and her body would be found in the morning, or maybe even during the night, by wild animals . . .

They came to a round room, stone walled, of course, and without windows. Here there was a dim light from a lantern set at the back, away from the stairs, standing on what looked like an altar. The staircase continued upwards, spiralling into the darkness.

'Sit you down,' Gwen told Lisbie, not unkindly. 'There, facing the lamp . . . And Neil, you sit down beside her; she's still afraid.'

Later, when she tried to remember what had happened, the next hour was a blur to Lisbie, although she tried to concentrate. Gwen read some passages from a worn old bible, passages Lisbie didn't recognise, but which sounded Old Testament, and from another book also, and she and Neil said things together in a low chorus, words she didn't understand, and Gwen did something to the lamp and a sweet-scented greenish smoke came out. Suddenly Lisbie felt relaxed and at ease, almost detached, watching the scene as if she were outside it, above it, sitting on a cloud.

Lisbie hardly remembered getting down the hill; the last thing she remembered was Gwen putting the light out, and it was as if she had extinguished the whole world, the entire universe.

She managed to drive all right, and took Neil home. There was a police car a few yards beyond the house, and as Lisbie pulled up to let Neil out, somebody climbed out of it and came over towards her. It was Douglas Niven, and he had an expression on his face that Lisbie had never seen before.

'Get out, the two of you,' he snapped.

Shaking, Lisbie got out and almost fell. Douglas caught her, and looked over at Neil, who had got out of the passenger side. He looked suddenly very scared.

'I think we'd better go into the house,' said Douglas to Neil. 'I need to talk to your father about you.'

Neil hesitated, and for a moment Lisbie thought he was going to run for it, but he didn't. For the first time, Lisbie saw Neil in a different light; now, he had no superhuman strengths, he was just a scared kid in a lot of trouble. Neil went up the steps and rang the bell. A light went on, and the door opened. In the doorway stood a rather short, thickset man a few years older than Doug, with the physique of a boxer and a craggy face that had obviously taken many a hard punch. His hair was dark, swept back, with a sharp widow's peak. He looked relieved to see Neil, then surprised when he saw Doug and Lisbie with him. He opened the door more fully and stood there, hesitating, seemingly unsure about asking them in.

When Douglas caught sight of the person standing anxiously just behind Neil's father, he took a sudden, shocked breath; it was Renée Stroud.

'I'm Detective Inspector Douglas Niven,' said Doug

heavily, not bothering to take out his identification. There were enough people there who already knew who he was. 'If you're Mr Mackay, I'd like to have a word with you about your son.'

'Come in, then.' Ken Mackay spoke with a strong Glasgow accent. He stood aside and Doug followed Neil and Lisbie into the house. As he passed Neil's father, Doug felt a wave of antagonism emanating from him. As a policeman, Doug was used to such a reception, but didn't expect it here.

Doug got straight to the point.

'We got a report of lights up on Kinnoull Hill,' he said, once Ken Mackay had closed the door. 'A squad car found Miss Montrose's car in the parking area at the bottom of the hill . . . We have reason to believe that your son and Miss Montrose illegally broke into the locked tower at the top.'

Doug glanced at Lisbie; she was as white as a ghost, and trembling. Everybody else was looking at Neil.

'Well?' said his father.

'We didn't break in,' said Neil. He was looking equally scared; all his poise and confidence had evaporated.

'But you were inside the tower?'

Neil and Lisbie both nodded at the same time. Neil told Doug a modified version of the truth, without mentioning Gwen.

Doug addressed Ken. 'We've had a few reports of lights up there, and at night it's a really dangerous place, right on the edge of the cliff . . .' He turned to Neil, and his face became stern. '. . . and it certainly is not a good place to be taking a young lady. I won't ask you how you got in, and I won't pursue the matter now, but I want your solemn undertaking that this won't happen again.'

Neil nodded.

'I never want to go up there again in my life,' said Lisbie in a tiny voice, and Douglas wanted to smile and hug her as he'd done many times before. But he didn't; both those kids needed a lesson.

From the moment he saw Renée Stroud in the hall, and even while he was talking to Neil, Doug had been wondering what she was doing there; was she Ken's girlfriend? She was looking at him with that strange, flickering gaze, but said nothing, and Doug couldn't tell what she was thinking.

'Now we've dealt with that problem,' said Doug, 'Lisbie, I think you'd better go home now.' He hesitated for a second. 'I had to call your mother when we found the car, so she knows where you were . . .' He looked at her as sternly as he knew how. 'And if she gives you a good skelping, you deserve it.'

'I'm eighteen,' said Lisbie, with a certain dignity. 'And *nobody* skelps me.'

Neil followed Lisbie out to her car, and when they had gone, Douglas looked curiously at Renée and Ken, both of whom had stood silently while Doug was dealing with Lisbie and Neil. Without saying anything, Ken showed Doug into the front room where they all sat down.

'It's a small world,' Doug said to Renée, a hint of sarcasm in his voice.

'Now you've frightened those two bairns out o' their wits, is there anything else you're needin'?' Ken Mackay looked at Doug with a truculent expression.

Doug looked steadily back at him, saw the dangerous glint in the man's eye, and said, remembering what Jean Montrose had told him, 'I understand your son was in Morgan Stroud's class.'

There was a gasp from Renée, and he saw her bite her lower lip.

'Well, what of it?' asked Ken, in a suddenly quiet voice.

'Well, Neil made some comments recently I'd like to talk to him about,' said Doug. 'But I'll be coming up to the school tomorrow, and I'll see him then.'

Out in the hall, there was the sound of the front door being closed very quietly, and then Doug heard Neil's footsteps going upstairs.

He paused. Both Ken and Renée were sitting on the couch, and she had taken hold of his hand and was hanging on to him so tightly her knuckles were white. So that answered one of his questions.

Doug got up. 'I'll be on my way now. We'll be checking that tower in the morning, and I'll let you know if there was any damage done.'

He turned at the door. 'You must have been really angry at the way Morgan Stroud treated your son, Mr Mackay,' he said quietly. '*Really* angry.'

He nodded to Renée, and went down the steps to his car.

All of a sudden, the case of Morgan Stroud was getting interesting.

As soon as he got home he went straight to the phone and called the Montroses' house. Jean answered.

'Did Lisbie get home all right?'

'Yes. Between what happened on Kinnoull Hill and talking to you, she was scared out of her wits, poor child.' Jean did not sound too happy with him.

'Well, I just didn't want her to get into too much trouble when she got home . . .'

'Douglas Niven, why should she get into *any* trouble? The only thing she did wrong was not tell us where she was going, and I think that's our business, don't you?'

'Jean . . . Never mind. Everything ended all right, and I just wanted to be sure Lisbie got home safely.' Douglas sounded so woebegone that Jean laughed.

'Well, no harm was done, and I'm sure you had reasons of your own . . . We're seeing you tomorrow, right, you and Cathie, about seven?'

When Doug put the phone down, he sighed heavily. Jean would understand when he explained it all to her, but she certainly was very protective of her family.

'Well, you look like the cat that ate the cream, then found it was sour,' said Cathie, who had been half listening to the conversation. She opened the oven and took out his dinner.

'Here's your mealy jimmies and chips, fine and warm.' She looked doubtfully at the dried-up chips. 'They look a wee bit dry . . . Here, put some ketchup on them . . .'

Doug sat down and, between mouthfuls, told her what had happened, only noticing what he was eating when he came across a chip he couldn't break with his teeth. He finished by telling her about finding Renée Stroud at the Mackays' house.

'Some coincidence, eh?' he said, wiping his mouth with his napkin. Cathie shrugged.

'It doesn't take much to get you excited, does it?' she said. 'Not in that direction, anyway.'

He looked suspiciously at her, but her back was turned so he couldn't tell if she was joking.

'Well, don't you think it's an interesting coincidence? Stroud taking it out really viciously on the boy, just because his estranged wife is seeing Neil's father?'

'It didn't sound as if Jean Montrose was too happy with you just now.' Cathie started to put away his dishes. 'I bet she didn't tell Steven, though, because he wouldn't be amused one bit. And I'd have thought Lisbie would have more sense than to go traipsing up there in the middle of the night like that . . . Do you want some more tea?'

Doug shook his head.

'I told Lisbie her mother should give her a good skelping. I would have, I think, if she was my daughter.'

'At the rate you're going, my lad, you'll never know,' replied Cathie acidly, putting his cup down with a bang. 'Remember how you used talk about "your son and heir"?'

'Well?' said Doug as usual on the defensive when this topic came up.

'The way things look now, by the time he can walk, he'll be pushing you around the nursing home,' said Cathie cryptically. She wiped the inside of the sink with a wet cloth then hung it between the taps to dry.

*   *   *

'It's a heat rash,' said Jean. The morning surgery was more crowded than usual. 'Keep the baby out of the sun, give him cool sponge baths often, and let him go naked as much as you can . . . Let me know if it isn't better in a few days.'

Jean closed the door after checking the waiting room; Mrs Lindsay and her baby were her last patients, so she went over to see how Helen Inkster was doing.

'I'm going to take a couple of weeks off, and go to Saudi Arabia to cool down,' grumbled Helen. 'The radio said there wasn't any sign of rain in the offing for East and Central Scotland.'

'Mrs Thatcher even said something in Parliament about the heat wave.' Jean flipped through the medical journals on Helen's desk.

'I didn't think she knew anything *existed* North of Leeds,' said Helen, sounding unusually tart. Then she grinned, as if to excuse her abruptness. 'Anyway, I'm thinking of planting some date palms in the front garden, and maybe a few cactuses.'

'Great, I love dates,' said Jean absently; she had stopped at an article that interested her. 'I wonder if Malcolm Anderson read this,' she said, speaking almost to herself.

Helen's voice went on, '. . . The roof of the prison was set on fire this morning,' and Jean pulled her attention back to what Helen was saying. 'They're demanding air conditioners in their cells . . .'

'Well, a hole in the roof'll improve the ventilation for them, anyway,' said Jean sharply. 'I'm sick and tired of hearing about those criminals and their demands. *I'd* like an air-conditioner too . . .' It took Helen's astonished expression for Jean to realise that she had spoken out of character; usually she had sympathy for everyone. 'Sorry,' she said, feeling embarrassed. 'The heat must be affecting me too.'

Chapter Thirteen

Next morning, Douglas drove out to St Jude's; he hadn't been out in the countryside recently and he was shocked at the dry, brown appearance of the fields and hills on the way. Even the trees, normally easily able to withstand the worst of weather, had their leaves turning brown at the edges, although autumn was still a long way off.

He negotiated the sharp bend in the road, but the turn into St Jude's drive caught him by surprise, and he half skidded, half slid around the corner, thinking it was a good thing there wasn't any other traffic, and happy that he was in a police vehicle, not his pampered old Austin Atlantic, which would never have made it without turning over. He crawled slowly through the narrow gates, and even at that speed he raised a cloud of dust that followed the car all the way to the front of the school.

He parked in the area marked 'Visitors', and went in through the front door. Mr Wardle, the headmaster, had agreed to put a small room on the third floor at Doug's disposal for interviewing the boys, not without some reluctance. Space was at a premium at the school, he explained, and he hoped Douglas wouldn't need it for very long.

'I don't think so,' Doug had said. 'I just want a brief chat with the boys who knew Mr Stroud; they aren't suspects.'

Mr Wardle's laugh was so shrill Doug held the phone away from his ear.

Doug was a shrewd if untutored psychologist; he decided to see the boys together rather than individually, thinking they would be more likely to talk freely in a group, and would reinforce or disagree with each other, so that he could better evaluate their responses.

He made sure the boys had been in the room for a few minutes before he came in, in order to encourage their feeling that he was a visitor to the school rather than an authority figure. When he wanted to be, Douglas was very good at getting people to talk; he provided a quiet, unobtrusive interest to which the boys seemed to respond.

'So what kind of a person was Morgan?' he asked them, deliberately using Stroud's christian name.

'He was okay as a teacher,' said Billy, hesitantly. 'He was strict and sarcastic, but he made sure you learned the stuff.'

'I don't think he *cared* about a lot of things.' Terry Drummond was sitting straight up, looking very neat and tidy in his grey blazer and red-and-blue tie. His eyes blinked behind his round glasses. 'He didn't care how he looked, or the way he walked . . .' Terry glanced at the others, then said rather helplessly. 'He was very fat . . .'

'And he certainly didn't have much feeling about other people,' said Dick Prothero, who had always tried to stay on the good side of Morgan Stroud. 'Boys or teachers or anybody.'

'Yes he did,' interrupted Neil quietly. 'He hated everybody, and everybody hated him right back, including us.'

A silence followed Neil's words, and Douglas looked thoughtfully at him. He seemed to have completely recovered his composure after the events of last night; and there was something a bit disconcerting, an emotional awareness that was surprisingly sharp and direct in someone as young as Neil Mackay.

'Anybody in particular who hated him?' asked Doug, casually. He was sitting among the boys rather than behind the teacher's table, although the smallness of the desk forced him to sit sideways.

'You mean besides us?' Neil gave a slight smile, as if he

enjoyed trying to draw the fire of suspicion.

'Besides you.' Doug's glance included all of them.

'He didn't talk to anybody, hardly,' said Billy. 'People just avoided him.'

'He talked quite a bit to Mr Elmslie . . . and Mr Townes too. I think those two were the only ones who ever said anything to him,' said Terry.

'Was there anybody who had a particular dislike of Mr Stroud?' asked Doug.

The boys looked at each other and grinned. 'Big George,' said Billy and Dick together.

'That's what we call Mr Elmslie,' explained Terry.

'What about Mr Townes?' asked Doug, to change the subject.

'They seemed to get along okay,' said Billy.

'He's a lot cleverer than the other teachers,' said Terry, as if he'd just realised that fact.

'He helped to set up a shelter for abused kids in Perth,' said Billy. 'He's very hot on that.'

'The way he's different,' said Neil, 'is he talks to us as if we were real people, not just stupid kids he's paid to teach.' Billy and Dick nodded; Neil always seemed to be able to put their thoughts into words. 'But we only see a tiny bit of him, the surface part. Underneath, he's very sad and reserved, and sometimes he just sits by himself, as if he was really miserable about something.' Again there was a short silence; Neil had summarised everything the other boys were thinking, and more.

Douglas moved in his seat and stretched his legs out in front of him. 'I've heard that some of the boys here play at . . . magic; you know, spells, that kind of thing.' Douglas felt suddenly uncomfortable; he was more at ease asking direct, factual questions, because he was good at detecting lies and subterfuge. Part of his discomfort was due to the fact that he didn't know what were the right questions in this context.

The boys were looking at him with suddenly blank expressions.

'Not any more,' said Neil, very quietly.

As the boys were leaving the room, Doug crooked a finger at Neil, indicating that he should stay behind.

'We checked the tower first thing this morning,' he said. 'The lock was on and everything was all right . . .' He paused, trying to get some insight into this tall, immobile boy in front of him. '. . . Renée looked pretty upset, last night.'

For a moment he thought Neil was going to respond, but he just said, 'Can I go now?'

'In a moment,' said Doug. 'But first,' he said, in a kind tone of voice, 'tell me a bit about you and Stroud. I hear he really persecuted you.'

But Neil just shook his head. 'He's dead now,' he said, 'there's no point in talking about it.'

It wasn't until Doug had a talk with Mr Wardle that he learned that Mr Mackay had driven up to the school on two occasions this term to complain about Stroud's treatment of Neil.

'Mackay Senior came across as rather a boor, a bit of a ruffian, I'm afraid,' said Mr Wardle, dabbing at his nose with a handkerchief. 'I simply can't imagine what kind of school *he* went to . . . I believe he was brought up in Glasgow . . .' He said it as if that explained everything, ignoring Doug's own fairly marked Clydeside accent. He hesitated, not wanting to seem to be witholding information.

'And last week, the second time he came up, he cornered Stroud and actually threatened him with physical violence, if you can believe that,' he went on, shaking his head. 'You know, Inspector, like yours, our profession is being treated with less and less respect these days. It's a sign of the times, I suppose . . .'

*   *   *

'Did you get one of those?' George Elmslie held up a flimsy official-looking letter and Angus Townes glanced up from his papers.

'It looks like one I got from Inspector Niven,' he said. 'Is that who it's from?'

George nodded. 'I suppose it's about our late colleague,' he said, 'but of course that's just conjecture.' His voice sounded odd, and Angus looked up at him again. He was looking out of the window. 'That police car's still there . . .'

'Why, what else have you been up to, George, besides bumping off poor old Morgan?' Angus grinned; for some reason he took a perverse pleasure in teasing George.

George made a sudden movement and Angus moved back, startled, noticing suddenly what a big man his colleague was.

George glowered at him. 'That's not funny, Angus. Anyway I thought the case was closed . . . Have you heard any different?' George's heavy, usually rather expressionless face was flushed, and a thin line of sweat ran along his hairline, but that could have been the heat, which in the small, airless commonroom was stifling, in spite of the open window.

'There's no reason to suppose our two invitations are related,' said Angus, watching George with some interest. 'Maybe they've noticed the condition of my car; that would be grounds for suspicion, at the very least, don't you think?'

George didn't answer; but Angus was aware of the man's fear, his acute discomfort, and it made an uneasy contrast with his fine physique. Angus gazed thoughtfully at him; why should George be so concerned about having to go and talk to Douglas Niven, particularly when he knew that Angus had also received a similar summons?

'Yes, I think the case *is* closed,' said Angus. 'Spontaneous human combustion, they think it was. So they must be after you for something else. Your income tax, maybe? Let me know if I can help; I can't afford to bail you out, but I'll be happy to give you a character reference.'

George closed his book with a bang, scowled unpleasantly
at Angus, bounced to his feet and went out, slamming the
door behind him. The heat, thought Angus, it must be the
heat. And if it hadn't been so hot, he probably wouldn't
have been tempted to tease George so unkindly, either.

As soon as the door closed, all the weight of his sadness
came down on him again. Angus felt that his life was like
pushing a huge rock up a hill; by using every ounce of effort
he could just keep it in motion, but if he relaxed even for a
moment it threatened to roll back and crush him.

But it *wasn't* quite the same; the thought of that pleasant
cup of coffee he'd had with Jean Montrose in the little cafe
opposite the nursing home crossed his mind, and suddenly
there seemed to be faint outlines in the fog, some movement
. . . a feeling that life might at some point contain more for
him than just pain.

George felt better after slamming the commonroom door
behind him. His watch showed that he still had a couple of
minutes before his class was due to start. He went in to the
staff toilet and locked the door; there was just enough time
to work a bit on his deltoids, so he stripped off his shirt, and
tensed his arm and chest muscles, staring intently into the
small, fly-speckled mirror above the sink. With his right
elbow held in to his body by his left hand, he strained against
the resistance. The deltoid came up quite nicely, but it
wasn't as well defined as he would have liked. Then the bell
went, and a moment later somebody rattled the doorknob.

'Just a moment,' he said, pulling his shirt over his head
and adjusting his tie. Not bad, he thought, turning his
shoulders from side to side, but those deltoids and trapezius
muscles need some work.

He went down the narrow stairs towards his classroom.
Now that he was the head of the department, he had been
given a slightly larger classroom, with windows on two sides
which gave some cross-ventilation. He pushed his way

through the little knot of boys and opened the door with his key. The boys filed in, some of them saying good morning, others still talking to each other. It didn't take long for George to tell what kind of homes those boys came from. Neil Mackay was talking to his friend Billy Wilson, but stopped speaking as he came into the room and looked at George for a second, but didn't say anything. What peculiar eyes that boy has, George thought; they seem to glow . . . And he had a strange expression, too, or was that just his imagination? Maybe . . . George shrugged to himself. He'd assiduously avoided touching any of the boys at the school, but he felt an old familiar stirring; maybe it was the heat, or maybe getting into the photography again had started him thinking along those lines. And now that Morgan Stroud was dead, he felt a new freedom, an almost ecstatic liberation . . .

Once the thought had rooted in his mind, he wasn't able to dislodge it; during the entire class, although he was perfectly able to discuss and teach them about movement and acceleration on inclined planes, the sight of Neil Mackay, the way he moved behind that small desk, the smoothness of his skin . . . All of it lit up fires which he thought were now extinguished, or at least dormant.

'Drummond, can you tell me the rate of acceleration of a body in free fall?'

Terry Drummond shook his head. He knew that he'd never be able to understand the principle of acceleration, especially after Mr Elmslie had informed them that acceleration could occur when a body was following a curved path, even though its speed remained the same.

'Mackay?' The tone of George Elmslie's voice changed, but so little that Neil's friend Billy Wilson was the only one who noticed.

'Thirty-two feet per second,' replied Neil promptly. He liked this stuff, especially now that Stroud was no longer there to take the fun out of it with his sarcastic comments.

'With what limits?' asked Elmslie. With a kind of perverse delight, Billy kicked Neil's leg from his place at the next desk. He wished he could say, 'Hey, Neil, the bloke's giving you the come-on, don't you see what he's doing?'

Neil ignored Billy, but made a mental note to beat the daylights out of him during break. He had enough problems of his own without getting into trouble with Mr Elmslie.

'Limits?' he asked, hoping to gain a little time.

'Well, suppose a person jumps out of an aircraft at thirty thousand feet, do you think he'll keep on accelerating until he hits the ground?'

George put his elbows on the desk and cupped his chin in his hands, waiting for an answer, his eyes fixed on Neil. A strangled snort came from Billy, who was unable to contain himself any longer, and to everyone's surprise, George ignored the interruption, unlike Morgan Stroud who would have laid into the culprit without mercy.

Neil's mind went blank; normally sensitive and quick on the uptake, he could feel there was something in the air, something going on around him, but he had no idea what it was.

Finally, George turned to Dick Prothero, the sycophant, but Dick hadn't the faintest idea even of what the question had been.

'Air resistance,' said George, addressing Neil, 'will slow the acceleration until a fixed terminal velocity is reached at around two hundred and twenty miles per hour . . .' He sighed. 'You'd better stay after class and I'll attempt to make you understand this a little better.'

'What should I wear?' asked Cathie, looking at the clock. It was already after six, and they were supposed to be at the Montroses' at seven.

'Nothing too fancy,' replied Douglas, without thinking. Cathie shook her head at him. 'Douglas Niven,' she said, 'you know as well as I do that I don't own a single thing that's even a *little bit* fancy.'

Dinner at the Montroses' was always an event; the food was good, there was plenty of it, and conversation never flagged. The only potentially discordant item was Fiona, who didn't like Cathie Niven. 'It's got nothing to do with Doug,' she said angrily once when Lisbie challenged her. 'I just don't like her. She's . . . Well, it's that she's . . .'

'Married to Douglas! That's the only thing you don't like about her!' interrupted Lisbie loudly, and ran before Fiona could catch her.

Before the guests arrived, Jean sternly warned Fiona to behave and be polite to Cathie, 'And what's more, Fiona Montrose,' she said pointedly, 'I think you're being very silly about the *whole thing*.'

Angus Townes arrived first. Only Jean had met him before, so she came to the door to greet him.

'Come on in,' she said, with that warmth and good-natured friendliness that she always radiated. 'You must be roasting, with that jacket and tie!'

Angus Townes was indeed uncomfortable, and not only from the heat of the day, which was just now beginning to die down. It had been a long time since he'd been invited to someone's home for dinner; the last time had been several months ago, a duty dinner with the headmaster and his wife. For years, Angus had avoided social occasions, as they always seemed to reopen his wounds. Not that he didn't like to see people being happy, and he certainly appreciated the give and take of family life; those occasions just reminded him too painfully of his own losses.

'Steven, this is Angus Townes,' said Jean. 'Girls, come and say hello . . . This is Fiona, my elder daughter, and behind her is Lisbie . . .'

'The younger, and of course the prettier,' said Lisbie, quite recovered from her adventure of the night before. She tilted her chin at her sister.

'Well, she's certainly the more impudent,' said Jean, who was quite used to this. 'And she's also the best at setting the table, aren't you, dear?'

With a forced sigh, Lisbie went off.

'Would you care for a sherry?' asked Steven from the table near the window, where he was serving drinks. 'Or would you prefer a gin and tonic?'

'Sherry would be fine, thanks,' replied Angus, going over towards him. 'Dry, if you have it.'

Douglas and Cathie Niven came soon afterwards, and Cathie picked up a glass of sweet sherry before following Jean back into the kitchen.

'Jean tells me you teach at St Jude's,' said Steven. 'This is Doug Niven, by the way, if you haven't met: He's the long arm of the law around here.'

They talked for a while about the weather, the initial topic of every dinner, every cocktail party, every luncheon in the area these days.

'The golf course is about burned up,' said Doug, glumly. 'It's a real shame, even the greens are like dried hay, and the ba' just rolls on for ivver.'

'Do you see a lot more crime in a heat wave like this?' asked Angus. 'It certainly seems to make people very aggressive and irritable.'

Doug held out his glass for another sherry. The glasses were very pretty, cut crystal, maybe even Waterford, but they didn't hold much.

'Well, some people think that the heat's responsible for a lot of things,' replied Doug cautiously. 'And I must say, there have certainly been some strange goings-on around here recently.'

'Are you referring to my colleague Morgan Stroud's death?'

'Well, yes, but that's not all of it, not by a long chalk . . .' Doug went on to give a recital of the fires, accidents and other unusual events that seemed in some way to be connected to the heat wave.

'There's supposed to be a black magic ring working somewhere around here,' said Steven. 'My manager, Bob Mackenzie, a very sensible chap, was doing some stargazing with his telescope just last night, and happened to see some very strange lights, right up at the very top of Kinnoull Hill.'

'Probably a vagrant,' said Doug, without batting an eyelid. 'We hear about these lights every so often, and we've given up checking them out, because there's never anything suspicious there.'

'Well, the word around town is that there *is* a coven, or whatever they call it,' said Steven. 'And they do strange things, and maybe that's all connected, more than the heat.'

'Talking about heat,' said Douglas, taking the opportunity, and addressing Angus, 'Jean tells me that you're quite an expert on burns. Have you ever heard of *spontaneous human combustion*?'

'I've heard of it,' said Angus slowly, 'and I know there have been cases reported, especially during heat waves, several in America. It's supposed to occur when the fuels in the human body combine in a certain way. Chemically, I must say that it makes sense.'

Steven raised his eyebrows. 'In the paper they said that's what Morgan Stroud died of,' he said, looking at Douglas. 'But I must say that sounds to me like what Jean calls a last resort diagnosis.' Douglas and Angus stood looking at Steven, politely waiting for an explanation.

'I don't know what that means,' said Angus finally, sounding apologetic.

'What Jean says,' said Steven, 'is that when a patient is dying in the hospital, the only thing they're not allowed to do is die without a diagnosis, so sometimes the doctors pull one out of the sky, invent one, just to have something to write on the death certificate . . .'

Douglas flushed slightly; it might have been the three glasses of sherry he'd swallowed within a matter of minutes.

'I'd like to remind you that that wasn't a police diagnosis,' he said. 'It was made by Dr Anderson, the police surgeon, who's well qualified and well respected around here.'

'It makes sense,' repeated Angus, speaking quietly. 'When I heard that's what they thought, I did a few calculations . . .' He looked at his companions, not wanting to bore them, but they seemed pretty interested. 'In the human body, there's a fair amount of fat, and that was particularly true of our unfortunate friend Morgan. He probably weighed about fourteen or fifteen stone, and probably something like thirty-five percent of that was fat.'

'That much?' asked Doug. 'That seems an awful lot.'

'It was maybe more,' said Angus. 'A really obese person can be up to forty-five percent fat.'

'Hold it,' said Steven. 'Jean should be listening to this.' He went off and brought her back into the living room. 'Angus was saying that Morgan Stroud was thirty-five percent fat,' he told her. 'Go on, Angus.'

'Well, I'm sure Jean knows more about it than I do,' he said modestly, smiling uncertainly at her.

'I'm sure I don't,' said Jean. 'I may have known about it a long time ago, but I've certainly forgotten by now.'

Doug looked at Jean to see if she was joking, but her face was completely straight. He knew Jean *never* forgot things like that. She's a deep one, he thought, then went back to listening to what Angus was saying.

'Well, the fat . . . That adds up to about seventy pounds of fat.'

'My goodness,' said Jean, 'that *is* a lot. Doesn't fat contain nine calories per gram, or something like that?'

'Exactly right,' smiled Angus, and Doug grinned to himself; yeah, how come she hadn't forgotten that too? 'It's really a huge amount of energy,' went on Angus, 'in the neighbourhood of 300,000 calories. He paused, and the others could see him going through the calculations in his head. 'That's enough heat energy to bring *over eight hundred gallons of ice-water to the boil.*'

'My God,' said Douglas, astounded at the numbers, and remembering what Malcolm Anderson had told him. 'If you put all that energy in a suitcase, you could blow up the Houses of Parliament, no trouble.'

Angus smiled faintly. 'I don't know about that,' he said, 'but it would certainly be more than enough energy to burn a hole in the floor.' He looked questioningly at Douglas. 'And that's really the question we're asking, isn't it?'

Lisbie came in and held a brief, whispered conversation with Jean.

'I hope you're not all famished,' said Jean. 'There's been a small delay.' She smiled at her daughter, and Angus thought how special Jean Montrose was, taking every problem in her stride, and never seeming to lose her patience. He was astonished at the warmth of his thoughts; this was the first real feeling of kinship he'd had with a human being for years, and it made him faintly nervous. This was not the time to be getting attached to anyone.

Lisbie went out and Jean's face developed a frown. 'But it would need more than just the fuel, wouldn't it?' she asked. 'For instance, you need a detonator to set off a bomb, don't you?'

Angus smiled. 'You're quite right, Jean,' he said. 'And, from what I've read, there's more than enough phosphorus in the body, and more than enough potentially explosive methane gas to do the trick.'

'Are you saying that the only thing that keeps us from burning to a crisp is that the fuel and the detonators are kept far enough apart?'

'That's about it,' said Angus. 'You summarised it better than I could have.'

'The thing that bothers me,' said Steven, breaking the long silence that followed, 'is if all that's true, why doesn't it happen more often?'

Angus's answer was almost identical to Malcolm Anderson's when Douglas asked him the same question on the day of the discovery of Morgan Stroud's body.

'Why are rare diseases rare?'

Soon afterwards, they sat down to dinner and the conversation became general. Douglas was unusually silent, in spite of Fiona's efforts to get him to talk. Angus, on the other hand, was lively and entertaining. He sat next to Jean, who watched him with pleasure; he hasn't had this good a time for years, I bet, she thought, and Jean thoroughly enjoyed the courteous attention that he paid her throughout the meal.

Afterwards, when everybody had gone home, Lisbie went down with Fiona to her basement room.

'Did you notice Angus with Mum?' asked Lisbie.

Fiona was more concerned about Douglas's silence, which had lasted almost throughout the meal. 'No, I didn't,' she replied.

Lisbie said nothing, until Fiona sat up and said in an annoyed voice, 'Well, what about Angus? Why can you never finish what you're going to say?'

'Well, I think he's in love with Mum,' said Lisbie very solemnly. 'And what's even funnier, Mum really likes *him*.'

'That's bullshit . . .' said Fiona, but her voice trailed off. 'Well . . . you're maybe right. He *was* looking at her with a really stupid expression . . .'

The two girls looked at each other with growing astonishment, and were still speechless with laughter several minutes later when Steven called down to find out what all the racket was about.

Chapter Fourteen

George Elmslie sat back in his armchair and read the note again. It had come in an official OHMS envelope, and that had already unnerved him. 'Please report to the Central Police Station at 0930hrs on Wednesday . . .' He checked the date; that was tomorrow. He was requested to go to the third floor, where he would be interviewed by Inspector Niven. There was no indication of the matter to be discussed, only a long list in small print of the rights of the recipient of the letter, including the right not to attend the proposed interview.

George wiped his forehead with the back of his hand. There was no way he could tell if there was a threat lurking in this letter; did the Inspector want to ask him about Morgan Stroud? Or were there other things on his mind?

He got up, walked over to the window and looked through the small telescope. He could see the bridge traffic so clearly, even the face of a cyclist coming towards him on the far side of the bridge, although with the naked eye he could barely make him out. George loosened the polar axis and declination clamps and moved the 'scope around until it was pointing at a house set on the side of a slope about a mile away. He peered through the eyepiece; the window had been closed, but the black splash of smoke was still clearly visible on the wall above it. George smiled grimly, although even now he could feel a wave of hatred surge through him at the thought of Morgan Stroud. That smoke on the wall; George wondered what part of Stroud that had been – his face, maybe . . . Anyway, the widow would have to get that mess cleaned up before she could even think of selling the house.

He returned to his chair and scanned the letter again. It was one of those impersonal, computer-generated missives, and George simply couldn't get any kind of feel for what it might be about. Anyway, he would go; if he didn't, it would certainly arouse suspicion. But still, maybe he should stop doing the photography sessions for a while. George pondered that; the only problem was that he needed the money to set up a studio where he could do colour movies for home video cassettes; nowadays that was where the market was growing fastest, and he would be able to demand several hundred pounds a copy for a really juicy one. He glanced at the small pile of catalogues of photo equipment; the colour studio would be really expensive to set up, what with the cameras and lighting and sound recording machines.

He really had to do it, for his own pleasure as much as anything, and he felt a hot stirring in his groin at the thought. Movies . . . so much better than the frozen stills, although these were pretty erotic, and sold well. Suddenly a thought struck him, and he froze. That kid's mother . . . After they'd finished the last session, he'd had a little fun with the younger boy, and in the excitement he'd accidentally hurt the kid. The mother had somehow found his telephone number and phoned, half drunk, and shouted and screamed at him, threatening all kinds of retribution, including reporting him to the police. Then the phone was taken away from her, and Alec got on, sounding very apologetic. 'I'll take care of *her*, George,' he said, 'don't worry about a thing.' George had been so shaken he didn't wonder until later how the woman had managed to get his phone number.

George went into the walk-in cupboard he'd turned into a dark room, and took a series of prints off the drying rack. He brought them back, about three dozen of them, into the living room, and sat down in his chair to examine the pictures in comfort. They were good; very good, in fact, although he said it himself; he felt that activity again, that heat in his groin as he scanned his work. He was a real artist, he recognised with some complacency; there was no doubt about it.

Jean felt a bit guilty about engineering the meeting, but she knew that Gwen usually spent the hottest part of the day at the North Inch, down by the river, and it was really important that she talk to her. Jean drove along the park several times, and the third time, she saw Gwen coming up the path towards the street. Jean stopped the car and waited till she came up. When she was parallel with the car, Jean called out to her.

'Gwen!'

Gwen stopped. Rather reluctantly, it seemed, she came over to the kerb, and Jean leaned over and opened the passenger side door. 'Jump in, I'll give you a lift,' she said. Gwen shook her head, but Jean insisted. 'I want to talk to you,' she said, 'about Kinnoull Hill.' Jean's voice brooked no refusal, and Gwen resisted the impulse to run, and climbed in awkwardly.

Jean fastened Gwen's seat belt for her and pulled away from the kerb. Gwen sat in the corner, hard against the door, as far away from Jean as she could get. Jean could see that Gwen kept her eyes on the dashboard and realised that the sight of the shops and cars speeding by was making her dizzy.

'Lisbie told me about her midnight visit to the old tower,' said Jean, trying to keep her voice flat and unemotional. 'What's going on?' Jean noticed a strong odour coming from her passenger, and wondered if she'd be able to scrub the smell out of the seats. Once, when Jean's brother Charlie was visiting from the States, he'd smoked a cigar in the car and the odour had lingered for weeks.

Gwen said nothing, and Jean suddenly got the feeling that she might jump out. A dreadful memory leapt to her mind; once, not very long ago, she'd had a young woman patient, who suddenly got out while they were stopped on the bridge, climbed over the parapet and jumped to her death. Jean looked across at Gwen, and it was then that she realised that the woman was simply petrified with fear from being in the car.

'Let's stop for a cup of tea,' said Jean. They had just passed Kennaway's bakery, so Jean pulled over and they got out. Again Jean had the feeling that Gwen was a wild bird, still for a moment, but bound to escape in a sudden flurry of wings; so she held on to Gwen's arm with a friendly but firm grip as they walked back to the restaurant.

'Is she with you, Dr Montrose?' asked the pretty young waitress, eyeing Gwen with distaste.

'Yes, Katie, she is,' replied Jean, firmly enough to make the girl blush. Gwen made a sudden movement, and Jean thought she was going to run for it, but the moment passed, and they followed Katie to a table near the back. Curious eyes followed their progress; Jean Montrose was known to many of the patrons, and most of them had at some time seen Gwen striding along the streets of the city clutching her ever-present bible.

'We were talking about the old tower on Kinnoull Hill,' said Jean briskly as soon as they sat down. She'd sneaked a look at her watch on the way to the table, and knew she didn't have much time.

Gwen kept her head down, and for a moment Jean thought it was going to be a waste of effort, that she wouldn't get anything out of her, but Gwen raised her restless eyes and spoke hoarsely across the table.

'There's no harm,' she said. 'The boy's learning what he needs to know.'

'I thought St Jude's was supposed to take care of his education,' replied Jean, her eyes not leaving Gwen's face.

She tried to keep the acid out of her voice. 'And the old tower seems a strange place for a classroom.'

'He has a gift,' said Gwen.

'What about Lisbie?' asked Jean. 'Does she have a gift too?' In spite of herself, the anger was creeping into her voice. What right had this woman to frighten these young people like that?

'No, she does not,' replied Gwen. 'Just him. God chose him.'

'And God told you about it?'

'Yes.' Jean felt suddenly abashed by Gwen's directness. Her voice was honest and without guile; the woman seemed to believe what she was saying.

The waitress came with their coffee, while Jean steeled herself to pose the next question. Gripping the handle of the cup tightly, she tried to sound matter-of-fact and calm.

'Does any of this have to do with your brother's death?' she asked, and sat back quickly, not knowing what kind of answer to expect.

'Morgan? God killed him,' said Gwen, raising her left arm to scratch her armpit. 'He struck that evil sinner down with a thunderbolt.'

Jean's eyes widened. 'But if God had done that,' she asked, feeling a sudden tightness in her chest, 'wouldn't the whole house have gone up in flames?'

Gwen stared at Jean, who could feel an unexpected strength emanating from this strange woman. Her upper lip curled back to show the gap where her front teeth had once been, making the canine teeth on each side look longer than they really were. Gwen leaned across the table and Jean forced herself not to move back.

'You don't know your bible, Dr Montrose,' she said. She took her tattered bible, put it on the table and opened it without looking. 'Look you there, Doctor,' she said, pushing the book across the table. 'Chapter six, verse twenty-seven.'

Jean saw that it was opened at *Proverbs*, and the print on

the greasy page leapt out at her. She took a deep breath and
read the words out slowly. 'Can a man take fire in his
bosom, and his clothes not be burned?' The significance of
what she was reading struck her like a blow, and suddenly
Jean felt she couldn't breathe, and put her hand on her
chest. She looked fearfully across the table, but Gwen was
already on her feet.

'God's answer to that question is "Yes!" ' she said, and
leaned over to take the bible out of Jean's hands. A moment
later she was gone, slipping between the crowded tables like
a wraith.

Doug put some papers back in the filing cabinet, then took
out a bunch of keys on a long chain attached to his belt. He
selected one of the smallest ones, locked the cabinet and
checked around the little office. Even the walls seemed to be
sweating, and the metal desk was warm to the touch. The
small tear in the green leatherette back of his chair had got
bigger, and the whitish stuffing was visible. Doug couldn't
imagine how it had happened; it must have been something
some careless cleaning woman had done. The large-scale
map of Perth hung limply on the back wall, and even the
pages of the Rossleigh's calendar on the filing cabinet were
curling, hiding part of the picture, an elegant country house
with a couple getting out of a Rolls-Royce in front of it. The
illustration offended Doug's class-conscious sensibilities,
but he didn't have another calender to replace it. He walked
down the corridor and found Constable Jamieson coming
out of the toilet, blue cigarette smoke billowing out after
him.

'I'm going over to Mackay's dry-cleaning shop on South
Street,' he said. 'Meanwhile, you go out there and interview
Gwen Stroud, see if you can find out what she was doing the
night he died. And by the way . . .' Doug hesitated, 'try to
find out about the black magic I'm told she's into, and who
she does it with, okay?'

Doug strode forward, not wishing to get into a discussion with Jamieson. He went down the back stairs, two at a time, hoping that would make him feel young and energetic, but he almost missed the last step and lurched into the back door at the bottom of the stairway.

Using an expression Cathie would not have approved of, he pushed the metal bar and went outside. It was only a five-minute walk to Mackay's shop, but it would be hot and tiring, and for a moment he seriously considered taking the car.

Ken Mackay's dry-cleaning place had large red-and-white advertising posters on the window, and the sign above the door still looked fairly new. A little bell rattled when Doug opened the door and walked in. There was a bare plastic-topped counter with a ribbed metal railing around it which stretched the width of the shop; at the far end a small hinged section of the counter was raised. The floor tiles were square, old, white with sea-green swirls, left over from the previous occupants. Or the ones before. Behind the counter was a long rack with a row of transparent plastic covered clothes, hanging like a queue of ghosts patiently waiting to get out. The shop had the usual faint warm smell of chemicals and steam that all dry-cleaning shops have; Doug recognised it as petroleum solvent, the most commonly used dry-cleaning agent.

There was a girl behind the counter; she looked up at Doug with faint surprise, as if a customer was the last thing she expected to see.

'Mr Mackay?' he asked.

'He's in the back . . .' She hesitated, her eyes uncertain. 'What name shall I say?'

'Niven,' said Doug. '*Inspector* Niven.'

She came back after about a minute. 'He's in the middle of doing a batch,' she said. 'Can you come back later?'

'I'll wait,' said Doug. He positioned himself opposite the double curtain, which separated the shop from the work

area, but he couldn't see anything. The girl pulled a
magazine from under the counter and started to read it.
There was a sudden snapping noise and Doug's head swung
around. The girl was chewing bubble gum; she must have
had it parked in her cheek when he came in.

A few minutes later, the line of light where the curtains
almost met darkened, and Doug could feel the presence of
someone watching him from the other side. Then the curtain was drawn and Ken Mackay appeared, looking just as
aggressive as usual. Quick as a flash, the magazine was back
under the counter, and the girl was looking over at Ken out
of the corner of her eye.

'Yes?'

'I'd like to speak to you for a few minutes,' said Doug
easily. 'Privately.' He glanced at the girl.

Ken jerked his head back and pulled the curtain open.
Doug went to the end of the counter and through the open
gate. Ken was obviously a man of few words. In the back,
the smell of cleaning agents was stronger; Douglas followed
him through a short maze of hanging clothes and empty
racks on one side and a row of metal drums and a steam
press on the other, into a small, cramped office. Inside, the
heat was almost unbearable, although it didn't seem to
affect Ken one bit. There was a small metal desk with a
telephone, a calculator and a pad with a monthly calendar
squared off on it.

The front two feet of the desk were on a small piece of
ancient carpet, which also supported the wooden visitor's
chair. Three metal shelves on the wall projected into the
room, heavy with well-used catalogues, mostly of industrial
chemicals.

Doug sat down.

Ken stood in the doorway, short, stiff, muscular, watchful.

Doug got straight to the point. 'I'm told that a week or
two ago you came up to St Jude's to talk to Morgan
Stroud.'

'So?'

'What did you want with him?'

Ken didn't answer immediately; he looked as if he was trying to decide how much Doug already knew.

'I told him to lay off Neil,' he said finally. 'He persecuted the kid, in front of all the others.' Ken's fists knotted at his sides.

'How? I mean, how did he persecute him?'

'Sometimes he sneered at the way he spoke . . .' Ken's lips tightened. It was obviously a sore point. 'He didn't think Neil sounded "cultured" enough for St Jude's. And sometimes Neil stammers, and Stroud . . . Well, he imitated him, and that made it worse.'

'Did you ever threaten him?'

Ken's eyes flickered. 'I was angry. Maybe I said something that sounded, well, as you say, threatening, but I never . . .'

'Do you remember your actual words?'

'No, I don't. As I said, I was very angry.' And he was getting angry again, Doug could see. He'd even started to sweat. Doug mopped his own brow with the back of his hand.

'Did you ever see Stroud again, after that?'

'No . . .' The answer came too fast, too emphatic. Doug felt sure he was lying.

'You didn't go to his house after he'd been baiting Neil again? The night he was killed?'

Ken stepped inside the office, which suddenly felt very small. Doug could tell that the man was a born fighter; every time something happened that he didn't like, up came his fists in an automatic reflex.

'No, I just told you . . .' Ken's quick fury showed on his face.

'How long have you lived here in Perth?' asked Doug, quickly changing the subject.

'About a year,' replied Ken after taking a big breath. 'Why?'

'Just wondering,' said Doug, moving in the chair. He stretched his legs under the desk.

'Where were you before you came here, Mr Mackay?' he went on.

'All over . . . I was in Cumbernauld for a year, and before that in Dundee. I was the area rep for a chemical company.'

'That seems rather different kind of work from dry-cleaning.'

'Not really. It's all chemical processing . . .'

'What made you decide to come here? I mean to Perth?'

'My wife died, and I'd been away from Neil for a long time. He was at school in Glasgow, staying with my aunt, and I wanted him to get a better education.' He laughed, but there was no humour in the sound.

Doug made the appropriate sympathetic noises.

'That's tough.'

'We get by.' Ken hesitated, and Doug waited, his eyes bright on Ken's.

'I maybe made a mistake sending him to that snob school,' he went on. 'And to be paying for that kind of crap, the insults he . . . that we *both* got up there . . .' Ken made an effort to hide his anger, but it was all too evident.

'What does Renee think about it?' asked Doug smoothly, thinking he'd done a clever job of bringing her name into the conversation without it looking too forced.

'None of her business,' replied Ken brusquely. 'That's between Neil and me.'

'What sort of chemicals do you use for the . . . process here?' asked Doug, suddenly changing the subject.

Ken pointed at the drums outside the office. 'There, you can read the labels,' he said. 'Now I need to get back to work. I have a batch coming out in three minutes.'

Douglas got up.

'Were you with Renee the night before Stroud was found?' he asked, following Ken out of the office.

'Yes.'

'Did you drive up to Tomintoul to pick her up?'

Ken stopped, and turned to face Douglas. 'Yes,' he said after a moment. 'That afternoon.'

On the way back to the station, Douglas went over in his head what Ken had told him, and tried to separate the lies from the truth.

Chapter Fifteen

George Elmslie put down his packages and opened the front door of his flat. Carefully he brought the boxes inside, all the new equipment he'd bought to set up the improvements in his photographic studio. It was late, because he'd had to go to Glasgow after school; the local shops didn't carry the kind of sophisticated gear he needed. Fit as he was, George was sweating profusely. The evening was humid, breathless and oppressive.

The phone rang just as he was closing the door behind him, and he went into the kitchen to answer it. There was a brief silence at the other end, followed by the click as the receiver was hung up. George stared at the phone for a moment, then shrugged, but it left him with an uncomfortable feeling.

He soon forgot about it in the excitement of unpacking. There was a new tripod, very sturdy, with a mechanism for moving the camera up and down without altering the settings, several large blue lightbulbs for colour photography, a dappled white-and-blue background sheet, a new exposure meter, a couple of filters . . . everything he needed to convert to a first-class colour studio. With the money he made with this, he'd soon be able to afford movie equipment, and then he'd really be in business. At that point, he might give up teaching altogether, but then he'd miss working with the boys, especially boys like Neil Mackay . . . Now that was an interesting young fellow – and George had the feeling that he might become a lot more interesting, if he played his cards right. Maybe he'd invite him to the flat, with a friend, of course, the first time . . .

Suddenly he heard the shrill sound of the front door buzzer, and George almost jumped out of his skin. He wasn't expecting anybody, and very few people ever dropped in. He hesitated, tempted to ignore it, but after a moment he went to the door, lifted the phone which connected to the front entrance of the building, and listened.

'Yes?' His voice was deliberately abrupt.

'George? Hello, it's Alec.'

George's mouth opened in shock. Alec! Alec from Glasgow, Alec of Alec and Sally, the people who brought the kids . . . What did he want? Neither of them had called since that little bother they'd had with that drunken woman whose child he'd played with, so he'd thought he'd heard the last of them.

The buzzer rang again, for a longer time.

'All right,' said George reluctantly. 'You can come up.' He pressed the button which allowed the downstairs door to open.

Sally came in with Alec, and George wondered briefly why he hadn't mentioned that she was with him.

George wasn't feeling at all hospitable. 'I wasn't expecting you,' he said after closing the door.

'It's hot even up here,' said Sally. 'I'd have thought on the sixth floor it would be cooler.'

They stood there, waiting for George to offer them a seat, and George sensed something strange about them. Neither of them would look him in the eye.

'Well, you'd better sit down, I suppose,' said George. 'The place is a mess, my cleaning lady comes in tomorrow . . .' Then it occurred to him they might be interested in his new equipment, and he brightened up.

'I just came in,' he said. 'Got some nice equipment for colour . . .'

'We've got a problem, George,' said Alec, and Sally nodded. She took out a packet of cigarettes.

'Nobody smokes in here,' said George, without looking at her. His eyes were fixed on Alec. 'What sort of problem?' His insides were turning over as he spoke; George had a fine physique and talked tough, but he wasn't nearly as brave as he looked.

'That kid's mother,' said Alec in a regretful voice. 'The one who called you. She seemed so nice and cooperative the first time we met her.'

'What about her?' George had difficulty keeping his voice steady.

'Well, you know the kid was hurt, not much, I know, but he was bleeding . . .' Alec shook his head at the duplicity of women. 'She's talking about going to the police, naming names, that sort of thing.'

Sally lit her cigarette and stared at George, sensing his fear. 'She needs money,' she said, and puffed a defiant cloud of smoke towards him.

Suddenly George felt very calm. 'How much?' he asked. Alec and Sally exchanged a quick glance. This was going to be easier than they'd thought.

'She's talking about a thousand pounds,' said Alec quickly. 'Maybe she'd take a bit less, but I doubt it. She knows how much trouble she can get you into.'

'The bitch,' said Sally, and sucked the smoke into her lungs before exhaling it as a blue cloud. She smiled, showing her teeth. There was something frightening about Sally, George realised suddenly, something bloodthirsty and wild. She looked like a starving alley cat, ready to take on anything for a meal.

'I don't have a thousand pounds,' said George. 'Not anything like it.'

Alec grinned, and sucked in his thin cheeks. George waited while his visitor picked at something that seemed to be stuck between two teeth. 'Come on, George, you're a man of property.' He looked pointedly round the flat. 'And you have a very nice car outside, and a job . . . Most banks would love to lend you money, George, and if not, well, I know a chap in Rutherglen we can ask.'

'I'll need to think about it,' said George. 'How can I be sure that that would be the end of it? What's to prevent her from doing this again? And again?'

'She knows better,' said Sally, and laughed hoarsely.

'You see, George,' said Alec, taking the cigarette from Sally and taking a long pull, 'we agree she and the kid should get some compensation. They deserve it. But only once. That's what I said to her, honest. Any nonsense, I said to her, and there'll suddenly be another orphan on the Glasgow social security register.'

Sally laughed again, then coughed, a hard, racking cough.

George didn't say anything, and when Sally finished coughing, she and Alec looked expectantly at him. 'I can get the money,' he said finally, 'but it'll take me at least a week.'

Alec and Sally stood up simultaneously. 'Good,' said Alec. 'We'll come by next week. Same time, same place, eh?' They both laughed; George thought they sounded relieved, and had the sudden impression that they'd done this kind of thing before. Maybe he'd made it too easy for them.

He smiled to himself.

'Right,' he said. 'See you then.' George showed them out and locked the door behind him. He looked at his watch; it was almost nine o'clock.

Although meal-time conversation in the Montrose household was usually general, sometimes it went in two layers, each at right-angles to the other. Steven and Jean, facing each other across the table, had their conversation going and so did Fiona and Lisbie.

'There's a new glass-colouring method we're going to

try,' Steven said. 'It's really exciting, just been developed in Germany, and avoids an entire step in the manufacturing process. I got some samples, you should see the colours!'

'What's that blue called, the one in very old stained-glass windows, the colour they can't reproduce any more?' Jean had taken a lot of trouble to learn about the glassmaking process, and had spent hours watching the glassblowers working at the plant.

Fiona was saying something quietly to her sister, who made a quick retort, and as usual, their voices got louder.

Steven couldn't hear what Jean was saying.

'Do you mind keeping it down a bit?' he asked the girls. 'Otherwise we'll go back to having just one conversation at a time.' Jean gave the two girls a reproving look.

'I started talking first,' said Fiona. '*He* interrupted *me*.'

'That's enough from you,' said Jean, looking warningly at Fiona. 'And don't call your father *He*. He does have a name, you know.'

'Quite right, Mum,' chipped in Lisbie. 'You should be ashamed of yourself, Fiona!'

'Who asked your opinion? You're the one who should be ashamed, baby-snatcher!'

'One more word out of either one of you, and you finish your meal in the basement.' Jean's reactions were almost automatic; the girls argued like this at almost every meal, and it amazed her that she and Steven still noticed. Maybe it was only when they got too loud . . . Anyway, it was all quite inoffensive, and once they had some food inside them, everybody settled down. She looked over at Steven.

'Would you like some more chicken, dear?'

'May I speak now?' asked Fiona.

'And at the podium we have Fiona Montrose, the new Miss World,' announced Lisbie in a loud voice. 'She will now say a few words. Miss Montrose, you have the floor. Ta-rah!'

'Thank you, thank *you*!' Fiona stood up, holding her

napkin in front of her. 'Unused as I am to public speaking, I would nevertheless like to thank y'all for selecting little ol' me for . . .'

'Enough!' Steven, when particularly tired from his day's work, occasionally lost patience with his daughters. 'Why do you girls have to turn every meal into a circus? Sit down, eat your food, and I don't want to hear another word from either of you.'

There was a long silence, broken only by one poorly suppressed giggle from Lisbie.

'That was a lovely dinner,' said Steven, when he'd finished his chicken and mashed potatoes. He sat back, feeling sorry he'd spoken so sharply to the girls.

'They're making me some bead samples of that new glass,' he said to both of them. 'The colours are just wonderful, and there should be enough for two rather nice necklaces.'

A moment later, Steven remembered something.

'I hear the *Courier* is getting a clairvoyant.'

'To join the paper?' asked Jean, surprised.

'No, I shouldn't think so,' replied Steven. 'They say this woman's from Edinburgh. They think she'll be able to solve the Morgan Stroud business. That's what I heard, anyway.'

'They don't need a clairvoyant when they've got Douglas Niven right there,' said Fiona indistinctly. 'He'll solve it.'

'Don't talk with your mouth full, dear,' said Jean. She looked around the table. 'Does anybody want any more chicken? There's only a small piece, and I don't want any leftovers.'

Lisbie passed up her plate. 'Neil said Mr Townes was talking about you,' she said. 'He said you look after his daughter.'

'Well, sort of . . . here, you can finish the potatoes while you're at it,' she said, scraping the dish on to Lisbie's plate.

'Neil says Mr Townes really likes you, Mum.' A quick glance passed between Lisbie and Fiona.

'Well, that's very nice, dear,' said Jean, sounding a little complacent. 'As a matter of fact, he asked me out for coffee tomorrow morning, if I finish my surgery in time.'

Both girls looked over at Steven for his reaction. He was looking at the paper, and slowly folded it.

'By the way, Jean,' he said, 'that reminds me . . . I've been hearing your name taken in vain . . .' Steven looked suddenly uncomfortable. Jean's eyes opened wide, but she said nothing. 'People seem to be thinking that you're . . . that there's something going on between you and Angus Townes . . . Oh dear,' said Steven. 'It's so silly, I'm embarrassed even to mention it . . .'

'I don't need to tell you,' said Jean steadily, 'that there's nothing to those rumours. I had coffee with him a couple of times . . .' She took a deep breath and made a decision. She was not going to jeopardise her home life or her good name, although the last thing she wanted to do was hurt Angus Townes.

Douglas was standing in the kitchen, watching Cathie wash the after-dinner dishes in the chipped enamel sink. The kitchen was neat, frugal, well scrubbed and very old-fashioned. The only modern touch was a tiny refrigerator tucked under the counter by the window. A big, black, four-burner stove sulked in the corner opposite, one burner glowing under the kettle.

Douglas had told Cathie over dinner about his encounter with Ken Mackay, and she'd been thinking about it.

'He's got a chip on his shoulder, that man,' she said. 'He's like you, he hates the hoity-toities, but he'd like his son to be one of them rather than like him.'

'Nothing wrong with that,' said Doug. 'In any case, he can have a barrelful of chips on his shoulder for all I care. What I want to know is if he had anything to do with Stroud's death.'

'Did you hear the *Courier*'s hiring a medium?' asked

Cathie. 'I've never heard of anything so stupid.'

'Waste of money,' said Doug. 'But I suppose it'll help their circulation. That's all *they* care about.'

'Maybe he'll be able to find out what happened, though,' said Cathie with a sly look at Doug. 'You can't say that the police investigation's been too successful so far.'

Douglas started to put the dishes away.

'When did *you* become an authority on police work?' he asked. 'How do you know what progress we're making? I don't necessarily tell you everything that's going on, every avenue we're exploring . . .'

'I always know how things are going,' replied Cathie. 'I just need to look at your face when you come in through that door. You don't need to tell me anything. Usually you know right away who's committed a crime, even if it takes you a while to prove it. And right now you don't really have any idea. Admit it . . .' She put her arms around Doug's neck, and he pulled away for a second, irritated, but not long enough for her to let go.

'I'm really working hard at it,' said Doug, sounding misunderstood and aggrieved. 'Where do you think I am when I'm not here? What d'you think I do for a living, sit on my hands, or chase pretty quines around town?' He ducked out of her embrace.

'I know very well what you do,' replied Cathie. 'Because you tell me. Now if you'd just move out of my road so I can put the dishes away . . .' Doug went over by the window, out of Cathie's territory.

'Well, I apologise if I bore you with my work . . .' Douglas's huffy tone was assumed; he was deliberately misunderstanding Cathie. She smiled at him, a knowing, loving smile. She knew Douglas far too well to let him get away with something like that.

'What do you think *really* happened?' she asked. 'Do you think there's any way he could have, well, just burst into flames?'

Douglas shook his head. 'Cath, I honestly don't know what to think. This is so . . . far from what I was trained for. Shootings, knifings, drownings, street accidents, you know I can handle a' that, nae bother. But this . . . I don't know . . .' Douglas raised his head. 'And anyway Dr Anderson says that it was a natural occurrence and he can prove it. A murder without a killer, that's what he calls it.'

'Aye, but what does our Jean Montrose think?' asked Cathie. 'I'd listen to her a lot sooner than to that Dr Anderson.'

'Come on now, Cathie,' exclaimed Doug. 'He's a specialist, a pathologist, this is the sort of thing he's supposed to know all about.'

Cathie's shrug left him in no doubt about her feelings on the matter.

'It seems a strange coincidence,' she said, 'that so many people hated that man and then he goes and dies of something natural.'

'Maybe it wasn't natural,' said Doug darkly.

'Maybe it wasn't.' Cathie turned the gas off under the kettle. 'There was no fire in the house, and no petrol or anything on his body, the lab proved that . . .'

'I suppose all your girlfriends know exactly who did it, and how,' said Doug, his voice dripping with sarcasm. 'What have they told you, or is that classified information?'

Cathie was great at finding and reporting what people around town had to say; and on this particular topic there was much discussion.

'There was this woman at the bakery this morning,' she said, hanging her apron on the hook behind the door. 'She was saying some people can will themselves to concentrate heat in their bodies until they burst into flames, especially in this kind of weather, she said.'

'Well, I must say I was almost bursting into flames myself today,' replied Doug. 'There wasn't a breath of wind in the office, even with the window and the door open.'

'After she'd gone, Mrs Findlay said the woman works up at the crematorium, so she should know.'

'If that was really true, it would be in the books,' said Doug, shrugging.

'Well, it isn't exactly the BMA library you have access to, is it?' asked Cathie, referring to the small collection of books at the hospital for the use of the doctors and nurses. Doug had been given permission to go there after Jean Montrose got tired of taking books out for him.

Cathie hesitated. 'Have you heard the talk about black magic that's going around?'

Doug shook his head. 'That's all we need now,' he said. 'A bit of witchcraft thrown in.' Douglas's voice was getting bitter again. 'That's it, of course. Stroud was really a war-lock himself, and he did something bad to the other witches so they pointed their fingers at him, said "Pooof!" and the bugger just went up in smoke, right?'

'There's no need to use language,' said Cathie, primly. 'My father always . . .'

'Do you know Renée, his wife?' asked Doug suddenly. Next to Jean Montrose, Cathie knew more people in and around Perth than anybody.

'Yes, I do,' said Cathie. 'She's a really nice lady, who's put up with a lot more than I ever would, I can tell you that.' She glowered momentarily at all the males of the universe.

'Did you know she's partly blind?' Doug started to pace, but soon gave up as he kept bumping into her in their small, crowded kitchen.

Cathie hesitated. 'Yes. Apparently he, that is Morgan, had some kind of lab in the basement. Don't ask me what he was doing, because I don't know, and nor does she.'

'You mean there was an explosion or something?'

'That's what I heard,' said Cathie, and shuddered.

'Sounds like a lovely person, Stroud, doesn't he?' said Doug. 'Just the sort of person you'd like your daughter to marry.'

'Well, *you* won't have to worry about that problem, anyway, will you, the way things are going?' Cathie's voice was snappy, and she spoke as if the words had come out by themselves.

Doug shrugged defensively. 'We *both* decided it was better to wait, if you remember.'

'That was quite a while ago,' said Cathie, who hadn't seriously wanted to bring the matter up at this moment. She put out two cups with a clatter. 'Anyway, it seems that this Morgan Stroud was a really evil character . . .'

'Thinnest-looking tea I've ever seen,' said Doug glumly, looking at his cup, which Cathie was filling up with a light yellow brew. 'And it's got things floating in it! What . . . ?'

'It's a' right,' said Cathie. 'It's a free sample I got through the post. For only three pounds and ninety-nine pence, you get a pound of this tea and four of these little china cups, the kind with dragons and no handles . . .'

With a suspicion born of long experience, Doug picked up the cup and took a sip. He barely had time to taste it before a look of disgust came over his face.

'No wonder the Chinks look the way they do, if that's the kind of rubbish they drink.' He stood up. 'D'you still have some ordinary Lipton's?'

'In the blue sugar jar where it always is,' replied Cathie wearily. Maybe she should have mixed a little of the new tea with some of the usual tea at first, then gradually put in more . . . That way he could have got used to it before he realised it was different.

When Doug came back to sit down with his Royal Wedding mug full of strong fresh tea, it took him a moment before he saw that Cathie was watching him, smiling and pulling the corners of her eyes up and out, in a parody of a slit-eyed, oriental look.

He stood up and looked out of the window into the darkness of their garden. A moth smacked into the glass, slithered down, then fluttered away, an untidy whitish blur.

It was strange, Douglas thought; he could recognise some of Ken Mackay's feelings in himself, that helpless anger he felt towards people who were more cultured, or in a higher social class. And he had a lot of sympathy for Mackay's furious reaction when these same people made fun, not so much of him, but of his son . . .

Chapter Sixteen

Next day, first thing, before even going to his office, Doug went back to Morgan Stroud's house; Cathie's chance comment about Stroud's wife being blinded in a home lab accident had hit him hard, although he made sure Cathie didn't notice. A lab in the basement! He shook his head. Maybe they'd lived in a different house when it happened, because to his recollection there was no basement in the house in Pitcullen Lane. Doug drove more slowly than usual, feeling a strong reluctance to go inside that house again. That smell . . . Doug drove along East Shore Road, keeping in the right-hand lane to avoid the bridge traffic, and started up the hill towards Pitcullen Lane. It was already getting hot; people driving to work had their windows open and most were in shirtsleeves, one arm out of the window.

There was a big padlock on the front door of the house, and a large printed police sign forbidding entry was stapled to one panel. Doug took the padlock key out of his pocket, and for a moment wished he'd brought Constable Jamieson. Even from the outside, the house gave him an eerie, frightening feeling, and Doug laughed at himself. Surely after his years on the force, he couldn't let something like this get to him. The door creaked as if it had been closed for years. The burglar alarm system had been deactivated by the dealer, so he didn't have to worry about that. The smell was faint but still there; Renée would have to get rid of that odour somehow or she'd never be able to sell the place.

The silence in the house was oppressive, as if something

was lurking there, waiting for a new victim. Doug closed the front door behind him, irrationally wishing he could leave it open, then walked past the dining room through the narrow, dark hall to the kitchen, and stood there for a moment. Never had he needed a cigarette as he did right then, and he was fumbling in his pockets when a sudden noise right behind him made him leap to the other side of the kitchen with one jump, whirling around as he did so. But it was only the refrigerator coming on, noisily.

Doug sat down suddenly in a chair. This place . . . it really gave him the creeps. But he was right, there was no basement. Then Doug remembered that the house was on a hill, and the garage was under the house; there was no direct communication between them. Before going down to the garage, Doug went into the living room, now deserted-looking, splashes of whitish dust still showing where the fingerprint people had been busy. Doug's eyes went irresistibly to the black-edged hole in the carpet and the charred timber beneath. With a tremor of unearthly apprehension, it occurred to him that through that black hole Morgan Stroud's evil soul must have gone straight down to Hell.

The garage was large, big enough for two cars; Stroud's blue Ford, with a red police tag still taped on the windscreen, occupied one space. There was a partition wall separating off about one third of the garage, with a central door made of the same kind of panelling, partly hidden by the car. If he hadn't been looking for it, Doug might not have noticed it. Douglas took a torch out of his pocket, pushed the door open with his foot, and flashed the beam around the little room, not sure what he was going to find. There was a bench along one side, with two anglepoise lamps. That was all he needed to see for a start, and he went in and switched the lights on. In the centre of the bench, between the two lights, was a piece of equipment that looked a bit like two old-fashioned projectors facing each other, two metal cylinders about eighteen inches apart, with lenses, mirrors and a small platform. Attached to

the main instrument was a red and white label which said
DANGER CO2 LASER.

Alongside the equipment was a pair of thick goggles with
dark lenses, the kind used in hazardous environments. To the
right of the second anglepoise lamp, within reach of a person
sitting in the chair, was a pile of school notebooks, a Keiller's
marmalade jar full of pencils, pens and a wooden ruler; a
large electronic calculator, and half a dozen letters tied
together with a rubber band, stuck between two bricks.

Doug gazed at the laser. He wondered if it had anything to
do with Renée being blinded . . . Had she been fooling
around with the machine, trying to work out what kept her
husband down here hour after hour? Had she switched it on
by accident, while looking into the lens? Or had something
more sinister happened? Doug knew that the intense light
beam from a laser was enough to blind a person in a fraction
of a second.

Doug picked up the top notebook. It appeared to contain
records of experiments, in Morgan Stroud's rather sprawling
script. From what he could gather, Stroud had been trying to
accelerate certain chemical reactions by exciting different
molecules with laser beams. He shook his head. All that kind
of thing was far beyond him.

Then he turned to the letters, wondering if he should put
them in a plastic bag and take them straight to the forensic
lab, but on reflection he decided to examine them himself
first, taking care not to destroy any evidence such as fingerprints. He cut the rubber band with a pair of nail-scissors
from his pocket, then noticed that all the envelopes were of
the same kind, cheap, white, letter-size. Holding the envelopes by the edges, he saw that they were all postmarked
Perth. The dates weren't clear on all of them, but the earliest
he could identify for sure had been sent two years before. The
forensic lab wouldn't have any trouble with the others. The
name and address were the same in all of them, in clumsy
block capitals, written in pencil, Mr Morgan Stroud, 13

Pitcullen Lane, Perth. With great care Doug opened the top
envelope, which was postmarked a few days before Stroud's
death, and took out the contents, touching only the edges of
the paper. There was one sheet only. Doug put it on the bench
and carefully opened the single fold, using the backs of two
pencils from the marmalade jar. In letters of different sizes,
apparently cut out from pages of newspapers and glued to
the paper, were the words, on two lines, *He that lives by fire,*
will die by fire. Doug examined the letters that made up the
message; some were capitals from a headline, others were of
different fonts and sizes. He sat there, staring at the words
and tried to visualise the writer painstakingly putting the
words together, driven by an unendurable hatred . . . Was it
a man, or a woman? His wife, Renée? Doug had a sudden
vision of Gwen, Stroud's crazy sister, with that bible of hers
. . . Or could it have been somebody at the school, a boy he'd
tormented, or perhaps another teacher, someone whose
hatred he'd earned?

With scrupulous care, Doug opened the other letters. They
were all similar, each with a biblical quotation, each with a
reference to fire, and each, in retrospect, frighteningly
appropriate. After carefully returning the letters to their
respective envelopes, Douglas put them all in a plastic evidence bag and sealed it, then wrote out the label, leaving
blank the space marked 'witnessed by'. He hesitated for a
moment, then decided to call Constable Jamieson to come
and witness the removal of the material, otherwise if it ever
came to a trial, it might not be admissible as evidence. Doug
locked the garage up behind him, and walked up the short,
steep drive to the road. Back in his car, he called Jamieson on
the radio, and waited for him there. There was no point going
back into that house.

Lionel Wardle, the Headmaster of St Jude's, sat in his room,
tapping his teeth with the end of his pencil, feeling very
annoyed at Morgan Stroud. It was incredibly difficult to find

a replacement teacher in the middle of the term, and the candidates the agency had sent . . . He shuddered. Even for St Jude's, and nobody could say they were too fussy, they were beyond the pale. At least there was one bright spot. Angus Townes, who'd earlier said he would be leaving at the end of the term, had changed his mind and decided to stay. Townes' whole attitude had changed, too. From a rather carelessly dressed, almost pathologically silent person he had come out of his shell and started to take part in some of the school activities such as rugger and the dramatic society, and had bought himself a new wardrobe of quiet but well-cut clothes. The headmaster was always on the lookout for changes in the behaviour of his staff, because it often meant that they were going back on the bottle, making money selling drugs, or stealing from the school. Alcohol, drugs . . . The headmaster shrugged. These frailties were all part of the great fabric of humanity. But stealing from the school, that was something else. When Angus started to perk up so suddenly, the headmaster had checked around very carefully. Angus didn't hold any of the school accounts, so he didn't have to delve into that, and food certainly wasn't being stolen in greater quantities than could already be accounted for by the cooks. Nor did Angus have the bright-eyed, febrile high spirits of the drug taker. The headmaster had seen plenty of those, and he could recognise the signs a mile away. There really was no obvious explanation. Actually the whole matter was of total indifference to him, so long as Townes wasn't stealing from the school.

But Neil Mackay had a pretty good idea what had effected this dramatic change in Angus Townes' personality. The night before, when Lisbie and he were talking on the phone, she'd told him about how Angus was sweet on her mother, and they'd both laughed and felt embarrassed. It was a bit disgusting to think that old people like them were still interested in that kind of stuff.

Chapter Seventeen

'I think we should go,' said Neil.

'You're nuts,' replied Billy Wilson. 'He's a homo if I've ever seen one.'

'I'm not so sure,' said Neil, thoughtfully. 'I think he's just being friendly. Some of the other teachers have boys over to their homes, and nobody thinks a thing about it.'

'Those are the *married* ones.' Billy started to hop up and down on one foot. 'I bet you can't do that a hundred times,' he said. 'I did eighty-one yesterday, and I thought my leg was going to fall off.'

'We're going,' said Neil. When he saw that Billy was about to refuse, he went on. 'If he tries anything, we just get up and leave, okay?'

'He could kidnap us,' said Billy. 'Keep us as slaves to do his bidding.'

'Chained to the walls . . .'

'Fed on slops . . .'

'Tortured . . .'

'I'm not going,' said Billy.

'Yes you are,' replied Neil. 'I'll meet you outside his place at seven.'

At a couple of minutes past seven, Neil was outside the foyer of George Elmslie's building, but there was no Billy. At five past, just when Neil was about to leave, Billy appeared, breathless. 'I've been thinking,' he said, 'let's go to the cinema . . .'

'I've been thinking too,' said Neil. 'And I agree with you.

I think he probably *is* a homo. If he is, that's okay with me, it's his business. But if he's fooling around with kids like us . . .'

'Corrupting our morals,' said Billy, wide-eyed.

'Right. You and I can handle it, but supposing he started on somebody weak, or who wasn't doing well in his class?'

'He'd have them instantly in his power.'

'Billy, you've been reading too many comics. We're going to go up there like two innocent kids, okay? Take your lead from me. Don't panic or I'll knock your block off.'

The next morning the two boys discussed the events of the evening before.

'Big George said it would cause a lot of trouble if we said anything,' said Billy, looking around nervously. They were walking in the school grounds; their next class was not due to start for another ten minutes.

Neil laughed. 'The trouble's all going to be for him,' he said.

'You know, Neil, you led him on,' said Billy accusingly. 'The way you looked at him, and everything.'

'Remember, we were there to find out about him,' said Neil. 'If you don't put bait out, you'll never know if there's a fish.'

'In the photos, do you think those little kids knew what they were doing?' asked Billy. 'They were smiling, and everything . . .' His voice tailed off. He stopped in the middle of the path. 'I think we should tell somebody,' he said. 'I don't like it.'

'I think we should take the matter into our own hands,' said Neil. His eyes had that peculiar glow again, but he could see that Billy was getting really upset.

'Who do you think we should tell?' asked Neil, to pacify his friend. 'The Head?'

'My God, no,' said Billy. 'He'd take Big George's side

and we'd be in deeper trouble than ever. You know, Neil, you really piss me off sometimes. We should never . . .'

'Why don't we talk to Angus?' interrupted Neil. 'He's a lot older, and he's sort of sensible, for a teacher.'

'Good idea,' said Billy, brightening. 'We've got him next, and we can stay and talk to him after the class. He'll know what we should do.'

Angus Townes seemed to be in a particularly good mood during class; he even made some jokes, which astonished the boys.

'He won the pools,' whispered Dick Prothero. 'That's why he's so happy. He got the big jackpot.'

'That's bullshit,' sneered Terry Drummond from behind his desk. 'He's got a girl friend. And I know who it is, because Mrs Alexander in the kitchen saw them.'

After the class, Neil and Billy hung around until everybody else had gone.

'The two of you look as if you've been up to something,' he smiled, pulling an old briar pipe out of his pocket. He sat down at his desk and filled it.

'What kind of tobacco is that, sir?' asked Billy, sniffing. 'It smells so good . . .'

'It's called Balkan Sobranie,' said Angus, 'But I'm sure you didn't stay behind to find that out.'

'Last night Mr Elmslie invited us to his flat,' said Neil. 'He showed us some dirty pictures and wanted us to do weird things with him.'

Angus tried not to look surprised, his thumb suddenly stopped packing the tobacco into the bowl of his pipe. 'Are you quite sure?' he said, lost for words. George Elmslie! His astonishment was replaced by a quiet anger when the boys told him in detail what had happened.

'Let me think about it for a while,' he said finally. 'In the meantime, don't go to his place again, and don't talk to anybody about it, all right? I'll make a few inquiries, and we can get together again. Let's see, today's Wednesday

. . . Friday, after class, all right? I'll have a better idea what to do by then.' He grinned reassuringly at the boys and tapped his pipe on his heel. 'You both look as if you'd been caught robbing a bank,' he said. 'Everything's all right, no harm's been done. Now get going, and remember what I said.'

'That's a load off my mind,' said Billy, relieved, once they were outside again. 'I really like Angus, he's so calm, and he didn't blame us or anything.'

'I still think we should handle the problem ourselves,' said Neil. 'What do you think?'

'Count me out,' said Billy hurriedly. 'We should have never got into this in the first place.'

'Please yourself,' said Neil. 'I don't need you anyway.'

Angus Townes had planned to use the rest of the day to do some long-postponed repair work on his house. He'd bought the little bungalow when he first came to Perth a couple of years before, because the mortgage payments were less than an average rent. Angus soon found out why. The roof started to leak within a few weeks of his buying the place, and at that time he could afford to make only temporary repairs. When it rained more than just a little, Angus had to distribute pans and buckets in the kitchen and the bedroom. In addition, the paintwork on the bungalow was flaking badly, especially around the windows.

With all the recent dry weather, the roof hadn't been a problem, but now was the time to do something about it before the drought ended and he was back putting buckets all around the house and sleeping with his galoshes on. And with his new-found general lightness of spirit, cleaning up his house seemed a natural way of working off his excess energy. And who could be certain that he wouldn't soon be entertaining a visitor?

The heat and the dryness had made the paintwork look even more shabby, and Angus decided to start with that; at the weekend he'd be able to get somebody to help him with the roof; maybe he'd ask Neil and his friend Billy. They could probably use a little extra pocket-money. The house was old, with a slate roof, and he needed help to carry the heavy new slates up.

The day before, on the way back from school, Angus had bought three one-gallon cans of paint and a can of thinner, which he estimated would be enough for two coats all round. The other things he needed – brushes, a scraper, a blowlamp to burn off the paint – all these he had already, together with a small stepladder.

Angus was feeling very cheerful in spite of the heat. The next day, Thursday, was the day he'd arranged to have coffee with Jean Montrose, and the thought made him whistle with an unaccustomed zest. What a marvellous woman she was! Businesslike and efficient, she still found the time and the energy to be gentle and caring. There was nothing sloppy or sentimental about Jean, and that was just what he liked. With Jean Montrose, you knew exactly where you were, because there was no pretence, no maybes, no grey areas.

The old paint on the outside woodwork had been a dark, lavatorial green, and Angus decided that white, a good matt white, would look bright, clean and cheerful. To think that only a couple of weeks ago he would probably have chosen black . . .

First, though, he had to get the old paint off. About a year ago, he'd bought a new-fangled device, a kind of whirling metal brush, but it hadn't worked well, so he was going back to the old tried and true methods. He put on an old pair of jeans, an ancient shirt that dated back to his Cambridge days, and a pair of tennis shoes most people would have consigned to perdition long since.

The scraper . . . He found it with the paint-brushes, the paint rags, the masking tape, all thrown together in an untidy pile in the cupboard under the sink. The blowlamp

. . . That was in the garage, he remembered, in a bag. Finally he assembled all his equipment and carried it outside.

All the time he was doing this, as a background even to his pleasant thoughts about Jean Montrose, was the worry and disgust about what Neil Mackay and Billy Wilson had told him. At first he thought they were exaggerating the situation, that George had just been friendly to them, but he knew Neil and Billy pretty well; they were both reliable, and neither would make up that kind of story, he was quite sure of that. Still, Angus wanted to double check and called a friend in the Scottish Education Department; then he had an informal chat with Doug Niven. Doug remembered Angus from the time they'd all had dinner at Jean Montrose's house, and had liked him. The information he gave Angus was guarded but unmistakable. The information from his friend at the SED was less guarded but also unequivocal. George Elmslie was bad news and they told him why. The thought made Angus sad and sick. Pornography and child molesting! And George's responsibility was to teach and influence young minds . . . It went against everything Angus believed in, and a deep distaste at the man settled like a lead weight in his stomach.

Angus pushed those thoughts aside; he had to pay attention to what he was doing. There was only a little fuel left in the lamp, so he filled it up, pumped the air with the shiny brass handle, flipped his lighter, opened the valve a little and the lamp lit with a pop and a hiss, and was soon burning with a cheerful blue flame. He held it with his left hand, passing it over the dry, flaking paint until it was hot and soft, then scraped the paint away with his other hand. It was tiring work, and Angus soon felt thirsty and dry, but he persevered, and by lunchtime he had got three windows down to bare wood.

Weary, hot, and with aching arms, Angus went in to have a shower and make himself a sandwich. He put the paint and tools on the kitchen table, and on his way to the bathroom looked around the living room, and suddenly saw how shabby it was. He'd get some new furniture, he decided, and some nice curtains . . . Angus could almost see Jean sitting on his new sofa, looking so pretty in that bright dress she was wearing last time he'd seen her. Maybe she'd even help him choose the patterns; maybe . . . Angus laughed gently at himself, faintly embarrassed at his own fantasies, but, he had to admit, stranger things had happened, and he felt pretty sure she was interested in him, too.

So Angus was not prepared when Jean phoned. She was cancelling their date, she said quite bluntly, because there had been gossip after the last time and her husband Steven had not been pleased.

'I'm sorry,' said Jean, 'but I'm sure you understand.'

Angus was struck by a misery as acute as any he had suffered in the past. Every second of the afternoon seemed to drag, every minute was an eternity of sadness. It wasn't the first time Angus's world had fallen in, and the grey horizons were nothing new to him. But it *was* more painful, because things had just started to get better, he was just slowly picking himself off the floor when a boot kicked him in the head again. This time, he thought, I'm down for the count.

He couldn't even blame Jean. He'd mistaken her kindness and concern for something else – how stupid could he get? With his mind locked in a painful numbness, Angus slowly ticked off the things he had to do before going to see his daughter. Poor Deirdre. They made a pair, she and him. All his thoughts were back to half-speed again; he realised that he needed to go to the supermarket for provisions, and to buy some mango juice and grapes for Deirdre, but all kinds of other thoughts came diving in at him like screeching gannets, interrupting him, instructing him, pecking at his mind with their sharp beaks.

He went into the kitchen to wash his hands. On the table

were the tools he'd been going to use to beautify his house. The paint . . . He put the unopened cans under the sink; maybe one day he'd get up the energy again to use them. Then the scraper, the paint-brushes . . . All dead, lifeless tools now, with no future, no excitement, no utility. And the blowlamp; Angus topped it up mechanically, walked like a robot into the garage and put it into the boot of the car before going back into the house for a shower. Deirdre. Deirdre of the Sorrows . . . Angus had only heard that expression years after she had been baptised, and it certainly fitted, now. But not then, when she was little and lively and beautiful, and ran up in her little pink dress to meet him on the steps when he came home from the College.

Angus had some trouble starting his car, but finally the motor caught, and with a puff of oily smoke he started off towards the centre of town, then along South Street to the crossroads, chugging along to the big supermarket where he did all his shopping. Today was the day for basics, flour, vegetable oil, sugar, a big tub of lard, shoe polish; he picked those up and put them in the trolley before going over to get Deirdre's mango juice and grapes.

At the nursing home, he parked in the same place as when he'd met Jean; it was the only space left, and his heart contracted at the memory. He sat, immobile, nerving himself as he'd done a thousand times before going in to see his daughter. Most of her young life, now, she'd been like this, in a kind of waking coma, unresponsive, eating only when fed, not recognising anyone, not even her father. If, somewhere in that damaged brain, there was a vestige of memory of what her father had looked like then, it certainly wouldn't register now. Angus looked at himself in the car mirror; he was old, worn, a faint shadow of the man in the photo he carried in his wallet, the one of him and Deirdre taken in the garden of their home in Cambridge, with her arms so lovingly around his neck. Angus remembered how he had been, enthusiastic, idealistic, full of plans to right the wrongs in the world. Well, there weren't too many wrongs he could still right at this point in his life, maybe just one or two.

Deirdre had had a good day so far, the nurse told him, but when he went into her room there was spilled food on the sheets and an odour of faeces in the air. Angus called the nurse back and helped her to change the sheets. Deirdre's legs were so thin, it hurt him to look at them.

He fed her some grapes, holding each one by the stem to put it in her twisted and puckered mouth, and she sucked it off the stem, automatically, like a baby. Did she taste anything? Was that a face, that tortured, twisted rind of red and white scar tissue? Was that still a person, lying there, unable to make purposeful movements, forever unable to think, to sing, to smile, to kiss, to love?

Angus slid down on his knees by the side of Deirdre's bed, and for the first time in many years, he put his head in his hands and wept with the abandon of total despair, his harsh sobs rising and falling as the daylight slowly faded outside the window.

At that moment, Jean, coming to visit an old lady who had recently been admitted to the nursing home, pulled up next to Angus's car in the parking area outside, and noticed that his boot wasn't properly closed. She opened it to slam it shut, but some of the groceries fell out and it took her a moment to put everything back in. She slammed the boot, took a deep breath and walked towards the door of the nursing home. She really didn't want to meet Angus, because she felt so badly about cancelling their coffee meeting. It hadn't been easy, because she really liked him, but in a town like Perth, one couldn't take chances with one's reputation, especially as she was a doctor, and, without meaning to be, something of a public figure.

Chapter Eighteen

Doug sat back and watched George Elmslie come into the office, ushered in by Constable Jamieson. Doug had been taught to use every moment of the time spent with suspects; instinctively they would think that an interview started when they sat down opposite the interrogating officer, and finished when he said 'Thank you, that will be all'. But it was before and after those times, when they weren't on guard, that could be the most revealing.

'Have a seat, Mr Elmslie.' George came in, straight-backed, arrogant, confident-looking, and, it seemed to Doug, very conscious of his physique. He sat down in the metal chair placed opposite the desk with its back against the wall, a symbolic touch lost on most of its occupants. George was a big man, and made the office seem even smaller than usual.

'Now, Mr Elmslie,' said Douglas in his slowest voice. 'First, I'm going to tell you your rights, including your right to remain silent and your right to have a legal representative . . .'

He's heard this before, thought Doug as he enunciated every word, watching George carefully the while. George shifted irritatedly on his chair.

'There's no need for all that, Inspector. Of course I know my rights. I'm here on a completely voluntary basis to discuss a serious matter with criminal implications. All right?' He looked challengingly at Doug, as if he might just change his mind and walk out.

'Just routine, sir,' said Doug mildly. 'I didn't mean to
upset you.' In the space of a minute he had learned that
George Elmslie had prepared for this meeting and knew
exactly what he was going to say, that his apparent confidence was spurious, and that he would probably not be too
difficult to rattle.

Doug pulled a ruled police notebook in front of him,
made a few little circles in the corner to make sure his
ball-point pen was working properly, and very deliberately
held his pen poised over the paper. This too was a routine,
designed to give the impression that he was ponderous and
maybe even a bit slow-witted.

'Well, Mr Elmslie,' he said, settling into his chair with a
sigh, as if he were forcing himself to submit to the tedium of
his task, 'let's start with your full name and address . . .'

George gave it, obviously contemptuous of the painstak-
ing and methodical way Doug wrote everything down.
Doug was still writing when George, unable to control his
impatience, started right in. 'I'm a spare-time photographer, you see, and these two people came to me with a
proposition . . .'

'Would you happen to have their names and addresses?'
The tip of Doug's tongue showed as he laboriously pressed
hard on the paper.

George, getting really irate at what he considered Doug's
delaying tactics, slapped his pocket and said, 'Yes, of
course, but what possible . . .' He suddenly realised that
he'd spoken too fast, and could have bitten his tongue with
annoyance. 'I mean, yes, they told me where they came
from . . .'

Doug was looking at him, his blue eyes suddenly neither
sleepy nor stupid.

'Please tell me about the proposition, Mr Elmslie,' he
said.

'There were two of them, a man and a woman, named
Alec and Sally Govan, from Glasgow,' said George, his

voice somewhat subdued. 'They came wanting me to do some child portraits, and offered good money, so of course I . . .'

'How did these good people find you, Mr Elmslie? Through their local church? Or were they going from door to door, or perhaps you're in the Yellow Pages?'

'Not at all, Inspector,' said George smoothly, ignoring the sarcasm. He had the answer all prepared. 'I take my film to be developed in Glasgow, it's a special process for certain contrast effects . . . They got my name from the people who run the lab.'

'Go on, Mr Elmslie.' George noted that Doug had stopped taking notes; Constable Jamieson had unobtrusively taken over that function.

'Well, they came with these three children and their mother . . .' George wrinkled his nose. 'She'd been drinking, quite heavily, I would say. Anyway it soon became obvious that they wanted me to . . . photograph the children in various unspeakable poses.' Here the pitch of George's voice went high with righteous indignation.

'When I protested, and said that I had no intention of participating in this revolting business, the woman, the mother that is, became insolent and abusive. Apparently she makes her living in this way . . . Ugh!' George's big frame quivered with disgust. 'Anyway I put them all out, as quickly as possible. Those poor children! The mother was shouting drunkenly that she'd get me . . . It was *so* embarrassing . . .'

There was something in his voice that made Doug glance sharply at him. 'I'm sure it was,' he said, slowly. 'In a nice, middle-class building like the one you live in, the neighbours must have been very put out. How many do you have on your floor?'

'How many what?'

'Neighbours, Mr Elmslie.'

George hesitated for a second. 'Actually the walls are

pretty thick – none of them have actually said anything, or complained, that I know of.'

Doug assumed an expression of bored irritation. 'So, Mr Elmslie, what do you expect me to do? Put out an All Stations for them? Call Scotland Yard?'

'I'm very disappointed in your attitude, Inspector,' said George, huffily, although he had done all he wanted to do, which was to provide himself with a defence if Sally and Alec proceeded with their blackmail scheme.

'I'll get in touch with the Glasgow police,' said Doug, leaning back. 'If there's anything like a pornography ring there, they'll know about it. Thank you for letting us know about your . . . experience.'

George looked at him suspiciously but this time there was no trace of sarcasm in his voice. Douglas lined his pen up with the bottom of the pad and got up; the interview was over. He resumed his non-official way of speaking, as if he were relieved that it was finished, and they could be just man-to-man again.

'Incredible weather we're having here, aren't we?' he said, opening the door for George. 'I understand it's even hotter in Exeter, if you can believe it. Oh and by the by, I'd like to talk to you about Morgan Stroud, because I think you may have killed him.' George was staring at him with an expression of astonishment mixed with fear.

Doug smiled, and his teeth showed just a little. 'Tomorrow, Thursday, Mr Elmslie, here at four in the afternoon, so it won't interfere with your classes. Now I have one piece of advice for you.' Doug's voice was friendly, confiding. 'Prepare your story more carefully than today, please. And remember one thing. If you lie to me tomorrow, and I'll know it the second you do, I'll book you and have you in handcuffs before you have time to say "spontaneous combustion"!'

George went pale and his mouth dropped open with shock. A moment later, he found himself outside the closed door of Douglas's office, speechless, not even realising that he was cracking the joints of his fingers, one after the other.

'Why didn't you take him in now, sir?' asked Jamieson, a worried look on his face. 'He could be hundreds of miles away by tomorrow, even abroad.'

Doug shook his head. 'A man like that wouldn't run, Jamieson, because he knows we'd catch him.' Doug tapped his fingers on the desk. 'No, he'll be up all night tonight worrying, wondering what we know, what we don't know. By four in the afternoon he'll be a mess, ready to spill everything he's got. We won't have any trouble with him. Besides I need to get some information on him, and it'll take till tomorrow afternoon to get it.'

'I thought he was going to faint when you mentioned Exeter,' said Jamieson. 'Is the weather really that much hotter there?'

'For him, Jamieson, yes, it could be,' said Doug, grinning. He put his pad and pen back in the drawer.

'Well, I'm glad I don't live there, I can tell you,' said Jamieson, wonder in his voice. 'It's certainly bad enough here. Are you ready for a mug of tea, sir?'

Jean Montrose went off to work as usual that morning. Every time she passed Lochie Brae, the steep road that led up to the last abode of Morgan Stroud, she shivered. The whole ghastly business repelled her, but to her mind what was worse were the ugly complications that the burning of Morgan Stroud had slowly dragged into the light with it.

Jean turned into the right-hand lane, in preparation for going over the bridge, but she couldn't take her mind away from the house on the hill. It was like lifting a stone and seeing all the centipedes and creeping things scuttling away for safety. There was more to the whole situation than anyone knew, she was quite sure of it, and the awful thing was that it wasn't over yet.

From the bridge she could see the river below; even it

seemed to be sluggish and exhausted; the grass of the North Inch was parched and there were great expanses of brown on the playing fields. The oaks and chestnuts around the park stood stoic but obviously suffering from the continuing drought.

Jean looked at her watch. There was just time to go and see her mother, who had been in a nursing home since fracturing her hip some months before. She pulled in to the car park outside Marks and Spencer's and dashed in to buy some grapes. She picked up a bottle of Chablis on impulse; her mother liked an occasional drop of wine with her meals.

One of the nurses met her at the door. 'Mrs Findlay's nae been so well this morning,' she said. 'She was a bit upset about something and . . . Well, she threw her porridge at the nurse . . . anyway she's resting now.'

'I'm so sorry,' said Jean, feeling terribly embarrassed. 'Tell me the nurse's name and I'll get her something . . . I really am sorry.' Jean went into her mother's room. Mrs Findlay had her eyes closed but Jean knew she was wide awake.

It was a nice room, large, airy, with a comfortable easy chair, a table covered with books and papers and a big window which looked out over the garden with its pergola and little fountain. Jean put the grapes and the wine on the table.

'Don't think I didn't try kindness first,' said Mrs Findlay, her eyes still firmly shut.

'What happened?' Jean sat down beside the bed. Her mother was usually polite, if authoritative, with the nurses.

'She wanted me to get out of bed,' replied her mother. 'And I said, "For once, I'm going to have a long lie in," and she said, "Now Mrs Findlay, you know the routine, it's time to wake up," and I said "Be off with you, I'm going to sleep another half an hour," and she said, "MRS FINDLAY YOU HAVE TO GET UP AND EAT YOUR BREAK-FAST," and I said . . . Well, actually I didn't say anything.'

'That's when you threw your porridge at her.'

'Yes. No young chit like that tells *me* what to do. I pay good money to stay here, as much as a hotel . . . But there's no ill feeling, just as long as she comes back in here and apologises.'

Jean opened her mouth to say something then changed her mind. Mrs Findlay opened her eyes wide, and stared at her daughter.

'Aren't you going to shout, carry on, heap reproaches on my head?'

'No. I brought you some grapes and a bottle of Marks and Sparks Chablis.'

'Aren't you afraid I might lurk behind the door holding that bottle and crack the next nurse that comes in over the head?' Mrs Findlay looked at her daughter with a defiant glare.

'No.' Jean smiled at her mother, who was still feeling aggressive and enjoying it. 'Because you'd see yourself in that mirror by the door, and you'd see how dam' silly you looked, standing there in your nightie with that bottle raised above your head . . .'

Mrs Findlay exploded with laughter at the thought.

'You looked just like your father, right then,' she said. She dabbed her eyes with a handkerchief, weak with laughing. 'And that's exactly what he would have said, in these circumstances.'

Jean helped her mother get out of bed. It was a real effort; the old lady was very weak, and her hip still hurt a great deal, but finally she got her into the easy chair.

'Do you want to look at the newspaper?'

'No. It's all rubbish. Do you think I want to read about the weather, which I know about by looking through the window, or see photos of unknown pimply youths on the back page, holding up trophies? Humph!'

'Steven's got a group of Japanese going around the works today,' said Jean. 'There's some talk . . .'

'That poor Steven,' said her mother. 'I don't know how he stands for it, you being out of the house all the time the way you are. A man needs a wife who stays at home, not one who gallivants all over town, getting mixed up in things that don't concern her.'

'So you *do* read the paper,' smiled Jean. There had been a piece in the previous day's *Courier* about the heat wave, and Jean had been quoted on the medical effects.

'No. I'm talking about that teacher who got burned up. That was the Lord's work, and nobody should interfere with that. The best thing you can do, my lass, is stay out of it, mind your own business. Remember what happened to Lot's wife! *She* was told not to be nosey, but she looked back . . .'

'Oh, Mother!' said Jean, beginning to lose patience. 'I don't have anything to do with it. It's entirely a police matter . . .'

'Right. And don't you forget it. Just because I've been locked away here, out of sight, doesn't mean I don't hear what's going on.'

Jean stood up. 'I have a surgery to do, so I'd better be off . . .' Her voice was flat, and Mrs Findlay, looking up, suddenly remembered with a guilty feeling what a weight was on her daughter's shoulders, with all the domestic and medical responsibilities she had to carry. She knew it was far more than she'd ever had to deal with in her time.

'I'm sorry, dear,' she said. 'And thank you for coming. You've made me feel much better.'

Chapter Nineteen

The only people who seemed to know anything about Eloise Martin's arrival in Perth were the reporters on the *Perth Courier and Advertiser*, and they made sure their knowledge was not kept to themselves. The headline, 'POLICE BEG FOR MEDIUM'S HELP' made Doug go puce with fury, but that was nothing compared to his rage when the Sunday tabloids got the story a few days later. The headlines became 'GHOUL KILLING TERRORISES HIGHLAND TOWN', and 'FIERY FIEND FOXES FUZZ' (full story on p 2).'

Eloise was remarkably independent. She didn't need to visit the scene, she said. The emanations were all over Perth, she said, stronger of course near the 'house of horror'. She said she would just walk round until the spirits told her what had happened and why. She acknowledged that she might not be able to name a guilty party, if there was one. Eloise asked for a lock of the victim's hair, a shoe, something personal, but none was available. Eloise and the reporter who was escorting her tried to find Renée, but she was nowhere to be found.

The newspaper reporters and Grampian television came for Douglas, but he saw them coming, and left hurriedly down the back stairs and out through the Town's Lane entrance, telling Constable Jamieson as he left to take care of them, meaning get rid of them. But Constable Jamieson took him more literally, and spoke to the media to such good effect that he occupied a two-minute segment of the local evening television news, at which Doug, watching from the comfort of his own easy chair, almost had a stroke.

The announcer introduced the spot by saying that local citizens had been concerned by a wave of strange occurrences in and around the city of Perth, culminating in the horrific burning death of a teacher who worked at a local private school.

'Am I right in saying the police are baffled? asked the announcer.

'Shut up, Jamieson!' Doug shouted at the screen. 'Don't you say a word! Get off that television screen!'

Cathie put a restraining hand on his arm; she didn't want to miss Jamieson's reply.

'Ay, we're baffled,' said Jamieson, and Doug put his head in his hands. 'But that disna mean we don't know what's going on,' Jamieson added loudly, pointing at the camera, just as it was switching over to Eloise.

Eloise was a bright-eyed middle-aged woman wearing a silk aviator's scarf above a yellow dress with big black circles, the hem down almost to her ankles. The interviewer asked about her previous successes, which, according to Eloise, who spoke in a prim, precise Morningside accent, were numerous and spectacular.

'There is a menacing aura over the city of Perth,' she announced, flinging the scarf over her shoulder. 'Fire begets fire . . . The present heat wave is only a reflection of the malign influences now at work in this fair city . . .'

'Do you think there could be black magic involved in the burning death of Morgan Stroud?' asked the reporter, pushing the microphone into Eloise's face.

'The Devil is more at home in a hot environment, of that there is no doubt . . .' The cameraman, in a moment of sheer inspiration, panned to the heat haze over the town behind her, and the point was made.

'When will this all end, can you tell us that, Eloise?'

'There will be more deaths . . . You can expect nothing but trouble here until the weather breaks . . .'

At this point Doug turned the television off with a vicious jab at the remote control.

'Bloody fool!' he said, referring to Jamieson; he could not have verbalised his thoughts about Eloise.

Cathie slipped quietly into the kitchen; she had no desire to act as a lightning conductor, not that night anyway. Her friend Moira, the wife of the news editor of the newspaper, had said that Eloise was well known in Edinburgh, and came well recommended. Moira seemed to know quite a bit about the woman, and said that Eloise had been on the right track more often than not, although as a good Presbyterian, Moira herself certainly didn't believe in that kind of stuff.

What was it Eloise had said? That dreadful things were going to go on happening until the weather broke? More deaths! Cathie put her hand up to her mouth and nibbled on a hangnail. If this went on much longer Doug would be ready for Murray Royal, the local mental hospital. He had been showing signs of stress for a while now; no wonder, because this wasn't the kind of case he'd been trained to deal with, poor man. There seemed to be nothing for him to hold on to, just a lot of nasty people doing strange things that probably had nothing to do with the Morgan Stroud business at all. Like that George Elmslie. Cathie gave a shiver of disgust. Doug had told her briefly about George's appearance at the station that afternoon, and he didn't try to hide his instinctive dislike of the man.

'Do you really think he could have killed Morgan Stroud?' Cathie had asked. Doug had shrugged and wouldn't look her in the eye. Then he said he'd asked the Exeter police to teletype all they had on Elmslie; he wanted the material in his hands tomorrow, before talking to him again.

In the living room, Doug was still fuming. This case was

really getting to him, he knew that. Normally he was a
pretty calm kind of person, and he knew he was over-
reacting to Jamieson's television appearance. Under different circumstances, he might have been annoyed for a short
time but he'd have simply decided to give Jamieson a
reprimand, without losing sight of the humour of the
situation.

But what could he do? He got up and paced about the
small room in his agitation. It gave him a headache thinking about the case. Had there been a crime? Was the
burning of Stroud related to the other strange things going
on, Gwen Stroud and her black magic, that boy Neil Mackay
who was going out with Lisbie, and who Jean had indicated
was an 'unusual' person, George Elmslie and his photographs, Renée, Stroud's wife . . . And now this clairvoyant
woman getting the media all excited, as if Perth was in the
grip of some kind of plague . . .

'WHAT THE HELL IS GOING ON IN THIS TOWN?'
he shouted aloud, his voice hoarse with frustration. Cathie
came through from the kitchen and put an arm around
him. 'Why don't you go out and take a wee walk?' she
asked gently. 'It always helps when you go around the
North Inch, it clears your head.'

Doug put his arms round her. Cathie always knew just
how to approach him when things weren't going well, what
to say, and always in just the right tone of voice.

'D'you want to come with me?'

'You're better off going by yourself,' she said. 'Anyway
I have some letters to write. Off you go now, and I'll see
you in a whilie.'

When George Elmslie got back to his flat he went straight
to the cabinet in the living room and poured himself a stiff
vodka, which he gulped down in one swallow. He gasped,
then coughed; he rarely drank spirits because he knew it did
bad things to his body, but tonight he needed something

really strong to steady him. The liquid burned its way down his gullet and he felt suddenly nauseated, and sat down.

Exeter . . . He could have died when Niven mentioned the place. How could he have known about that? Or was it just a shot in the dark? He'd been found not guilty, so there was no criminal record he could have checked up on.

It was really strange, because at first everything seemed to be going like clockwork; he'd even felt a conscious pride in the way he'd told the story. 'They wanted me to photograph those children in various unspeakable poses . . .' A nice turn of phrase, and he'd practised the simultaneous wrinkling of the nose in front of the mirror. And that stupid policeman, sitting there, writing it all down, so solemnly . . . right up to the last minute, when George thought everything had gone nicely, that he was home free, then the bastard dropped that bomb shell on him. And that wasn't even the worst. My God! When he started about Morgan Stroud . . . George wondered if his shock and fear had shown on his face. And he thought that by now the whole nasty business was dead and buried, so to speak. If that was going to be brought up again . . .

The phone started to ring, and George jumped as if he'd been shot. Who on earth could that be . . . ? He let it ring until he couldn't stand it any longer, then went into the kitchen and picked the phone off the wall hook.

'Yes?'

'George, I'm glad you were home.' George recognised Alec Govan's voice. 'Me and Sally, we were talking . . .' Alec cleared his throat, a long, drawn-out hawk. 'It occurred to us you might try to double-cross us, and I just wanted to let you know we're not far from you right now, and we're thinking about you.' For a few moments, all George could hear was a muffled sound while Alec had a brief conversation with somebody at the other end, presumably Sally. 'Right, sorry about that,' he said when he came back on. Then his voice changed from his usual nasal whine and became soft but very clear. 'George, do you remember Gogs Murray?' George caught his breath and gripped the phone tightly. Yes, he'd heard of him, or to be more exact, he'd read about him in the papers. Gogs Murray was a minor underworld character whose body had been found floating in a disused Clydeside dock some months before. Nobody knew who it was until some children found his head ten days later on a rubbish dump, loosely wrapped in paper towelling inside a plastic bag.

'Gogs used to do some work for us,' went on Alec. 'Nothing too complicated, just delivering film, taking it around to different places, stuff like that. But he wasn't honest, George. He made copies of a whole lot of our films, ones we'd entrusted to him, and he went into competition with us . . .'

'So?' said George calmly, but his mouth was suddenly very dry. Alec didn't answer; he'd hung up.

George went back into the living room, shaken, but only for a moment. He looked in the long mirror by the door and was reassured by what he saw. That little runt Alec! George couldn't help laughing. If he got his hands on him, he'd break him in half. And the front door was always kept locked; there had been an attempted burglary a few weeks back and everybody in the block was very conscious of security. He'd use his bicycle to go to school for a while, it would be a good ride, great exercise. Alec would have a hard time putting a bomb on his bicycle.

Then a sudden thought crossed his mind. Why had Alec called now, tonight? And why did he say he was close by? Did he know about the visit to the police station? George sat down suddenly, his brow covered with sweat. The noise of his knuckles cracking was like breaking chicken bones, but he didn't hear them. Gogs Murray had known the risks he took, but that hadn't saved him . . .

His whole frame trembling, George put his head in his hands. What should he do? Suddenly the fear of death swept over him like a slimy tide, and he started to weep with terror, great sobs racking his heaving, muscular body.

As soon as he had regained control of his voice, he looked in the phone book, and called Doug Niven at home to demand protection.

Chapter Twenty

That morning, when Jean slid quietly out of bed, already uncomfortable with the heat, she had a feeling that it was going to be a bad day. Before she had finished in the bathroom, the phone rang and Steven answered it. 'It's for you!' he said, before flinging himself back on the bed. 'I'm sorry, dear,' she murmured, although Steven couldn't hear her. The call was from Mrs Dornoch's daughter, saying that her mother was having trouble again with her leg. The old lady had been having leg problems on and off for years, so Jean didn't feel that she needed to postpone her surgery and go out there immediately, and said she'd call at around eleven.

Jean was feeling listless and lethargic, and it was an effort to rouse Lisbie and Fiona out of bed. They'd been out together the night before, and Jean wasn't sure when they'd got home. The day was hotter than ever, and the morning paper had a front page article about Eloise Martin, her prediction of future horrors, and her assertions about a mantle of evil hanging over the city. The article included a picture on page three of Constable Hector Jamieson confessing, in so many words, to the total bewilderment of the police in the case of Morgan Stroud.

'Oh dear,' said Jean, looking at the photo, in which Jamieson's expression personified the bafflement of the entire police force. 'Poor old Jamieson, he'll be in for it, just as soon as Douglas Niven sees this!'

The newspaper was open on Eleanor's desk, and Eleanor

and Helen were discussing the story when Jean came in.

'It's a scandal,' said Eleanor, always easily influenced by what she read. 'A city this size, and they're so inefficient. Is this what we pay our taxes for?'

'Now that's not true,' replied Helen sharply. 'What do you want them to do? Go around arresting people just for the sake of it? It's not even certain that a crime was committed.'

Jean didn't want to get involved in the discussion, and asked how many patients were waiting. Rather guiltily, Helen folded the paper, but flung a final shot at Eleanor. 'If it was an act of God, and *I* think it was, what do you think they should do, subpoena Him?'

Jean picked up her small pile of post and went into her little office; she had made no comment after Helen's last sally, although Helen had looked across to her for support. Jean felt a dreadful sinking feeling in her stomach as she opened the letters, and realised that what she already knew would have to come out sooner or later. The death of Morgan Stroud was no act of an infuriated Deity, but a planned, carefully premeditated murder.

Eleanor opened the door. 'Mrs Dornoch's daughter called again,' she said. 'She's really worried about her mother . . .'

'Oh dear,' said Jean. 'Perhaps I'd better go and see her. How many patients does Helen have?'

'Just six,' replied Eleanor. 'Shall I ask her to see yours?'

'No, thanks, I'll ask her myself, said Jean, packing a few things into her black bag. 'If Bella's still on the phone, tell her I'll be out there in about ten minutes.'

Helen didn't mind seeing Jean's patients, at least until she came back; and although Jean hated to give her partner additional work, she just as often did the same for Helen.

In her little Renault the steering wheel was hot to her touch; Jean had forgotten to open the sun-roof, and the interior was airless and stuffy.

Although part of Jean's brain was dealing with the mechanics of driving her car, and another was concerned with Mrs Dornoch, somewhere at the back of her mind the whole question of Morgan Stroud was being sifted, evaluated, re-examined . . . Several factors convinced Jean that Gwen Stroud somehow had the key to the mystery, although she had trouble believing that poor, disturbed Gwen could have carried out a murder, particularly one which had involved such a frightening degree of cunning. But one never knew with mentally unstable people, they were sometimes capable of the most incredible actions. And of course there was Renée . . . Poor woman, thought Jean, her life wrecked by a single sadistic act, she certainly had plenty of reason to want Morgan Stroud to die in the most horrific circumstances. But shifting in the uncomfortable shadows of her mind, Jean saw Neil Mackay, dark eyes glowing; Neil, who knew that his essay was at the top of the uncorrected pile right next to Morgan Stroud's charred body; Neil who was involved in strange magical rites; Neil who had been victimised by Stroud, and who hated him. Then there was Neil's father, Ken, who'd been a boxer and was used to resolving problems by force. Jean thought about him for a minute. He was another of those socially resentful people, far too sensitive about real and imagined slights or sneers. Jean knew that he'd confronted Morgan Stroud and threatened him; she could just see Stroud's arrogant, contemptuous face, sneering at Ken Mackay's plebeian accent. That would really drive him up the wall . . . And then, of course, there was the large and frightening George Elmslie, victim of Stroud's blackmail which had cost him a senior job at St Jude's, and maybe more . . .

Jean shivered and swung her car into Minto Crescent. It was time to get her mind back in gear, back on the job, back on to Mrs Dornoch; she was a diabetic, and Jean had had difficulties regulating her insulin dosage. Jean was only too aware of the kind of problems Mrs Dornoch could encounter as a result of her unstable diabetes: everything from kidney failure to blindness.

Mrs Dornoch lived in what used to be a council flat up in one of the better estates; she and her daughter had bought it when the city council sold them off a few years before.

Jean pulled up outside the house, and saw the quick movement of the curtain in the front room. Bella Dornoch must really be worried about her mother, thought Jean as she locked the car door and went towards the house.

Bella was waiting, a faded, careworn woman who had once been quite pretty. She cleaned houses, and Jean had told her several times she was working too hard.

'Thank you for coming, Dr Montrose,' said Bella, wiping her hands nervously on her apron. 'She's in the bedroom.'

She followed Jean along the narrow hall. 'It started last night,' Bella said. 'You know she always had pain in that leg, so I didn't pay too much attention. I gave her a cup of hot milk with a wee drop of rum in it, because that usually helps . . .'

Jean opened the door. 'Well, hello, Mrs Dornoch,' she said, smiling. She put her bag on the chair by the window. 'Bella says you've been afa nae weel?'

The old lady smiled. 'Bella disna talk like that, it's only me that does . . .' She was pale, with a rim of sweat around her hairline. 'But aye, I've nae been weel since tea-time yisterday. I was sitting down tae ma tea when the leg, the right ane, started to pain me, then it became real weak and tingly-like . . .'

While she was speaking, Jean gently raised the sheet at the lower end of the bed. The leg looked all right, not too different from the other one, maybe a little pale, with some brown marks and whitish scars on her ankle from old, long-healed ulcers.

'Can you move your toes?' asked Jean. 'Wiggle them for me.'

The old lady did so, but with some difficulty. Jean

noticed how thick and brown the toenails were; the big toenail in particular was twisted up almost like a horn.

Jean touched the skin of the leg with the back of her hand to test the temperature; it was cooler than the other side. Her hand slid down to the foot; it was cold as ice. Quickly Jean checked the two pulses on the foot, and then compared them with the left side. Just as she had suspected, the pulses were completely absent on the right. Then she checked the pulse in the groin. Nothing.

Jean stood up slowly.

'We have a problem,' she said slowly, giving herself time to decide exactly what she had to do. 'The main artery to the leg is blocked,' she said. 'I'm afraid we'll have to get you into the hospital right away, Mrs Dornoch.'

'No, I'm nae gaen to the hospital,' said Mrs Dornoch with a shake of her head. 'I'm ower old already, and if I'm tae die, I'm going to do it here.'

'Now, Mrs Dornoch,' said Jean firmly. 'It's a blood clot, and they can take it out in the hospital and you'll be back home as good as new in a few days. If you don't go, it'll turn into gangrene, and you don't want that, I can promise you!'

Jean left the room to phone for an ambulance, while Bella got a few things together and put them in a small suit-case.

'She won't go,' said Bella after Jean had put the phone down. 'As soon as you're gone, she'll put her heid down under the bedclothes and she winna let onybody touch her. I ken her . . .'

So Jean had to wait until the ambulance came. They sat in the kitchen, and Bella made some tea. 'Nothing for your mother,' cautioned Jean. 'They'll be operating on her leg today, and they won't want anything in her stomach.'

Bella was trembling. She was the only daughter, and the two women only had each other in the world. Jean explained what they would be doing to her mother. 'They put a little balloon down inside the artery, inflate it and pull it back, bringing the clot out with it,' she explained but Bella was too upset to understand. 'Maybe I should have called you sooner,' she said, tears appearing in her eyes. 'Maybe that clot could have been dissolved with medicine – maybe that's all she would have needed . . .'

They heard the ambulance pull up outside, and the men put Mrs Dornoch on a portable stretcher under Jean's watchful eye before carrying her down the stairs. Mrs Dornoch didn't want to go, but didn't dare start an argument with the Wee Doc because she was a little afraid of her and knew she'd lose.

'I knew something like this was going to happen,' Bella burst out. They were standing at the back of the ambulance as her mother was heaved up into it under the fascinated gaze of half a dozen children who had materialised from nowhere. 'Everything's going wrong in this town now!' She was speaking fast, almost hysterically. 'There'll be nothing good here until the weather breaks, or until they catch whoever's put a spell on us, like that woman in the paper said.'

Driving back to her surgery, Jean's mind went back to the charred body of Morgan Stroud, and again she wondered about the sparing of everything else in the room, and those gruesomely unburned hands and feet . . . There *had* to be an explanation for all that, surely, one that didn't involve black magic or ball lightning or divine retribution. Jean's hands tightened on the steering wheel; if nobody else could find out, she would; she decided to phone Bill Wilson, her old chief at the burn unit. He was one of the top burn doctors in Scotland, and in addition a wise and knowledgeable man.

By the time Jean got back to the surgery Helen had seen all the patients, so she checked her messages and went home for lunch. On the way back she thought about Bella Dornoch's comments; it was not too difficult to believe, as Bella obviously did, that supernatural forces were at work, hovering silently and malignantly over the parched city. But if they did exist, was someone manipulating them? And if so, who was that someone?

Jean drove straight home and parked in the street as Steven's car was blocking the drive. Good, thought Jean. She hated eating lunch by herself.

Steven had made some vichyssoise, and served it with a flourish, even adding a sprig of parsley as a finishing touch.

'You always make the most delicious soup,' said Jean, tucking in. 'I could eat this every day.'

'It's the garlic that makes it different,' said Steven, pleased. 'Not everybody knows to put a wee bit in, not mashed, just cut up into little bits.'

'I had to send Mrs Dornoch to hospital,' said Jean. 'Poor thing, she may lose her leg.'

'Poor woman . . . Her daughter's going to be terribly upset.'

'I know. It's a shame for Bella. She never got married so she could look after her mother. Now it's too late.'

'Somebody from the *Scotsman* called, just before you came in. They want to know what you think about that clairvoyant woman's predictions.'

'The *Scotsman*!' Jean's soup spoon stopped in mid air. 'My, we're coming up in the world! I wonder why they're asking *me*?'

'That's exactly what I asked her. She said she'd covered the Lumsden business and talked to you then.'

'Oh yes, I remember her now. Well, I'm sure she'll call back.'

A few minutes later she slipped out of the room and went to the phone in the hall. She made a long distance call and then, with much sadness, she spoke briefly to Angus Townes.

'I wish he'd been a sergeant,' fumed Bob McLeod, the Chief Inspector. 'Then I could have demoted the imbecile!'

'It was partly my fault, Bob,' mumbled Doug. 'I told him to take care of the problem, and he must have thought . . .'

'You're giving him too much credit,' interrupted McLeod. 'Jamieson doesn't have anything to think with. But you're not exactly covered in glory in this case either, are you?'

Doug grinned at him. 'Then maybe you should ask Eloise, the fortune-teller woman. I'm sure she could solve the whole thing for you just like that, by looking into her crystal ball.'

Bob looked steadily at Doug, as if he were really considering that possibility.

'The press has been phoning all day, asking for news,' said Bob weightily. ' "No news," I tell them, "God is not giving bulletins on his actions." '

'I don't know . . .' Douglas rubbed the side of his nose. 'I wish I could be so sure. There's nothing under "Acts of God" in the pathology books I've looked at.'

'Well, I think it's the weather as much as anything that's getting people upset,' said Bob, opening his jacket. 'If this had happened in January, everybody would have just said he'd set himself on fire with an electric radiator, or something, then had a heart attack . . .'

'I wish Dr Anderson would get back from holiday,' grumbled Doug. 'He's supposed to be writing a paper about it, so he must have researched it pretty thoroughly, but we haven't had the benefit of his opinion, except right at the beginning.'

'He won't be able to help you anyway,' said Bob stubbornly. 'Like you said, acts of God aren't in his book.'

Doug took a deep breath. 'Shall we just close the case, then, and say it was an act of God?'

Bob shook his head. 'Doug,' he said, 'it's your case. Do what you think is right.'

'Thanks for your help,' said Doug, his voice heavy with unnoticed sarcasm. Bob McLeod notwithstanding, Doug was reasonably sure at this point that a murder had been committed, and he had painstakingly narrowed his list of suspects down to two. No, he corrected himself, not two, but three. There was nothing to help him decide whether it had been committed by a man or a woman.

191

Chapter Twenty-one

Jean and Steven both knew there was something wrong the minute Lisbie came in. Maybe it was a parent's sixth sense, maybe her step, or the way she slammed the front door, but they looked at each other and held their breath until Lisbie came running into the living room and flung herself into the vacant chair and started to sob as if her heart was breaking.

Steven opened his mouth to say something, but Jean quickly shook her head. Not now, her eyes said, let her cry for a while, she'll tell us when she's ready.

Steven got up and tiptoed out. This was obviously a time to leave the women to themselves.

After a few minutes, Lisbie looked up, red-eyed. Jean sat still, her sympathy showing in her eyes.

'Neil?' she asked quietly, and Lisbie's renewed wails answered for her.

'He doesn't want to see me any more . . .' Lisbie's words came out in little gasps, all disjointed.

Lisbie slid out of her chair on to her knees and came over to Jean and put her head in her mother's lap. Jean stroked her fine brown hair and remembered the first time she had felt the same way. It seemed such a long time ago, but she well remembered that horrible, end-of-the-world feeling.

'He said . . .' Lisbie choked, then went on. 'He said I wasn't mature enough to handle . . .' She sat up suddenly. 'Mature! Can you imagine *him* telling *me* that! And he's just a kid!'

Jean smiled, and Lisbie grinned through her tears. Jean

was relieved; it wasn't going to be as bad as she feared.

'He said I hadn't handled the events of the past few days in a mature way,' she said, now beginning to sound indignant. 'As if *I* were the child in this relationship!'

Jean smiled. 'Did he say which events?' she asked, noticing that her heart was beating fast.

'No, but I suppose he meant that magic stuff he's into,' replied Lisbie, sniffing. 'Do you have a tissue?'

Jean reached for the box, her hand not quite steady.

'Did you . . . do any of that magic with him?'

'Just up in the tower, on Kinnoull Hill.' Lisbie blew her nose hard, like a trumpet. 'And that was just boring, all these funny words, reciting, and that smoky stuff she burned.' She opened her eyes wide and dabbed at them with the corner of the paper hanky. 'Anyway his father is really mad at him, made him promise not to do any more of that stuff.'

'Have you met Mr Mackay?'

'Oh yes. And I don't like him either. There's something . . . I don't know, rough, or brutal or something. He was a boxer – there are photos of him all around the house, standing over people with his fists up . . . and a piece from an old newspaper that he has framed, that says Killer Mackay does it again, something like that.'

Steven opened the door a crack and looked in.

'It's all right now, Daddy,' said Lisbie. There was something so sweetly feminine about the way she spoke that both Jean and Steven smiled. He went over and gave her a big hug.

'Boys are no good anyway,' he said. 'Ask your mother. When she was your age, she knew more about them than anybody!'

'Hey, you!' said Jean, pretending to bridle. '*You* were the only boy I knew who wasn't any good!'

By the time they sat down to dinner, Lisbie seemed to have forgotten all about the Mackays, but Jean, sitting very thoughtfully at her end of the table, had not.

Fiona was all set to tease her sister, but Steven shook his head very firmly at her. Lisbie was putting on a good face now, he knew, but later, he felt pretty sure, she would cry herself to sleep.

'I got a letter from Buckingham Palace today,' he announced, not without a certain amount of pride.

'Going to tea with the Queen, then?' asked Fiona pertly.

'She doesn't live there any more,' cut in Lisbie. 'When Mrs Thatcher took the place over, she put her and Philip into a council house!'

Everybody laughed, but Jean kept looking at Steven. He wouldn't say something like that unless he was serious.

'We're getting the Queen's Award for Industry,' said Steven, trying not to sound too pleased. 'And Prince Philip may even come up for the presentation himself.'

Jean put her hand to her mouth, thinking instantly that she didn't have anything suitable to wear for such an occasion.

'Steven! That's wonderful!' Jean went around the table and hugged him. She had tears in her eyes. 'You've certainly worked hard enough for it,' she said. 'Oh, I'm so proud of you!'

Lisbie got up and rushed down to the basement. There was always a bottle of champagne in the refrigerator, kept for very special occasions, and she was stripping the foil off the top as she came back up the stairs.

'Don't shake it!' said Steven, surprised and delighted at the reception his news had earned. 'Here, give it to me, I'll open it.'

The cork shot up, hit the ceiling and landed in the spaghetti sauce and the wine fizzed over the top of the bottle before Steven could catch it.

'You see why I always let him do it,' whispered Lisbie to her sister.

'We'll have a toast to Daddy,' said Jean, raising her glass. 'This is the most wonderful day!'

'And to the end of Neil,' whispered Fiona. 'May his soul rot in hell!'

Lisbie stuck her tongue out at Fiona. 'I saw Mr Pratt's dirty fingerprints on your knickers,' she said loudly. 'So you shut up!'

'That's enough from both of you,' said Jean. 'We're toasting Daddy's Award, if you don't mind!'

They all drank to Steven, including himself.

'When is it?' asked Jean, thinking she'd have to go to Edinburgh to get herself a new outfit.

'When is what?'

'The Award. When will it be actually presented?'

'September,' said Steven, 'provisionally, anyway.'

'Well it certainly wouldn't be in August, would it?' said Lisbie. The others looked at her.

'And why not?' asked Fiona sarcastically. 'What do *you* know about the Duke of Edinburgh's activities?'

'Do you think he's going to stop shooting grouse to come down here?' Lisbie screamed at her. 'Are you completely daft?'

Jean watched Lisbie and worried. Not because she was screaming, but because she knew that Lisbie was saying these outrageous things about Mr Pratt and making all that noise just to keep her mind off Neil Mackay.

Later, after they'd all gone to bed, Jean hugged her husband and told him again how proud she was of his award.

'I just mentioned it to get the subject off Neil Mackay,' he said, rather apologetically.

Jean was very tired. The last thing she remembered, or maybe it was after she'd dozed off, she was telling Steven she was sure the next thing he would get was a knighthood, and then she would be Lady Montrose, but then she'd need a complete new wardrobe. She was feeling quite happy; not even the nagging worry about the Mackays was able to keep her awake.

* * *

The next morning, George Elmslie didn't show up for his first class, and the Headmaster was furious. After waiting for twenty minutes he decided to distribute George's pupils around the classes of the other teachers; Neil and his friend Billy finished up crowded in the back of Angus's room.

'I hope you won't mind doing physics twice today.' He grinned at the two boys. 'Maybe when Mr Elmslie finally does come in he'll take you all off my hands for the rest of the morning.'

The heat in the classroom became rapidly uncomfortable, and a few boys started ostentatiously fanning themselves with their notebooks.

'All right . . . Neil, you're tall enough,' said Angus resignedly. 'See if you can open that top window.'

Neil went over and stood on the sill, put his hands up on the window and was about to pull down on the frame when he froze. Coming into the small courtyard in a cloud of dust was a police car. It pulled up outside the main door and he saw two policemen get out and disappear into the school.

'Well, Neil, do you propose to stand up there all morning?'

'Sir, there's a police car . . .'

In an instant the boys were all crowding and pushing around the window. Angus waited for a moment, then said, 'All right boys, now you've all seen your very first police car, let's get back to work, if you don't mind!'

'They've come to arrest the Head,' said Billy, *sotto voce*. 'He's using this place for drug smuggling . . .'

'No, he sent the police to get Big George, and they had to drag him back here in handcuffs and chains.'

'All right, boys,' said Angus, with just a trace of impatience, 'that's enough of that. If you'll open your books at page forty-three . . . We've wasted enough time already.'

But the class never quite settled down to work; there was always someone trying to peer out of the window, and there was an undercurrent of whispering throughout the period, and Angus was glad when the bell rang and they all trooped out.

The next period passed in the same way, with all kinds of rumours and comings and goings. The boys passing the school office could hear the phone ringing almost continuously; there was a strange atmosphere of curiosity and excitement. The Head appeared several times in the corridor outside his office, but he had a drawn, distracted look and spoke to no one. The two policemen who had come in the car stayed for about half an hour, then left, but soon after that another car came and two more people were seen to enter the Head's office. One of them was carrying a portable phone, reported Billy, who had sneaked up for a closer look.

At about ten thirty, the Headmaster's secretary went round the different classes and whispered to each teacher that the Head had called a meeting of all the teachers for eleven o'clock, in the staff common room.

'What's happened, sir?' a boy asked Angus when the secretary had left the room.

'I have no idea,' replied Angus. 'All I can tell you is that nobody's learning anything at all this morning.' He banged his long pointer on the floor to get his pupils' attention, but there was too much in the air, too much speculation and uncertainty, and the class never really got going.

Angus got to the meeting a few moments late, and there was a tense, rather fearful atmosphere in the room. In the buzz of conversation, Angus could tell that nobody had the slightest idea what was going on. The door opened and the headmaster walked in. The conversation died instantly, and they watched him closely but could get no advance knowledge from his grim, drawn expression. But they didn't have to wait long.

He closed the door and stood with his back to it, his hands clasped together. His eyes were red-rimmed and his face haggard.

'Gentlemen,' he said, his voice showing the strain he was under. 'I have been informed that our colleague George Elmslie was found dead this morning in his flat.' There was an appalled silence, then everybody spoke at once. 'Please, gentlemen . . .' Mr Wardle's voice rose almost hysterically over the noise. 'I have been requested to ask that if any one of you has any knowledge or information about this tragedy . . .' the Headmaster's eyes flickered over the faces watching him, 'you must report immediately to Inspector Douglas Niven in Perth. I have his telephone number here . . .' Again his eyes went over the group but found no response, only white faces and shocked expressions. He took a deep breath. 'Inspector Niven will be personally contacting some of you, and he has asked that you all remain available. The school is hereby dismissed for the day, as soon as you have told your classes about this . . . this . . .' He couldn't finish, and almost ran from the room, trailing his black gown behind him like a crow with a dragging wing.

The teachers remained completely silent until the door closed, then a muted buzz of talk filled the room. It didn't last long. The teachers filed out and returned grim-faced to their classes, some of them wondering for the first time about their own safety.

'Oh no!' Jean listened to Doug's voice with growing horror. 'Doug, I can't . . . Where's Dr Anderson?' She looked around the office; Eleanor's beady eye was on her, curious, attentive. The clock indicated almost nine thirty, and there was nobody else in the surgery. Helen should be arriving any minute.

'All right,' she said finally, her sense of duty winning as it usually did. 'What floor is it on?'

The scene at George Elmslie's apartment was eerily similar to that she had seen at Morgan Stroud's house. But she soon found differences which were not immediately apparent.

First, the body was not nearly as badly burned, and was quite recognisable. The torso was partially charred, as was one side of the neck and head, but the arms and legs were almost intact, although they were stiff and bent. Had he been standing, he would have been in a position resembling a wrestler's crouch. He was lying on his back in the middle of the floor. Most of the face was intact, contorted by the contraction of the heat-damaged muscles, and a thin trail of smeared blood led from near the door across the room then back to the centre of the carpet, which was charred in spots beneath the body but not burned through. Elmslie had been wearing a cotton dressing gown over a pair of paisley-pattern pyjamas, and all the clothing over his chest and abdomen was charred.

And the smell was different . . .

'They're sending a pathologist over from Dundee,' said Doug. Otherwise the same crew was there; the fingerprint team had already left their grey dust on the doors and windows. The same young woman with long straight blond hair was putting away her photographic equipment. She smiled at Jean as she headed for the door, and Jean smiled back, absently.

Jean stepped gingerly over the plastic grid tapes and looked at the body. This time it was easier to see what had happened. 'The burns were made after he was dead,' she said. Jean was shocked at the strained, cracked sound of her voice.

'How can you tell?' asked Doug. He sounded subdued, but much more confident than he had been at the previous burning.

'There's no reddening or swelling at the margins of the burn,' she replied, looking for a radiator or other electrical appliance near the body that could have started the process. Of course there was none. The rest of the room was in a great disorder; pieces of torn, shiny photographic paper lay all over the floor, and by the window a smashed tripod lay on its side, one leg sticking uselessly in the air. Beside it was an aluminium reflector, crushed and deformed, fragments of blue glass and the remains of several large lightbulbs that had apparently been thrown on the floor and trampled on. A large projection screen had been ripped in half and the frame bent and twisted. Near the open door leading to the bathroom was a large stain on the carpet, and Jean could smell the acrid stench of chemical developers mixed with the strange burned smell coming from the body.

'Whoever it was really tore the place apart,' said Doug, watching her. 'I won't even show you the rest of it.' He shifted his feet. 'I spent a little time putting together some of the torn-up photos . . . He was quite a lad, this George Elmslie.' He looked to see how Jean was taking this, but she seemed quite unmoved.

'How long do you think he's been dead?' he asked.

Jean hesitated. 'It's hard to tell . . .' She overcame her revulsion and pulled up one of Elmslie's eyelids with her thumb, as gently as if he were still alive. The eyelid felt like a piece of wet wrapping paper, and the globe was dull and flaccid, its internal pressure already diminished.

'The heat speeds up the onset of rigor mortis, but I would guess about eight to ten hours.'

'That agrees well with our calculations,' said Douglas, grimly, and Jean could see that he had his confidence back. Although the death of George Elmslie was similar in some ways to the burning of Morgan Stroud, this time there were no distracting overtones of black magic or divine interference. He was confident this one was a plain, old-fashioned murder, the kind of thing he felt comfortable with. There were other major differences, too: the front door had been left ajar, the place had been wrecked . . . he was quite certain that the two murders had not been done by the same person.

'Who . . . ?' asked Jean, softly.

Douglas shook his head. 'We're looking for a couple of

people we think might be able to help us,' was all he would say. In spite of the horror of the situation, Jean couldn't help smiling to herself for a second; Douglas was much less communicative when he was sure of his ground.

Once again, Jean escaped as soon as possible, and made her way through the little crowd of curious onlookers around the entrance to the building. She was feeling stunned, almost distraught; this second killing had taken her entirely by surprise.

On the way back to her surgery, Jean turned for a short distance along South Street, past Ken Mackay's dry-cleaning shop. She had a sudden feeling of discomfort as she passed the rather tawdry premises, with the cheap, hand-lettered posters in the window, and without even realising it, she accelerated to get away from there.

Chapter Twenty-two

'Well, it saved the expense of one trial,' said Douglas. 'We flushed him out, all right, but so did the others, unfortunately.'

'They're quite a bunch, those teachers up at St Jude's, aren't they?' said the Chief Inspector, thoughtfully. 'So you think Elmslie killed Stroud, do you?' He didn't sound entirely convinced.

'I'm sure of it. He was being blackmailed by Stroud,' said Douglas. 'He'd found out about Elmslie's hobbies . . .' Douglas wrinkled his nose and glanced at the phone, willing it to ring.

Bob Mcleod followed his gaze. 'Expecting a call?'

'From Glasgow,' replied Douglas. 'I sent them an all stations to pick up that pair of . . . I don't know what you'd call them, child procurers maybe.'

'If they killed Elmslie, they'll be hiding out,' said Bob. 'Glasgow's a big place.'

'I know that kind,' said Douglas. 'I was on the force there for eight years, you remember. When they're on the run, that kind always stay close to home, where they know people who can hide them, bring them food and so on.'

'Still . . .' Bob had never worked outside Perth, and to him the vastness of Glasgow seemed a morass in which people could easily get lost for ever.

'Anyway they don't know we're on to them,' said Doug, and at that moment the telephone rang. Doug jumped for it.

'Alastair? Yes, it's me. Where? Lapadillo Street? Down there . . . ! Yes, I can . . .' Doug looked at his watch. 'About an hour, maybe more, maybe a bit less. Okay, see you then, at the Bannock Street station. Yes, of course I know how to get there. And don't lose those two, whatever you do!'

Doug put the phone down, his face full of grim satisfaction. 'The two of them are holed up in a house on Lapadillo Street, down in the Gorbals,' said Doug. 'I'm on my way . . .' He was out of the door before Bob could tell him to keep to the speed limit.

Doug was usually meticulous about obeying the letter of the law, but on the road to Glasgow, which for once wasn't choked with heavy lorries, he saw the speedometer creep repeatedly up to seventy-five, eighty, and the well-travelled road seemed unendurably long. The traffic got worse as he approached Glasgow, and by the time he turned into Bannock Street and parked outside the police station, almost an hour and a half had passed.

He left the car outside, and was out of it almost before it stopped, running up the steps into the familiar, grimy station with its wanted posters on a notice board, its dismal greyness and bare floor and walls. Doug felt a sudden warm pleasure; it was good to be back in Glasgow; there was something homely even about the grime and the smells. He showed his badge to the desk sergeant and passed through the reception area up the concrete back steps to the first floor, his heels clicking and resounding in the stairwell. He found Alastair Crimond, his old colleague and junior, at the water fountain on the landing, talking with a uniformed sergeant and a constable.

'And here comes our country cousin,' said Alastair, his foxy face lighting up. He grinned, and shook hands with Doug. He was still as slim as Doug remembered him, and his thinning red hair was plastered down on his head in tight little waves. Alastair had the kind of pink, freckled skin that didn't do well in the sun, and there had been a lot of it in Glasgow too, although it was pretty well filtered out by the time it reached the ground.

'This is Donald Watt,' said Alastair, indicating the sergeant. 'He found them. They're in number 97, third floor, above an Indian take-away place. We're still assembling information on them – that's quite a network they have . . .'

'Do you have a warrant?'

'Any minute now. They're not as easy to get as they used to be around here.'

'Even for suspected murder?' asked Doug.

'Right. We get them all right, but there's all that paperwork, it just takes longer. Anyway, the two suspects came in a Rover, the same colour and model as your man reported. It's still parked outside, on a yellow line, and we have surveillance from a car at the end of the street . . .'

The radio on the sergeant's shoulder crackled.

'Suspects entering car with several parcels,' said a voice. 'Request instructions . . .'

'Tell them to block them off at the end of the street,' said Alastair, but before the sergeant could transmit the message, the crackling voice came back. 'They're making a U-turn . . . Heading west, up towards St Mary's . . .'

Douglas didn't wait. He turned and ran down the stairs, and heard Alastair's footsteps right behind him. 'This isn't your area!' he was shouting. 'You can't . . .'

But by that time Douglas was at the door, and he went clattering down the steps.

'We'll take my car,' he shouted. 'It's here, and it's facing in the right direction . . .' Alastair hesitated, then jumped into the passenger seat, and a moment later a light green Rover sped past, going much too fast to be normal traffic. Far behind, Doug heard a police siren, and he pulled out with a squeal of tyres. Alastair started to tune the radio, but it wasn't set for the Glasgow frequencies.

'Damn!' he muttered to Douglas as he fiddled with the

set. 'As if we didn't have enough trouble of our own without
you coming down here . . .'

Douglas wasn't listening; he was trying to keep the Rover
in view ahead of him. It was travelling fast, and the street
was crowded, with pedestrians constantly crossing and
Douglas couldn't take the risk of killing somebody just to
catch up with the Rover. He swung fast round a parked car,
and Alastair had to hold on to the dashboard. 'Don't they
make you people wear seat belts?' asked Doug, without
taking his eyes off the traffic. Alastair growled and reached
up for the belt behind him. They heard the siren once again,
but it seemed further back.

'Jesus Christ!' said Alastair as Doug missed a delivery
van by inches. 'Do you all drive like that in Perth?' He
put his head down fast, and busied himself again with the
radio.

Douglas caught a glimpse of the Rover turning right
across the traffic at the next intersection, and immediately
swung into the outside lane, then across on the wrong side
of the street to get round a slow car. Doug drove like a
demon, full ahead for a few seconds, swerving, then
slamming on his brakes, sliding sideways, losing traction,
finding it again. The wheels squealed against the edge of the
pavement and people scurried out of the way. Doug heard a
woman scream as the car bounced out into the traffic again,
then they were sliding broadside across the intersection.
Alastair was thrown into the corner of the seat; everything
seemed to be coming straight at them, buses, trucks, cars
. . . he closed his eyes tight. Brakes screamed, drivers
shouted and frantically twisted their wheels to avoid the big
blue car, and a taxi went suddenly up on to the pavement
right in front of them. Douglas missed the rear of the vehicle
by a hair but now he was round the corner; he had turned
full against the lights and now they were only a few cars
behind the Rover, and miraculously untouched. Alastair
gripped the handle on the facia; his knuckles were white.

With all the jolting, he couldn't do anything with the radio; he just had to hang on and wait.

'I bet he's going to get on the M8,' said Douglas between clenched teeth. 'The turnoff's half a mile further along. I'll try to cut him off first . . . Hold on!'

With a forceful twist of the wheel that made Alastair gasp, Douglas leaned on the horn and cut out of the line of traffic into the oncoming lane.

'Flash the headlights on and off, and keep doing it,' he ordered, and Alastair obeyed. He might as well die doing something useful. But even Douglas couldn't get past. A big lumbering Dutch truck was directly in front of him, between him and the Rover, and the driver either didn't see Doug's flashing lights or ignored them. And Doug didn't have a siren or a flasher on the car, as it was normally used only by the detective section and not for patrol work.

Alec Govan, who was driving the Rover, must have seen the flashing headlights, because his vehicle leapt ahead, just making it through the next and last set of lights before the ramp up to the motorway.

'If you lose him here, we'll never catch him,' muttered Alastair, but Doug didn't need telling. The Dutch truck was slowing for the lights, and Doug swung out round him. A car making the turn just missed them and Alastair got a glimpse of a shocked white face staring at him, then with a hard swing back in front of the truck and a shuddering scream of brakes applied just for a moment, Douglas shot through the red lights, just missing a delivery van which swerved to avoid him. Alastair got a frozen glimpse of the van sideswiping a bus and bouncing off, leaving a dent and two wide streaks of black paint on its side. Then Douglas was through the traffic again, and they both saw the Rover turning on to the access ramp, fast, the car heeling over to the outside at a dangerous angle. For the next twenty minutes, the Rover zigged and zagged in and out of the thick traffic in front of them, then at over eighty miles an hour it suddenly swung from the outside to the inside lane, almost going out of control in the process.

'He's lost his nerve!' shouted Alastair, now totally caught up in the chase, and then a second later, in disbelief, 'Jesus! He's going to take this exit!' Douglas slammed on his brakes, knowing that if he tried to follow the Rover into the exit at this speed, the car would turn right over. The Rover turned, brake lights jammed on, into the curve of the exit, but it was going far too fast. It hit the railing, spun around, hit the railing again facing the wrong way, then the car rolled sideways on its right side over the railing and skidded on its roof on the packed earth until it hit the railing of the opposite ramp and came to a stop. Doug had slithered to a halt on the hard shoulder just past the exit, all four wheels locked, and Alastair and he both sat there for a second, shaking, unable to move.

'I'll get out on your side,' said Doug, undoing his belt. 'We don't want to get killed . . .'

They got out, both with their knees shaking. Other vehicles had slowed down, but the two policemen had eyes for nothing except the still-turning wheels of the upside-down Rover. A puff of smoke came from the engine compartment, then a flicker of flame ran back along the bottom of the upturned car.

'Bring the fire-extinguisher!' shouted Douglas. 'I'll try to get them out!' He jumped over the twisted railings and ran across to the wrecked Rover. He tugged at the door nearest him, but the roof had crushed it closed. He could see the two people strapped into the front seats; there was no movement from either of them. Vaguely he heard voices behind him, brakes, doors slamming. He ran to the other side and tried the doors. Then he saw a movement at the window, then a woman's face with blood all over it. The mouth was opening, and Doug could see that she was screaming, but he could hear nothing. The flames were now licking around the engine compartment, and Doug could feel the heat. The paint blistered and blackened suddenly on the edge of the bonnet. Then the whole of the bottom of the car was suddenly covered in flames, not high, not even frightening, but the sudden increase in heat made Douglas step back. Alastair came back with the fire-extinguisher, and sprayed it over the flames, making a thick, choking white vapour but it obviously wasn't big enough to douse the flames completely.

'We have to get them out!' shouted Doug desperately, but Alastair had run back to get another extinguisher from one of the parked cars, and nobody was there to hear him. He kicked at one of the back windows, but it was made of toughened glass and didn't even crack. Doug was about to go back to his car for something to break the glass with, when a burly man came running up with a truck tyre-iron, got on his knees and swiped sideways at the back window, smashing it with one blow. At the same moment, the flames roared up again and Doug saw Alastair coming back empty-handed.

'Get out of here!' said the burly man suddenly. 'She's going to go up!'

Doug dived to the ground under the back of the car, scrabbling around the broken rear window in a desperate effort to reach the two people inside. It was his fault, he'd chased them to their deaths . . . He was vaguely conscious of people around, somebody shouting to get away, a police siren in the distance . . . And then somebody caught his legs, his feet. He was being dragged away when there was a sighing noise, then he heard a loud 'Whup' and huge flames shot up and the blast hit him and he must have been unconscious for a few moments because when he looked again he was sitting on a piece of old concrete about twenty yards away. The car was a huge pyramid of flames, and the heat was coming at him in waves, hot on his cheeks and eyeballs.

*   *   *

In spite of his protests, Douglas was taken by ambulance to the Western Infirmary where he was treated for burns and cuts on both hands and wrists, and when he came out an hour and a half later with Alastair, they found the reporters and TV cameras waiting for him.

Alastair brought him back to his house for supper and to spend the night.

'I called your boss in Perth,' said Alastair after they'd got away from the reporters. 'The way I told it, he's very proud of you, instead of considering you for early retirement . . .'

'I suppose there wasn't much left of Sally and Alec?' Doug's voice was shaky; he felt as if he'd been run over by something heavy and his face was hot and raw as if it had been severely sunburned. Alastair had to open the car door for Douglas because of the bandages on his hands.

'No, there wasn't,' he said after strapping Douglas in. 'It was them all right. We've had them under observation since that killing about two months ago, you remember that guy who turned up in one place with his head in another . . . ? They did it, we're pretty sure of that. Tell me what they did in Perth.'

Doug told him about George Elmslie's fearful call that evening, saying that his life was in danger from Alec and Sally Govan, that they had phoned to threaten him with death if he betrayed them. Doug had immediately sent Constable Jamieson to keep an eye on the premises. He had seen these two suspicious characters, a man and a woman, hanging around and saw them get into a car but it was too far for him to see the number plates so he got in his own car and followed them. He never did get close enough, but he reported that it was a pale green Rover of the same year and model as the one in which Sally and Alec had died.

When Jamieson finally returned to George Elmslie's building, all was quiet, and nothing happened for the rest of the night. It didn't occur to him to check on Elmslie. It was only when Mr Wardle called next morning, very upset because George hadn't come to school and wasn't answering the phone . . .

Alastair was silent for a while. He drove sedately, like a little old lady going to church.

'Why did he let the buggers in, eh?' he said after a while.

Alastair's wife had made them a fine supper of bacon and eggs with lots of chips, one of Doug's favourite repasts. Because of his dressings, they had to feed him, to everyone's rather forced hilarity. For the rest of the evening the telephone rang incessantly; at first it was Alastair's boss, threatening him with everything from instant dismissal to putting him back on the beat. Doug could hear his voice from his comfortable seat in the living room.

Alastair came back grim-faced. 'He says you were acting outside your jurisdiction, and he's going to call your boss and get you fired,' he said. 'As for me, he says I'll be on point duty in the middle of Sauchiehall Street until I'm too old to stand up.'

Most of the later calls were from radio and TV stations in Perth and Glasgow, and Doug and Alastair saw themselves on the TV news at nine, where the burned out car was shown, still smoking, followed by a shot of Doug with his hands all bandaged, coming out of the hospital. They made it a very positive report, calling Doug's rescue attempts 'heroic'. Shortly after that, the Superintendent called to congratulate Doug and thank him for his efforts. Then Bob McLeod called, still not sure whether to fire Doug or recommend him for a bravery medal. When Alastair told him of the burns on Douglas's hands, and what the Superintendent's comments had been, he said he'd come down himself to pick Douglas up in the morning, and he'd bring a driver with him to take his car back.

Chapter Twenty-three

'It had better be a good story, my boy,' said Bob McLeod, as they drove back to Perth. He kept his eyes on the road. 'Your exploits have reached Chief Constable level, you'll be interested to know.'

'It's a good story, don't you worry,' said Douglas, trying to sound confident. 'All wrapped up in a pink bow. The Chief Constable's going to eat it up, you'll see.' He rubbed his nose with the back of his bandaged hand. The gauze felt stiff and alien. And his hands were painful; the burned fingers throbbed all the time, and he couldn't seem to avoid bumping them, and that *really* hurt.

'It's not only that,' said Bob with quiet relish. 'But you recklessly indulged in a car chase, endangering life and limb . . .'

'My car was commandeered by the Glasgow Police,' replied Doug calmly. Alastair and he had spent a full hour the night before perfecting a story which they hoped would ensure that they both still had a job when all the shouting was over. 'Under Detective Inspector Crimond's orders, we were able to intercept a pair of dangerous criminals, who not only ran a pornography ring, but were involved in child prostitution and murder . . .'

'*Intercept*! Is that what you call driving them off the road and getting them burned to a crisp?'

'I didn't drive them off the road,' said Doug, sounding offended. 'If he was stupid enough to take an exit at seventy miles an hour, you can't blame me. And as for getting burned to a crisp . . .' Doug held up his own elaborately bandaged hands.

The first thing he'd done that morning was to go back to the hospital where the doctor checked his injuries. Everything looked good, he said after cleaning them and applying a white burn cream which he told Doug was called Silvadine. He'd only need small dressings now, the doctor said, but Alastair was adamant that Doug's hands remain heavily bandaged.

'He does a lot of work with them,' he insisted. 'And we don't want them to get infected.' The doctor had grinned and done them proud.

Bob felt duly abashed, for about five seconds. 'That's not all,' he said as they went slowly through the village of Dunblane. 'Ron Crouch, who's bringing your car back . . . Well, he said the front alignment's all shot to hell, and there are bare patches on all four tyres. That's really going to cost you, my boy.'

Bob grinned wolfishly, and looked at his watch. 'Lunchtime,' he said, and they slowed and turned through the gates and up the drive of the Dunblane Hydro. 'For some reason your reckless and illegal actions seem to have taken the public fancy,' he said wonderingly, coming to a halt in the parking area facing the hotel. 'So you might as well be properly fed when you meet the press.'

That evening, Jean and Steven and Lisbie came running into the living room when they heard Fiona's scream.

'Look at him!' she shouted, jumping up and down. 'It's my sweetheart! Oh, look at his poor hands!' And there was Douglas on the evening news, very modestly reporting that with the cooperation of the Glasgow police they had been able to break up a criminal group which had been operating in the Perth area. 'And,' he said, his voice loaded with portent, 'these perpetrators were apparently also deeply involved in recent events concerning the death of a teacher who worked at a local educational facility.'

'Good old Douglas! And boo to that Eloise lady!' Fiona was so delighted she couldn't sit still. 'Do you think he'll come over tonight?' she asked her mother.

Jean had picked up a pile of post and had sat down to go through it. She put on her glasses, and replied in a distracted voice, 'I'm sure I don't know dear. Do you think you could turn the sound down a little?'

'I'd have thought you'd be pleased he solved the case,' said Fiona, clicking the remote control and sounding aggrieved. 'After all, he's one of our best friends . . .'

Lisbie lay down on the floor and laughed rudely, but her voice sounded strained. 'You'd like him to be your *very best* friend, wouldn't you, Fiona, haw haw haw?'

'That's enough, Lisbie,' said Jean automatically. Sometimes she felt she'd been born to be a permanent referee and peacemaker for her family.

Fiona got down and lay side by side next to Lisbie on the floor, facing the set.

Suddenly Fiona sniffed, and looked quickly at her sister. Lisbie was very still, pale from lack of sleep, and it was obvious that she was hurting, with Neil Mackay still very much on her mind. Fiona tightened her lips, but said nothing.

In the dining room, Steven had opened the big window at the back and set up a fan to blow outside air in. It helped to keep the room cool, but made a lot of noise, and they had to raise their voices to be heard over the hum.

Lisbie kept silent and hardly ate any of the tuna salad that Fiona had made.

'Here, take just a little, dear. Starving yourself isn't going to help anything,' said Jean, concerned about her daughter.

'Pick somebody your own age next time,' muttered Fiona.

'He was better than your Mr Pratt,' said Lisbie, turning like a cat toward Fiona. 'At least *he* didn't . . .'

'The weather's supposed to change soon,' interrupted Steven, throwing a warning look at Fiona.

'They've been saying that for a while,' said Jean. 'Pass your plate if you want some more, Steven.'

'That Eloise woman said that things would get better as soon as the weather broke,' said Fiona. 'But I think it's going to stay like this for ever.'

'What do you know about it?' asked Lisbie. Her voice sounded aggressive and a little slurred. 'Since when are you a weather expert?'

At the end of the meal, after they had cleared the dishes and Jean and Steven were in the kitchen, Fiona took a firm grip of Lisbie's arm and very quietly said 'You come downstairs with me, my girl!'

In the basement, with her bedroom door closed, Fiona sat down on her bed.

'You've started drinking again,' she said to Lisbie in a very grim voice. 'You promised . . .'

'I have not!' said Lisbie loudly, but she couldn't look her sister in the eye. 'Anyway you're not my keeper, you know.'

'Lisbie, we've been over all this before,' said Fiona. 'Every time something bad happens, you can't just reach for a bottle and think that'll make it better, can you?'

'Fiona, it's just killing me about N-N-Neil . . .' Lisbie dropped face down on the bed, and Fiona patted her shoulder rather helplessly.

'I know, Lisbie, but you can't just let yourself go like that. Do you remember how Mum was when Daddy went off? Well, she was sad, a lot sadder probably than you'll ever be, because they were married and had us and everything . . .' Fiona didn't quite know how to say what she wanted to say without making things worse.

'Anyway, you remember how she was? She took even better care of us, and worked hard to cheer *us* up. She didn't just give up and start drinking vodka, did she?'

'She's much stronger than me,' sobbed Lisbie. 'And anyway I think I feel things more deeply than most people.'

Fiona took a deep breath. 'Let's go hiking this weekend, up around Crianlarach somewhere. The exercise'll do us good, and there's nothing like fresh air to get boys out of your system.'

'I don't need any exercise,' said Lisbie, sitting up, red-eyed. 'And Neil . . .' She bit her lip. 'I don't think I'll *ever* get him out of my mind.'

But it didn't take very long to persuade Lisbie, and that bothered Fiona too. Lisbie was always too easy to convince; after a token struggle, she usually went along with whatever people wanted her to do. Fiona was concerned that Lisbie would always be a soft touch, an easy target for unscrupulous people who could manipulate her whichever way they wanted. Maybe this business with Neil Mackay would toughen her up a bit, force her to stand on her own two feet.

They talked for a while, then Lisbie went up to her own room, after Fiona had exacted a promise that she wouldn't touch a drop of alcohol except what they all occasionally had at mealtimes. Just in case, Fiona went up after her and locked the wine cupboard, then reached up to put the small key on the ledge above the lintel of the door. Nobody would find it there, or even notice the cupboard was locked, as nobody besides Lisbie ever drank in the house except at dinner time.

Chapter Twenty-four

The next morning, Doug got a note telling him to report to the Chief Constable's office at eleven o'clock that morning. Lew Thomas, the union representative, was in Doug's office when Constable Jamieson brought the note; Doug had met him before, a tough, aggressive little Welshman with a thin, triangular face and thick black hair that came far down over his forehead. The union would defend him to the hilt, he said, sitting on the edge of the chair, if there was any talk of disciplinary procedures, and Doug felt better about that. But when Lew suggested he come with him to the Chief Constable's office, Doug demurred. He'd handle this himself; it was an unofficial meeting, and if they wanted to fire him or demote him or anything like that, they would have to convene a full inquiry. Right now, Doug didn't think Lew's presence would help.

The Chief Constable, Colin McConnach, was already in his office talking with Bob Mcleod and Superintendent Graham Walsh, who was in overall charge of the Perth police force.

'What's this chap Niven like, McLeod?' McConnach pulled out a cigar from his inside pocket, but didn't light it. 'It always helps to have a bit of background on a chap,' he said. 'Learned that in the Army.'

'First-rate officer, sir,' said Bob. 'Conscientious, able . . . Niven's one of our best men, don't you agree, Superintendent?'

Superintendent Walsh nodded. 'Never had any problems with him, sir. You may remember how he handled the Lumsden baby case . . .'

The Chief Constable looked at his cigar and rolled it thoughtfully between his fingers. 'The media's certainly taken to him,' he said. 'Did you see the piece on Grampian television last night? Well, it's not often they have anything good to say about our people . . . something to bear in mind, don't you think?'

The two men said nothing. They would take their cue from him.

'I've gone very carefully over the report on the two killings,' he went on. 'Sounds as if Niven's tied it all up very nicely.'

Bob McLeod hesitated for a second but still he didn't say anything. He shot a glance at Walsh, who ignored the look and stared straight in front of him.

'A really satisfactory conclusion, *from every point of view*, in my opinion.'

'Yes, sir,' said Walsh and Mcleod, almost simultaneously.

'There's been a lot of unrest, a lot of anxiety in Perth. People will be able to sleep more easily now that it's all settled . . .' The Chief Constable looked at Walsh and McLeod, and then at his watch. 'Let's get him in here,' he said.

Douglas was waiting on the wooden bench outside, feeling as if he was about to go on trial, and not too happy about it. He'd done his duty, solved both murders in one fell swoop, and there they were, trying to pin some kind of disciplinary charge on him. He looked at his bandages and felt sorry for himself. Maybe he should be like Bob Mcleod, he thought: sit on his duff and look busy, never take a risk, and never really do anything except fill in reports and work out the monthly duty roster. That was how Bob had gone gently up the ladder, without anybody ever pointing the finger at him . . .

'Inspector Niven, please.' The uniformed clerk called through the open door, and Douglas got up. Inside were three people, the Chief Constable, tall, white-haired, in uniform, with his medals in two proud lines on his tunic. The Superintendent was there, looking over at Douglas with his short-sighted pale eyes, and Bob McLeod, staring grimly over Doug's head as he walked in.

'Come in, come in,' said the Chief Constable. 'Yes, take a seat there, please, Inspector.' He indicated a fragile-looking round-backed cane chair of the kind they used to have in church halls.

'I want you to know that this meeting is simply for informational purposes,' said the Chief Constable in his gruff way. 'There are two reasons for having you here . . .' He picked up a teletype sheet. 'I have what amounts to a complaint from my opposite number in the Strathclyde Sector, Chief Constable Elphinstone, concerning your recent activities in his territory. I'd like to hear your version, if you don't mind.'

Douglas gave them a concise, clear account of what had happened, only slightly modifying some of the details.

The Chief Constable leaned back when Douglas had finished and lit his cigar, turning it round to get it burning evenly, while three pairs of eyes watched him.

'Sounds as if you did the right thing, Inspector,' he grunted when the cigar was glowing to his satisfaction. He glanced at the other two on his side of the table. 'Good initiative, that sort of thing . . .' He pulled out a large handkerchief and sneezed aggressively into it, as if to teach it a firm lesson.

'Procedure, Niven, I think that's what they didn't like about the way you handled it. You have to do it by the book these days. Don't tell me, I know *they* chase people all over Glasgow every day . . .'

They all looked at Douglas as if they expected him to say something, so he said 'Yes, sir', but he really wanted to ask which book he should use when he had only one second to make a decision.

'All right, then,' said the Chief Constable. 'I'll see if I can pacify Elphinstone . . . He's actually quite a reasonable chap, although he spent a long time in the Gordon Highlanders . . . Shouldn't be too much of a problem, and I'll take care of it. Now . . .'

Everybody paused while he sneezed again. 'Now we've dealt with that,' he said, 'tell us about your conclusions concerning those two burning deaths.'

Douglas put his bandaged hands on his knees and told them what he'd found out concerning Stroud's blackmail of George Elmslie.

'This was a most powerful stimulus for Elmslie to get rid of Stroud, sir. He'd get the job he felt Stroud had stolen from him, and his death would eliminate the worry of further blackmail attempts . . .'

'Yes, but how did he do it?' asked the Superintendent, pushing a hank of thin blond hair out of his eyes with a long pale hand.

'Elmslie was a very strong man,' he replied. 'He wouldn't have any difficulty overpowering Stroud . . . And we found the remains of two high-powered infrared heat lamps in his flat,' replied Douglas. 'They were smashed, but I believe that these were used to set the body alight.'

'How did he get in to Stroud's heavily defended house in the middle of the night?' asked the Chief Constable, his military curiosity aroused.

'We discovered that Elmslie was one of the very few people Stroud ever talked to,' replied Doug. 'They shared classes, being in the same department. Elmslie evidently got in on some pretext . . . that doesn't present a problem.'

The three men exchanged a glance, but Doug couldn't tell whether it was of approval or not.

'And Elmslie's own death, Niven? What was the sequence of events there?'

'A good deal clearer, sir, because we already had him under surveillance. And he'd told us about the two child abusers, Alec and Sally Govan, the two who died in the car. They had threatened him with death, and we now know that they were responsible for at least one other unusual death in the Glasgow area . . . By decapitation . . .'

The Chief Constable raised his eyebrows and leaned over to whisper something to the Superintendent. Doug waited until their conversation was over.

'Their obvious desire was to connect the death with Stroud's,' he went on. 'There had been a lot of talk about Stroud's body spontaneously bursting into flames because of the heat wave . . .'

Again the three exchanged a glance, and Doug's eyes went from one to the other, but without getting any information.

'The Govans' motivation was very strong. They were scared that Elmslie would blow the lid on their pornography and child prostitution ring, and as I said before, they were used to dealing with such problems in a very radical way.'

'All sounds very circumstantial,' said the Chief Constable, after a pause.

'Sir,' said Douglas, beginning to bristle, 'the two of them were seen near the scene of the crime, and their vehicle was identified. The Govans were both living in Glasgow, and had no other possible reason to be here in Perth.'

'But why would Elmslie let them in to his flat, for heaven's sake?'

'Sir, I was not privy to Elmslie's thought processes at the time, but I would assume that he wanted to convince them of his good faith, that he wasn't going to betray them. If he could have done that, it would have been entirely in his own interest.'

After a few more minutes of discussion, Doug was asked to wait outside. When he was called back, he could tell instantly that he was in the clear. Just like a jury, he thought bitterly, if they look you in the eye, you're not guilty. And it wasn't because of his brilliant arguments, or the way he'd presented the facts, he knew that, but more because the solution happened to be very neat and tidy, getting rid of a total of four very unpleasant people, and of course the publicity had made the police force of both cities look good.

'We agree in principle with your findings,' said the Chief Constable after sneezing once more. 'And we further recommend that the case be considered closed at this time.'

He put his handkerchief away in the top pocket of his tunic.

'And just between us, Niven, that was a damned good show you put up yesterday, trying to get those people out of the car. I wouldn't be surprised if you don't hear more about it . . . Thank you, Niven, you can go now.'

By the time they had all stood up and patted him on the shoulder, Doug's cynical annoyance had quite disappeared. Wait till Cathie hears this, he thought. And they're really not bad chaps, those three; working on a good force has certain advantages; for one thing, you can be sure of a fair hearing if a problem ever arises.

Chapter Twenty-five

Jean had expected Doug to turn up that evening, as he usually did when there had been a breakthrough in a case. Doug always took great pleasure in giving her and Steven, if he didn't escape up to his bedroom, a blow-by-blow account of what had happened behind the scenes.

But Doug didn't come, to Fiona's acute distress, and Jean's secret relief. Although in a way Jean felt proud of what he had done, her views on the case didn't quite agree with his.

So Jean and Steven spent a quiet evening, she with her clinic records, which she was making a valiant effort to get right up to date, and he with plans for expansion of the glassworks. The news of the award had already brought him a lot of attention, and the recent visit of the Japanese delegation was bringing in some major inquiries.

'The girls are very quiet,' said Steven, looking up. 'I hope Lisbie's beginning to get over that boy.'

'They're all right . . .' Jean took off her reading glasses. They were new, and she wasn't accustomed to them yet. 'Fiona's really very good with her, you know, in spite of all their bickering.'

'Can you come over here a minute?' asked Steven, and Jean went over to where he was working. 'I'm going to put in at least two new high-temperature furnaces,' he explained. 'Okay, the old ones are here, and I was thinking if we break down that wall . . .'

Jean peered at the plan. 'If you put your new ones there,'

she said, pointing, 'will there be enough room for the workers to turn round, holding a lump of red-hot glass, without bumping into each other?'

'It'll be close,' said Steven, peering at the drawings, but after Jean went back to her chair, he took out the rubber and scrubbed vigorously.

'Do you really think that business with Stroud and Elmslie is over now?' asked Steven after a while.

'I was just wondering about that,' replied Jean. 'If Douglas thinks so . . . And he sounded pretty confident on the TV, didn't you think?'

'You're always giving Doug the benefit of the doubt,' said Steven, 'but I can tell from your voice you don't believe a word of it.'

'I've been going over and over the whole thing in my mind.' Jean pulled the big cardboard box containing her records up on to her lap. 'There are so many things about that whole business that I don't understand, it gives me a headache.'

'What about all that magic stuff? Everybody I've talked to seems to believe that there really *are* evil forces at work in town, and that somehow it's all tied up with the heat wave.'

'I suppose it could be that,' said Jean doubtfully. 'But it seems that Doug has solved the case without resorting to the occult.'

'Well, Douglas isn't always right,' said Steven. 'And maybe he knows things and isn't telling.'

'I'm going to make some tea,' said Jean. 'Do you want some?' She went out and called down to the girls, but there was silence. They had both gone to bed.

When she came back with the tray, Jean had obviously been thinking about Steven's comments.

'There are still a few things that don't quite fit in,' she said, pouring. 'Like Renée and Gwen . . . I'm sorry, there's no milk, it all went sour, but there's some of this powder stuff.'

'Renée? Somebody told me they'd seen her at the pictures with Whatsisname Mackay . . .'

'Ken,' said Jean. 'And he bothers me too, I must say. There's something so *violent* about him; I took your Harris tweed jacket there this afternoon, and he was shouting at the girl who works behind the counter. But as soon as he heard the door open, he was all smiles and what can we do for you, Doctor . . .'

Steven shook his head at Jean and grinned. There was no real reason why Jean should have taken that jacket now; he wouldn't be wearing it again until winter. She must have had some ulterior motive, or maybe she was just being nosy . . .

'Renée Stroud,' said Jean thoughtfully. 'It's funny how some women choose the same kind of men to get involved with, again and again, in spite of experience.'

'Is that true, what people are saying, that it was Morgan who blinded her?'

'I honestly don't know, but if he did, that would be a pretty good reason to . . . No, I don't see any way she could have done it. She might have wanted to, I'm sure, but I really doubt it, with her eyesight . . .' Jean shook her head and paused, stirring her tea thoughtfully. 'You may find this hard to believe, but one of the people I've really been wondering about is our young friend Neil Mackay.' Jean heard Steven's sharp intake of breath.

'You mean our Lisbie's Neil? Come on, Jean, your imagination's running away with you. My God, he's just a kid . . .'

'Do you remember when he first came to dinner? That was the very same day that Stroud was found. Do you remember what he said, as cool as cucumber? That he *hated* Morgan Stroud? And then his essay being on the top of the pile, and he *knew* it was there . . .' Jean put down her forms on the table. 'Another thing I didn't tell you about, and that was Lisbie's adventure up on Kinnoull Hill . . .'

Jean told Steven the story, and he went red with anger. 'Why didn't you tell me before? I'd have wrung the little bastard's neck!'

'That's exactly why I didn't tell you,' murmured Jean, 'but now he's out of range of your paternal fury, I think you should know about it.'

'They weren't messing about with drugs, or stuff like that, were they? Because . . .' Steven got up, really upset, and started to pace up and down the room. 'I wouldn't worry about Fiona,' he said, 'not for a second, but Lisbie's so suggestible, so easily led . . .'

'Don't worry,' said Jean reassuringly. 'He's gone now, and can't do any more damage . . .' A sudden terrifying thought struck Jean. Maybe he *could* . . .

To get that idea out of her head, Jean went back to their previous topic of conversation.

'Gwen Stroud,' said Jean. 'I haven't understood where she fits in, if anywhere. She hated her brother, and said that God was going to punish him, and she talked about thunderbolts, the fires of redemption and all kinds of things . . . And of course she *is* a bit crazy, although why . . .' Steven looked at her. Jean's voice had changed and she'd stopped stirring and was looking into the distance.

'Yes?'

'Nothing . . . Something just occurred to me . . .'

But try as he would, Steven couldn't get Jean to say anything more on the subject of Morgan Stroud, although he could see how hard she was thinking and re-evaluating her previous conclusions about the whole case.

They went to bed soon afterwards, but although Jean tried to lie still, she didn't go to sleep for a long time. And the longer she thought about the burning of Morgan Stroud and the death of George Elmslie, the worse she felt. All the vague ideas that had been going through her mind from the time of Stroud's death, all came wandering in to roost tonight, inevitably. And now George Elmslie . . . How blind she'd been! All that information, all those clues sitting looking her in the face and she'd simply not seen them . . . It was all there. By the time the eastern horizon was showing the faintest glimmer of light, and Jean had finally fallen asleep, it was obvious to her that the whole case was more horrible and more complicated that she could ever have dreamed.

When Jean woke up, Steven was bending over her with the big brass alarm clock. 'I was going to give you a taste of your own medicine,' he said, grinning. 'It's almost eight. I got the girls up, and the tea's made.'

Jean struggled out of bed. Eight o'clock! It was a long time since she'd slept that late on a weekday. Then everything came back into her mind with startling accuracy, and with a dreadful sinking feeling in her stomach she knew that this was going to be an agonisingly difficult day.

The one good thing about getting up late, Jean soon found, was that she didn't have to wait an age for the hot water to come through. She showered and dressed, forcing herself to think about all the things she had to do; she had to go and see old Mrs Dornoch, who'd had her operation and was doing well. They'd taken out a clot six inches long from the femoral artery in her leg; it had completely blocked the circulation, just as she had suspected. Before going up to the hospital, she had to do the well-baby clinic; she enjoyed that, seeing all those bouncy babies and their mothers, half of them petrified when their baby sneezed or coughed up some milk . . . Jean remembered herself as a young mother; she hadn't been so different. Then she had a surgery in the afternoon, then home visits . . .

Jean ran around the house like a busy mouse, getting clothes and sheets and towels together for Mrs Cattanach who came to do the laundry and some cleaning twice a week. She would be surprised to see Jean, who was usually long gone by the time she arrived. They normally communicated by notes left in an envelope on the hall salver.

Jean heard some angry whispering from the region of the bathroom. She thought she heard Lisbie say 'You locked it up, you bitch!' followed by a murmured sharp reply from Fiona, but she could have been mistaken. Those two girls, they had a life of their own, and half the time neither Steven nor she knew what they were talking about.

Chapter Twenty-six

When Gwen woke up in her little shack she could feel the rays of the sun already heating the thin wall next to her. She struggled up from her palliasse and scratched her head hard. Her hair was matted, and she could feel the coodies itching, moving around on her scalp. She opened the door a crack and looked out for a good minute. There was nobody around. Gwen went out, feeling the sun already hot on her skin. Everything was so dry, there hadn't even been any dew on the grass for what seemed like weeks. And the grass itself was burned to a lifeless brown. She slid down the bank on the slippery grass for a few feet towards the track till she was well hidden from everything, unless a train were to pass. She pulled up her tattered dress and squatted down. She gritted her teeth, then whistled a tuneless air, thinking that this was how she wanted her life to be, free and easy like this, now that the cause of her misery, of all the sharp pains in her soul that had made her almost lose her mind, now that cause was gone. Gwen wiped herself with some grass and leaves, looked along the burning, flashing track, then struggled back up the bank.

To her intense surprise and sudden fear Gwen saw coming towards her down the black cinder path, stumping along in that determined way of hers, none other than Jean Montrose.

Gwen's first thought was to run, to escape, but she was too startled to move, and was still trying to decide what to do when Jean came up to her.

She looks like a bird, thought Jean, a wild, fearful bird who's terrified of being trapped or locked up.

'Gwen, I need to talk to you,' said Jean without preamble. Her face was so kind, so devoid of any malice that Gwen's tense expression started to relax a little.

'Let's sit down here,' said Jean, indicating the bank.

They moved a little further along the path at Gwen's suggestion, then sat down. Gwen sat easily, straight-backed, in a lotus position, but Jean felt her own knees creak as she sat rather heavily in the grass.

'Gwen, there are a couple of things I'd like to ask you. You don't have to answer, of course, but I think it would make life a lot simpler for you if you did . . .' Jean put her hand on Gwen's arm; she felt it quiver for a second, then still. Jean's voice was full of sadness, but there was also an unmistakable kindness in it. 'You see, Gwen, I think I know what happened with your brother . . .'

The story went through St Jude's like a flash of summer lightning, but now they were talking about George Elmslie the monster, the sadist, the killer, and everybody had forgotten about the rather quiet, self-conscious person they had actually known.

'My father's coming to take me out of this school,' announced Dick Prothero. 'He's driving up from Manchester this afternoon.'

'Good riddance,' said Billy. 'Now you won't need your cap.' He made a lunge for Dick's headgear, but the boy was quick on his feet and fled.

'So Big George was the one who killed Stroud, and those Glasgow people killed *him*, eh? And they're both dead now . . .' said Neil reflectively. 'I suppose we won't need to bother doing our magic any more.'

'Come on, Neil, you know that was just a game,' said Billy in a superior tone.

'Well, yes . . . But I've been thinking about it a lot, Billy.

Do you know *why* we did it? Because it made us feel strong, it gave us something to fight back with, even though we knew it didn't *really* work . . .'

'You know what, Neil?' said Billy. 'You're *weird*.'

'Did you hear about what Big George did to that little boy?'

Billy hadn't heard, so Neil told him in the most graphic detail; the child's mother had come forward, and Neil had read the story in the papers. Billy's face twisted with pain for the child. 'Yuck! What a filthy monster,' he said. 'And you made me actually go inside his flat, and sit beside him! You're insane, Mackay!'

Billy skipped to avoid Neil's fist.

'There's Mr Townes!' cried Billy, looking back along the path. 'Hey, Mr Townes, are you leaving?' Angus was heading towards his car.

'School's cancelled for today, didn't you hear?' he said, as the two boys caught up and walked alongside him, one on each side.

'Soon there aren't going to be any teachers left here,' said Billy.

'Or pupils either.' Angus smiled, but he wasn't amused. 'A lot of parents are taking their boys home.'

'I'm leaving at the end of the week too,' said Neil suddenly. 'My father says I'm to go to the grammar school in Perth.'

They accompanied Angus to his ancient vehicle, and he started it up, backed jerkily, then drove off in a cloud of blue smoke.

'Air polluter,' said Billy, watching the back of the car disappear around the desiccated rhododendrons.

'I don't care,' said Neil. 'He's the only decent teacher in this entire place.'

Chapter Twenty-seven

Mrs Dornoch was sitting up in bed when Jean came to visit. She was in the middle of the ward, and there was a murmur of pleasure from several of the patients when Jean came in through the double doors. Jean recognised several people and spent a few minutes chatting with them before coming back to Mrs Dornoch.

'Well, it wasn't so bad, now, was it?'

'Not for you, maybe, Doctor . . . !'

There was a giggle from the patient in the next bed. Old Mrs Dornoch was never at a loss for an answer.

Jean rummaged in her bag and brought out a huge peach wrapped up in tissue paper. 'Here,' she said, putting it down on the old lady's bedside table, 'that shouldn't interfere with your diet . . . Are they feeding you all right here?'

'The food's just fine, Dr Montrose, and thank you . . .' Old Mrs Dornoch's eyes were brimming with gratitude.

After Jean left a few minutes later, Mrs Dornoch sat up and addressed the entire ward in a loud voice. 'That's the best wee doctor in the whole world, I want you all to know that.'

Jean had finished for the morning and headed her little car towards home. Today there was nobody in for lunch, which was just as well, because she had some phone calls to make, and she didn't want anybody listening in.

Her last call was to Angus Townes. He wasn't at school, and she finally tracked him down at home.

'Yes, Jean?' his voice was surprised, warm. 'I didn't expect to be hearing from you . . .'

'Well, Angus, something a little unexpected turned up and I would really be grateful for your advice.'

'Of course, any time.'

'How about this afternoon, about four? Let me take you for a cup of coffee. Are you going to be seeing Deirdre? Okay then, that little cafe opposite the nursing home, at four?'

Angus put the phone down slowly, a sudden feeling of hope lighting him up from the inside. At least she didn't hate him, if she was inviting him for coffee. Maybe . . . Maybe he could find a way of seeing Jean just occasionally without attracting too much attention, and then, who knew? Angus shook his head; he was having difficulty with these huge mood swings, one day in the pits of despair, then the next feeling on top of the world, just on the strength of a word or two from Jean Montrose.

Jean looked at her watch and gasped. As usual it was later than she thought, and here she was, with her surgery due to start in five minutes. One of these days Helen was going to lose patience if she didn't get herself organised.

She rushed back into her car with an egg sandwich, which she ate on the way down. It wasn't easy changing gears, but she made it without incident, and just on time.

It was a small surgery that afternoon, and Jean finished seeing her patients about three. Helen had half a dozen still to see, so Jean took a couple of them to help out. She was glad of the opportunity to take on some of Helen's load because she'd been feeling guilty about not pulling her weight in the practice recently.

Then she spent ten minutes looking through some old patient records, and particularly some transfer sheets with case summaries from the patients' previous physicians.

At a quarter to four, Jean felt a tightening around her heart and knew that it was time to go and see Angus. That poor Deirdre . . .

He was waiting, sitting at a far table away from anyone

else. Jean didn't know whether to be glad or sorry about that.

He got up when Jean came in. She could see the lines of tension in his face; the poor man probably always looked like that after spending time with his daughter.

'I'm so glad to see you,' he said, and Jean could see he meant it.

They sat down after Jean took off her jacket and put it on the back of the chair. She wore a white silk blouse underneath, and it felt much cooler without the grey jacket.

'What made you change your mind?'

The waitress came up and they ordered. Even in this weather Jean had a fondness for Penguin chocolate biscuits, as long as they weren't melted by the heat.

'Angus, I'm still working on the Morgan Stroud and George Elmslie business . . .' Jean laughed, a bit embarrassed. 'That sounds really pretentious, doesn't it? What I mean is I've been thinking a lot about the deaths, all the things that didn't add up . . .'

'Well, I suppose that you can finally relax now the case is closed,' smiled Angus. He desperately wanted to stretch out and touch Jean's hand across the table.

He paused until the waitress had poured the coffee and left. He picked up his cup and looked at her over it, almost as if he were proposing a toast. 'It's reassuring to know that finally it's all over,' he said. 'Stroud, and poor George Elmslie . . . and that those two Govan people won't be causing any more trouble.' His smile was so tired, Jean thought, the man is emotionally worn out. He looked at Jean over the top of the cup.

'Now Angus,' replied Jean in a slightly reproving tone. 'You know perfectly well that the Govan people didn't kill George, and that George didn't kill Stroud.'

Angus shrugged and took a sip of his coffee. 'I'll take your word for it, Jean. I'm just going by what the papers are saying.'

'You see, all the way along it just didn't add up.' Jean stirred her coffee vigorously, her mind elsewhere. 'Morgan Stroud died in a house that was alive with burglar alarms. If we discount the supernatural theory . . .' Jean raised her hand, seeing that Angus was going to interrupt, 'we have to assume that he let the murderer into the house.'

'I don't know how you can just discard the possibility of supernatural input,' said Angus. He pulled out his pipe. 'Do you mind?' he asked, pointing to it.

'Go ahead. Actually I rather like that smell.' Jean moved on her chair and looked quite stern. 'Now you, Angus Townes, you know better than to believe in supernatural causes, being a scientist. Especially when the facts can be explained without them.' Jean put her hands on the edge of the table. She looks like an eager student, thought Angus.

'What I'd like to do, if it's all right with you,' went on Jean, 'is to go over what I do know, and maybe you can help me with what I don't. Okay?'

'Okay with me.' Angus sat back and lit his pipe. When he had it going satisfactorily, Jean started again, speaking in her quiet but forceful voice. Angus could tell that she'd sifted a lot of information, and what she said, she was sure about.

'Let's start with what we found at Morgan Stroud's house. A locked door, burglar alarms that hadn't been set off, a dead, incinerated body in the middle of the room. Now, that tells me two things, although I must say it took me a long time to work it all out.' Jean smiled ruefully. 'It tells me that Stroud let the killer in, which means he knew him or her well. Secondly, the body was set on fire.' Jean stopped. 'Now you're an expert on burns, Angus. You probably know as much as or more than most doctors who deal with burns. So you are no doubt aware of spontaneous human combustion, a misnomer, because you and I know how it happens.'

'Yes, I've heard of it,' said Angus. 'It's usually caused by a person dying suddenly, and falling into an electric fire, or some such heat source, then the body fat melts, the clothes act as a wick, and the body smoulders, sometimes for hours, until it's completely charred . . .'

'Right. You see,' said Jean, looking triumphant, '*I* didn't know that until I asked my old boss in the burn unit. And you *do* know more about burns than dear old Dr Anderson, our pathologist!'

Angus shrugged modestly. 'The thing that makes me think that it *was* due to supernatural causes,' he said, 'is precisely that. There *wasn't* any electric fire touching his body, no petrol . . .'

'Exactly, Angus. Because the killer had *removed* the heat source after setting Stroud's body alight and making sure the wick effect had taken hold.'

They looked at each other across the table. Jean averted her eyes when she saw what was in his, and went on, a little hurriedly. 'That's all we really need to know to decide that a murder's been committed,' she said. 'All that other stuff about black magic and bolts of lightning from God is just so much nonsense.'

Angus had to agree.

Jean was getting into her stride; it had sounded clear enough in her head, but she hadn't been sure how it would sound when she discussed it with Angus.

'Now we've established that a murder was committed,' she said, 'the next thing is to find out who did it.'

Angus smiled at the stubbornness which showed in Jean's voice. 'And you forged ahead and found out, right?'

'Well, yes, but the thing that bothered me was that I didn't know exactly *how* or exactly *why* . . .'

'Some more coffee?' Jean nodded absently and Angus refilled her cup.

'The first question was *how*. Who would Stroud have let in, late at night, after deactivating the alarm system? He had no male friends, no girl friend . . .' Jean waited in case

Angus wanted to suggest who it might be, but he said
nothing. Coils of blue smoke were now swirling slowly
around the ceiling of the cafe.

'His wife, of course . . .' Angus looked startled, and
puffed a sudden cloud into the air. 'He'd sent for Renée to
pick up some domestic item; there was a big wall mirror
sitting by the front door . . . maybe it was that. And the
killer, whom she knew, came right in behind her before
Stroud had time to close the door, and probably got him
with a long, thin knife, in the heart. There were no bullets
in the body, no sign of poison . . . Renée *couldn't* have
done it; aside from killing him, it took somebody with an
extensive and specialised knowledge of burns to know
about the wick effect and how to get it going. Anybody
could have thrown some petrol over him and set him on fire,
but that wasn't what happened to Stroud . . .' Jean
shivered involuntarily, remembering the dreadfully charred
body in the middle of the living room floor. 'It took the
application of a powerful heat source for many minutes to
get the process going, and probably a long cut in the skin to
let the fat underneath run out, but once the combustion was
well under way, the killer knew that the body would go
smouldering on by itself for hours until it was totally
consumed . . .'

Angus nodded in sober agreement as she spoke; Jean
really knew her stuff, for a GP who didn't have day-to-day
contact with burn cases.

'George Elmslie didn't have that special knowledge
either,' went on Jean quietly. 'And anyway Renée despised
the man and would never had cooperated with him on anything.'

'But what about George's death?' asked Angus. 'It
seemed pretty clear that the Govans tried to simulate
Stroud's burning, but didn't know quite how to go about
it.'

'No. The difference was only in the kind of body George

had. He was muscular, without an ounce of extra fat on him, unlike the obese Stroud. So once George was dead, the killer tried to use the same technique, but adding fat, lard maybe, to substitute for body fat. He got the wick effect going, but it petered out after a while, after the killer had gone.'

'Don't you think the Govans could have worked it out and done that?'

'How would they know? It's the same problem, Angus, where would they get that specialised knowledge?'

'But what's the connection?' asked Angus. His pipe had gone out while Jean was talking, and he opened his book of matches. 'I mean, who would want *both* of them dead?'

'Well, let's start with Morgan Stroud,' said Jean. She took a sip of coffee; all this talking was making her mouth dry.

'I was going through some old medical records this afternoon,' she said. 'You know when a patient moves to a new town, their doctor fills in a summary sheet with the medical history, details of medicines, stuff like that, and sends it to the doctor at their new location. Well, I looked at yours, and also at Morgan Stroud's, and found you'd both lived in Cambridge. In fact in the *same street*.'

Angus lit his pipe, and Jean could see that the match was shaking.

'So today I had a talk with Gwen, Morgan's sister. She told me that she'd been brought up in Cambridge with her brother, and they lived a few doors away from you. And Gwen told me about her very best friend, Deirdre . . .'

Jean shook her head. 'You know, I'm so stupid . . . Every time I went to see Deirdre, there was a little bunch of wild flowers on her bedside table, and sometimes some blackberries. It took me ages to realise that it was Gwen who was bringing them. I asked the nurses, and they told me she came in to spend time with Deirdre every day. She doesn't go to see anyone else.'

Angus had turned quite pale, and was looking suddenly ill, but Jean went on with her story, keeping her voice down so that she wouldn't be overheard by the other customers in the cafe. There was a long silence, while Angus puffed at his pipe.

'Of course the reason for killing George Elmslie was quite different. I know you're very actively concerned with child abuse, and you helped to set up a rescue facility for abused children here in Perth. And with what Elmslie was doing, and him a schoolmaster . . . It would be enough to make anyone see red.'

'Sounds reasonable.' Angus's voice was calm, almost nonchalant. 'Now, to get back to Stroud, the most interesting question is *why*?'

'That was the hardest part to work out, as you can imagine. It all goes back, let's see, a bit over thirteen years . . .'

Angus started to tremble all over, and Jean, feeling very sympathetic, put her hand across the table on to his.

'It would really be easier if you told the story,' she said. 'Because I don't know all of it. Let's make it a hypothetical case, keeping people's names out of it . . .'

Angus sat immobile for what seemed to Jean to be a long time. He stared fixedly up at the ceiling, and for a while Jean thought the memories were going to be too dreadful for him to say anything.

'I know enough to know I might have done the same thing myself,' she said. 'The case is officially closed, and I can't imagine anyone would ever want to reopen it . . .'

Angus smiled. 'We don't really need to use a third person, but if it makes you more comfortable, we can do it that way.' He sat back, collecting his thoughts. 'About thirteen years ago, there was a very happy little family of three people who lived in a small house in Cambridge, where the husband was a lecturer. I think you know about how their little girl was found burned, and the mother later committed suicide . . . There was something you weren't told, however. The mother had employed a baby sitter, a neigh-bour's boy who at that time was aged about sixteen . . .'

'Whose name was Morgan Stroud,' breathed Jean, her eyes fixed on Angus.

'Right. When it happened, he wasn't with Deirdre, he was having sex with a girlfriend up in our bedroom. He knew that Deirdre, who was five at the time, was mildly epileptic, and he'd been told to be particularly careful about it. I ran in and pulled Deirdre away from the fire, turned it off, called the ambulance and then ran upstairs . . . I dragged Morgan out of bed and down to the living room to show him what had happened, and he seemed dreadfully upset. I was so paralysed with fury that I was absolutely incapable of doing anything more, and Morgan was so appalled, so apologetic, so tearful . . .

'The days after that were a nightmare. Nobody knew if Deirdre would wake up, and we sat by her, hoping she'd open her eyes and say something. Every time she moved her head, we'd say "Thank God, that's it, she's waking up!" but she never did. Then she was always going for opera-tions, even though she never became really conscious again . . .' Angus was gripping the tablecloth with an intensity that whitened his knuckles. 'You should have seen her, going to theatre, so tiny on the big trolley, her hair like . . . like a halo . . .' Angus was having a difficult time holding back his tears, and so was Jean.

'Gwen, who as you found out was Deirdre's inseparable friend, spent a lot of time at the hospital with us,' went on Angus, determined to finish his story. 'And often she'd come home with us . . . Sometimes she would cry as if her heart was breaking, and finally she told us why. That was just before Susan went into the hospital herself . . .'

Angus stopped, and Jean could see that something really terrible was coming, because the veins in Angus's forehead were swelling.

'Gwen told us . . . Gwen . . .' Angus's voice faltered,

and Jean stretched out her hand across the table to him. Angus took a deep breath and swallowed several times. 'Gwen told us how Morgan made jokes about it all the time. He'd be cooking sausages, for instance, and ask if Gwen wanted them done à la Deirdre . . .'

'Oh, no!' murmured Jean, aghast.

'That's when Gwen started to act really strangely . . . And that's when I developed a hatred for that boy I didn't know I was capable of. And when Susan committed suicide . . . I decided that come what may, sooner or later I would revenge our whole family, Susan, Deirdre, and myself. I used to lie awake, thinking of ways of kidnapping Stroud, torturing and finally executing him . . . But outwardly I was kind, considerate and understanding, swallowing my hatred, smiling, smiling . . .' Angus's voice got louder, and the people at the nearest table looked round. His voice dropped back to its previous level. 'And Stroud thought I had forgiven him, and that made him laugh all the louder . . . All that made Gwen completely desperate, and she left home and hung around the city parks, sleeping where she could, sometimes at my house when it was cold . . .

'Stroud went to university, got a poor degree, then a job at St Jude's. Gwen followed him up here, to pester and reproach him; she had become as obsessed as I was about Deirdre. Some time during the period I was . . . in hospital, Stroud got married. Renée was a nice girl, totally out of her depth with him. You know what happened to her eyes. So after Stroud had been up here for two or three years, I applied for and got a job on the teaching staff at St Jude's. Stroud was surprised, but only after I'd been there for a while did he realise that I was implacably hostile to him. That's when he put in that fancy alarm system, because he was in fear of his life. And that was when my revenge began, when he started to be afraid, mortally afraid . . .' Angus's voice had changed again, and Jean felt the first twinge of anxiety at the suppressed violence she could see in the man opposite her.

'I'd found Gwen as soon as I came up to Perth,' Angus went on in a less harsh voice. 'She made up some letters with biblical warnings about what was going to happen to him . . . then Renée joined us, and we formed an alliance with the sole purpose of terrifying Stroud. When Renée took up with that fellow Mackay, I thought it was going to ruin everything, especially when he started to get really upset with Stroud, but it didn't . . . Stroud had destroyed my family with fire, and his wife's eyesight with fire . . . And I decided to destroy him by fire too, in due course . . .' Angus's voice changed again. 'You were quite right, I came in behind Renée, though she didn't stay to witness the killing.'

Jean looked at her watch. 'There's one other thing, Angus, and that's about George. Last time I came to the nursing home here, I parked next to your car. The boot was ajar, so I opened it to slam it closed, and some stuff fell out, including a large plastic tub of lard. And there was a blow-lamp there on the back seat too. That was the evening George died . . .'

A change seemed to have come over Angus. His calm, thoughtful, professorial look had been replaced by a cunning, self-satisfied expression.

'They'd put a policeman outside the building, and I thought I'd have to put Elmslie's execution off, but the copper drove off and followed another car soon after I got there. George was so happy to hear my voice calling up on the intercom . . . That foul, filthy sod!'

Angus stood up suddenly. 'You're very clever, Jean, and I congratulate you. But it was partly your fault, you know, George's death.'

Jean's mouth opened in shock.

'Oh yes,' said Angus. 'After you called to say you weren't going to see me, I thought what the hell, I don't have anything to live for now, so I'll do the world a favour and get Elmslie off this planet . . . And if I got caught, I didn't care. I really didn't care.'

Jean's hand went to her mouth, and her voice was barely audible.

'I'm sorry,' she said. 'Oh, Angus, I'm so sorry.'

Angus smiled, but it wasn't the most pleasant of expressions. 'Thank you, Jean,' he said, and hesitated for a moment. 'But don't think they're going to reopen the case on the strength of what *you* tell them. It's all conjecture, and a good lawyer would make mincemeat of your theories . . .'

Jean stared at Angus's face and was afraid; his upper lip was twitching spasmodically to one side, giving him a weird, animal-like appearance. He laughed, and the sound sent shivers up Jean's spine, and several customers looked curiously at them.

Angus turned suddenly, almost upsetting the table, and walked quickly out of the restaurant. Jean went to the desk and paid the bill. She felt a rising panic; what was she to do now? She was pretty sure Angus was right about the police not reopening the case. *Nobody* wanted that, and all her evidence was circumstantial. Her mind was in a turmoil as she crossed the street to the car park; Angus was driving out and didn't give her a glance. The heat was so bad now that Jean felt faint getting into her car, and opened the windows before moving off, so the breeze came directly on to her face and hands.

She drove away, not remembering one bit of the ride, and by the time she got home Jean was trembling like a leaf and unable to decide what to do. Should she tell Doug everything? She knew that wouldn't help. If she kept silent, would Angus kill again, someone who had displeased him for some reason? The first one was the hardest, they said . . .

There was nobody at home, and Jean sat in the living room, twisting her fingers together, not even noticing the worsening heat, her mind in turmoil. Whichever way she went, whatever she did, would be wrong.

'Anybody home?' Steven's cheery voice rang out from the hallway, and Jean jumped up, ran out of the room and into his arms, so happy to see him she couldn't speak.

Steven just held her close. It didn't take long for Jean to tell him the whole story. He was appalled that she had taken such a risk, and held her so tight her ribs creaked.

'You have to do something,' said Steven. 'Suppose he goes out and kills somebody else?'

'You're right, Steven. I'll have to tell Douglas, but I just can't do it right now.' There were tears in Jean's eyes again.

They sat quietly in the living room until the girls came home. The heat was unbearable; the air was still and oppressive, and even the fans didn't help. They all sat together in the living room, sweating and uncomfortable, and Jean and Steven tried to keep things normal, asking about Fiona's day at the shop, and telling Lisbie what to do about a heat rash she'd developed.

The telephone rang, and nobody wanted to answer it. Jean finally got up and picked up the phone in the hall. It was Douglas Niven.

'Jean?' Doug's voice was strained. 'There's been another death . . .' Jean thought she was going to faint, and sat down suddenly on the hall chair. 'Up near St Jude's . . .'

Who could it be? Who had he killed now? Jean thought silently. She gripped the phone until it hurt; she couldn't stand the suspense.

'It happened down at the end of the drive that goes up to the school. The car was coming out, and it's a dangerous corner there; it looks as if the brakes may have failed, because a whisky delivery truck slammed right into him. He didn't have a chance . . .'

'Who was it, for God's sake?' she screamed. '*Who was it*?'

There was a shocked silence at the other end. Then

Doug's voice said 'Jean?' But Jean was weeping silent tears of frustration and couldn't answer.

'Jean, I'm sorry. It was Angus Townes. I thought I'd mentioned that already . . .'

At the very moment Jean put down the receiver, a massive clap of thunder rattled the windows, and then the sudden unfamiliar hissing noise in the street and on the windows made Lisbie and Fiona run to the front door to watch the rain as it came pelting down.

— C. F. ROE —
THE
LUMSDEN
BABY

A DOCTOR
JEAN MONTROSE
WHODUNNIT

When little Magnus Lumsden, grandson of Lord Aviemore, is found dead in his cot, there is no question of natural causes. As Detective Inspector Niven finds, there are plenty of suspects in the upper-class enclave near Perth where the Lumsdens live. But it takes Dr Jean Montrose's medical knowledge and her sympathetic but shrewd understanding of human nature to uncover the horrifying truth.

This new series of murder mysteries is set in Perth, where Jean Montrose, known to one and all as 'the wee doc', is a busy GP who also takes care of her lively and amusing family.

FICTION/CRIME   0 7472 3422 1   £3.50

A selection of bestsellers from Headline

FICTION

PARAGON PLACE	Harry Bowling	£4.99 □
THE BAD PLACE	Dean R Koontz	£4.99 □
LIPSTICK ON HIS COLLAR	Elizabeth Villars	£4.50 □
CHEYNEY FOX	Roberta Latow	£4.99 □
RASCAL MONEY	Joseph Garber	£4.99 □
THE DAMASK DAYS	Evelyn Hood	£3.99 □
LOYALTIES	Gavin Esler	£4.50 □
MONSIEUR PAMPLEMOUSSE TAKES THE CURE	Michael Bond	£2.99 □

NON-FICTION

LOSE 7LBS IN 7 DAYS	Miriam Stoppard	£3.50 □
SEXUAL AWARENESS	B & E McCarthy	£4.99 □

SCIENCE FICTION AND FANTASY

FLY BY NIGHT	Jenny Jones	£4.99 □
PUPPETMASTER	Mike McQuay	£4.99 □

All Headline books are available at your local bookshop or newsagent, or can be ordered direct from the publisher. Just tick the titles you want and fill in the form below. Prices and availability subject to change without notice.

Headline Book Publishing PLC, Cash Sales Department, PO Box 11, Falmouth, Cornwall, TR10 9EN, England.

Please enclose a cheque or postal order to the value of the cover price and allow the following for postage and packing:
UK: 80p for the first book and 20p for each additional book ordered up to a maximum charge of £2.00
BFPO: 80p for the first book and 20p for each additional book
OVERSEAS & EIRE: £1.50 for the first book, £1.00 for the second book and 30p for each subsequent book.

Name ....

Address ....

....

....